ASHES RAIN DOWN

A *Story Cycle*

WILLIAM LUVAAS

SPUYTEN DUYVIL

New York City

ACKNOWLEDGMENTS

"Ashes Rain Down" appeared in *Glimmer Train* #66 (Spring 2008): 21-35. **First Place Winner 2007-2008 Winter Fiction Open Award.**

"Spooks" appeared in *Chiron Review* #92 (Autumn 2010): 24-27.

"Heat Wave" appeared in *Serving House Journal* #3 (Spring 2011). **Nominated for a Pushcart Prize.**

"Out There" first appeared in *Phantom Seed* #2 (2008): 46-58. It also appeared in *Carpe Articulum Literary Review*, Vol. 3, Issue 2 (Summer 2010): 76-86. **Awarded Honorable Mention in the *Carpe Articulum* International Short Fiction Award Series.**

"Fever" appeared in *Saranac Review* #6 (2011): 60-77. SUNY - Plattsburgh.

"A Crack in the Pavement" appeared in *Essays & Fictions Journal*, Vol. VIII (Summer 2011): 48-58.

"Family Life" appeared in *The Ledge Poetry & Fiction Magazine* #34 (Winter 2011). Bellport, NY. **First Prize Winner 2010 Ledge Fiction Awards Competition.**

Library of Congress Cataloging-in-Publication Data

Luvaas, William, 1945-
Ashes rain down : a story cycle / William Luvaas.
p. cm.
ISBN 978-1-881471-17-2
I. Title.
PS3562.U86A93 2012
813'.54--dc23
2012025950

Ashes Rain Down

CONTENTS

Ashes Rain Down

from the sky, or fall in a steady blizzard, rather, drifting slowly down, some tiny, some the size of oak leaves,
individuated as snowflakes. Looking up through them at
a sun distorted by smoke, with a sickly, jaundiced com-
plexion, we wonder if the ashes come from brush fires
in the mountains or are sucked up into the stratosphere
from that conflagration halfway around the world–*The
Forever War* (some call it "Armageddon")–embers sucked
upward on furious thermals that rise off burning cities
and oil wells, an indiscriminate crematorium, cooling
to ash and falling earthward thousands of miles away.
Reaching out a hand, you collect upon it either remnants
of trees or of torched homes, vineyards, and human flesh.
We poke at the larger ashes, seeking clues to their origin,
dissect them, so to speak, wondering if they are remnants of jack pine and ponderosa or of Babylonia, citadel
of lost reason. Histories reside in this ash–the palimpsest
of a distant purposefulness. Ashes pile in drifts against
fences, turn our lawns calcium white, make a foul, ac-
rid soup of water in dogs' bowls. They sift down col-

lars, creep through walls and form a fine pellicle over the furniture. Myrna Haney says it's "a sign of God's anger... Sodom and Gomorrah." She may be right. We have a saying now: "If ashes burn your tongue, shut your mouth." Which is to say: "Don't talk about trouble, it will only get worse." Mostly, we have stopped complaining, not out of acquiescence or fatalism but simply fed up with unhappiness.

The other day at Yesterdays, a waitress told me I should get out the hose and water down my roof. "There's been live embers falling all day, there's fire trucks out."

"You don't wet down the roof until flames are atop you," I said. "What's the point?"

"Live embers can travel two miles, I heard it on TV," the manager said.

"Travel, do they? That's a lot of nonsense."

They turned away from me as a lost cause then and began talking to Henry Staidley about what they would do to the arsonist if they got hold of him. Makes me nervous hearing grown women speak of doing such things to a man. "Besides," I reminded them, "we don't have adequate water pressure. Even if we did, you wouldn't want to waste precious water on a roof."

"Never did have," Henry insisted, "not even when it rained enough. Never had the storage capacity over here."

"Henry, are you suggesting that we should go ahead and waste water, since we never had enough of it anyhow? You ought to run for political office."

Henry shielded his mouth with a hand and spoke to the women. "Ashes burn your tongue and all..."

"Oh bullcrap! Besides, I wouldn't call that fellow an 'arsonist.' I'd call him a 'homegrown terrorist.' We don't need to go abroad to find Armageddonists and such like. We have plenty of them right here at home."

"Will you listen to him!" the waitress cried.

"You better don't let my husband hear you talk like that," the manager warned me.

Henry Staidley frowned. "He just don't think there's anything wrong with setting half the damn world on fire."

"I didn't say that, Henry. I said we don't need foreign terrorists to do it to us; we can do it to ourselves."

Hopeless. Wet down my roof, for crissake. What idiocy. Am I supposed to wake up every hour on the hour to water down my roof? I paid my bill and left them muttering behind me, would surely have received anonymous phone threats but our phones are out, cells, too, mostly, along with email, and snail mail only four days a week. However, our grapevine remains remarkably efficient; seems we have regained our telepathic powers. Makes you wonder if all that instant ability to connect didn't encourage lazy mental habits. But that's another story. And this story is not about fire but family politics. Some say all politics is familial; the earth embroiled in a global family feud. Possibly. It's gotten nasty enough.

Maybe Two Weeks Ago

I delivered a load of firewood down to the gals at Chez Amie. Margie amazed I was still cutting wood, what with fires burning and all. "Oh," I said, "the forest service wants us to get in and thin out the snags. Besides, there's all the citrus orchards being antiquated out. That orange and grapefruit makes good hot firewood. No one expects their trees to survive the winter, cold as it's likely to be. Growers hope to salvage something out of them— one last crop and a few bucks for firewood."

"What a pity," Margie said, "burning up all our citrus."

"Pity," Carlie agreed. "We hope to be prepared this winter. Gawd! last was awful."

"Awful," Margie echoed, "bone chilling."

They're Mutt and Jeff, those two—or more like double Mutts. Both heavyset, but Carlie a straight-out porker. Maybe two-fifty pounds. But she can cook, I'm here to tell. Her pork roast with a hazelnut glaze and sage stuffing is to die for. And her cheesecake! Both carry their weight well. For a time there, I thought of dating Margie. Still might, even though I suspect those two are lesbians. What the hell! "Scarcity," I'm always joking with them, "is the mother of diversity."

"Whatever that means."

"It means," I say, "if you get horny enough you'll try anything."

"You, maybe, not me!" Carlie waddles to the stove to sample the contents of a huge steaming pot, indifferent to all sensations but taste. Her face relaxes in a smile, eyes ecstatically closed. Maybe I'm missing something: taste, the mother of all desires.

Anyway, Margie finger-motioned me aside that day, telling her partner, "Carl, I'm just going to pay Lawrence, okay?" Once we were outside on the porch, she whispered, "Carl's mother is dying; we may have to close next week and drive up to Oregon."

"I'm real sorry to hear that," I said. "I sure would like to tell her so."

"No, please don't. It's just a horror—" pausing to study my face "—just terrible the way that old witch talks to her. It's 'fatso' this and 'Why don't you lose weight, for God's sake' that, and 'Yuck, I hate fatties.' Not only her mother, but her brother, too. Carl was on the phone with her mom last night, saying how much she loved her and couldn't imagine a world without her, and wanted her to stay alive forever. Then she went quiet, and I knew, I just knew. Even on her death bed the old witch is abusive. Must've been a doozie, because Carl covered the receiver. Finally, she said, 'Well, I'm a teensy overweight, Mom, I admit. But I promise if you stay alive I'll lose one hundred pounds. Is it a deal?' Can you imagine Carl svelte? Wow!

It would be like Dick Cheney smiling. Well, no deal, anyways! The old bitch-witch is dying and Carl is staying fat. All there is to it."

"You know, I wouldn't say she's fat exactly. Maybe a bit plump—"

"I would. The thing is, Lawr, if we go, we would like you to take us. We'll pay you. You're the only person we know with a pickup." Turns out there were items they wanted to liberate from Carlie's mother's house before her brother got his hands on them—antiques, family heirlooms and such. "He'll sell them," Margie said, "but Carl will cherish them. It would mean so much to her if you would."

"Sure, I'll take you. But I won't take your money. You can pay for the gas and eats."

Margie clapped her hands and lit up. She bounced forward to buss me on the cheek. I turned and caught her lips full against mine, got my tongue into it a little—that scarcity I spoke about. Jeschrist! she tasted delicious. She pulled away and brought a hand up to wipe her mouth. "None of that." More surprise in her eyes than revulsion. "Okay, we'll feed you free meals for a month, too."

"Hot damn!" I said. Meaning both that kiss and the promised grub.

"The Old Witch," as I came to call her myself, died that night. Carlie cried nonstop from Banning to Tracy as we drove north. Then, puffy-eyed and cheeked, raw nosed, sprawled across the back seat of my Chevy 4X4, she said, "That's enough of that." And didn't let go another peep. *Character* is what I think when I consider that woman: *eighteen stone of Character.* Pot-roast-brewing, tear-spewing, no-nonsense character. So I understand why Margie loves her.

"You cried right past Anderson's Split Pea Soup," Margie scolded.

"I saw the windmill." Carlie sniffled and heaved upright in back, causing the truck to leap into another lane.

"Ooooh, watch that!"

"No matter," Margie said, "they were closed. Imagine Anderson's Split Pea closed. The world is coming to an end and no question."

"No question," Carlie sniffled.

"Careful!" I admonished. "You two are starting to sound like Myrna Haney and Hector Dario and the end-of-days crew! Ashes in your mouth and all."

"So what? I'm starting to feel that way. We counted sixteen fires en route," Margie said, "or maybe one continuous."

There was, at that moment, a distant glow of fire on hills to our west—a purple-red nimbus, eerie against utter darkness all sides. Made you wonder if the power grid was down in Stockton and the Central Valley. Margie had brought along her laptop, but couldn't get on the Web to find out. Traffic sparse, just a few interstate rigs. Spooky.

"Lawrence was telling me about his dad. He says they never got along either. What did he call you, 'spilled seed'?"

"What do you mean 'either'?" Carlie asked. "Do you mean me and my mom?"

Margie didn't answer.

"Yeah," I said, "'a little spilled seed.' I was an 'oops.' Mom was wearing a diaphragm but some sperm must've leaked past and...Watch out! Here I come! Neither of them was all too happy at my arrival."

Carlie made a repudiating noise with her lips. "Oh, get a life, Lawr! Half of us start out as 'oopses!' It all sorts out in the end. I'm sure they loved you—in their way."

"Well, they kept it a damned good secret then. My dad used to say 'Oops' whenever I entered the room. 'Look what the devil dragged in.' I believe he considered infanticide early on, but preachers aren't supposed to kill babies."

"Your dad was a minister? I didn't know that," Carlie said.

"Wouldn't know it from me." I laughed. "Believe me, it's no commendation."

"Funny," Margie said, "but I knew. You can't hate religion as much as Lawr does unless you bear a grudge." In the mostly dark I could make out her smug smile. "Anyways, I liked him a whole lots more after hearing about his father. I mean, I always liked you, Lawr. It's just...now I understand why a little better."

She had let me know about it, too, snuggled up to me while her girlfriend bawled in back and we smooched—what I could manage while driving. I even copped a feel. Magnificent tits, Margie, soft and firm at once. Finally, she pushed me off and said, No, she wasn't into guys, just wanted to take a nostalgia trip back to high school for a minute. Whatever.

"Is it that obvious?" I asked. "When do I ever mention religion?"

They both chuckled.

"Some day you and your dad will learn to forgive each other," Carlie said.

"I doubt it, sister. My dad's dead. I won't likely meet him in heaven."

"Oh, that's just terrible. People should reconcile with their parents before they die. I'm not judging you negatively, Lawrence, I just really believe—"

"You mean like you and your mom did?" Margie asked a little bitterly.

"I tried." Carlie sniffled; it worried me she would let go again. "I really tried."

I was about to begin trying, I told them, when Dad fell over in his plate one Sunday after church, dead as his prime rib. Heart attack. He bequeathed me nothing in his will but for two admonitory words: *Beware damnation.* "Only trouble with your theory, Carlie, is it takes two to make up." Funny, I felt like whimpering myself, rubbed leakage from my eyes. Margie placed a hand on my knee, Carlie on my shoulder: warm baker's hands. We drove on a while in silence, past a landscape fringed with fire.

We Arrived In Drain,

Oregon, about five next morning after driving all night. A Frosty Freeze and gas station with antique pumps about all that passed for "town." Carlie's mother's farmhouse had a screened front porch and huge weeping willow in the front yard; paint was flaking off and moss crept across the shake roof; a wisp of smoke curled up from the chimney, though it wasn't that cold yet. The place seemed to me a sad icon of a past that had survived into the present, or some old wound that had never fully healed.

Carlie's brother greeted us at the front door, a snake-thin, lean-hearted fellow with long arms and hatchet-sharp nose, eyes deep set either side, mouth a mere hole. None of his sister's generosity, her opposite even in coloring. Right off, I didn't like him. We trooped in the front door, greeted by a blast of heat that carried some taint on it, as if the garbage had begun to ferment in the kitchen. "You know Mom," the brother said, "she hates cold... dead or alive!" Snuffling at his joke, he reminded me of a skinny shoat at his slop, looking Carlie up and down like he might go for her next. "I suppose this is *the girlfriend*. How you doin'? I'm brother Zack. No doubt you've heard

what an asshole I am. Right?" Snuffling again, then draw-
ing up ramrod straight, gesturing at me. "Who is this
joker?"

"Lawrence," Carlie said, "this is Zack. Zack, this
is our good friend Lawrence." You could tell she didn't
much want to enter the house. Me neither. Zack's hand
didn't grip mine; rather he pulled his palm across my
outreaching one and shot up his hand in a high five gesture; I slapped at it, but only caught a piece of his thumb.
Awkward.

"Mom's laid out in bed," he said. "I told the funeral-
home people to hold off picking her up until you arrived.
They said it wasn't a good idea. Maybe not."

"Well, I agree...my goodness." Carlie touched a finger
to her nose.

"I sprayed with air freshener. Guess we'll need to
again. Hey, I'm just trying to keep everybody happy here.
Okay!"

"You know what they say," Carlie said.

But we didn't. Not me, anyhow. I'm always fascinated
to watch grown friends relate to their birth families—all
those unresolved grievances and faded hopes, cloistered
anger and psychic chatter. It's always both alien and familiar—an unknown territory that you know all too well.
Margie gripped Carlie's elbow, steering her past brother
Zack as if she knew the house layout, though she'd never
been in the place in her life. Led us back to Mom's bed-

room through the dark living room–dawn light creeping around edges of drawn blinds–along passageways carved through a clutter of stacked boxes and dowdy furniture, the glass eyes of–were they dolls?–watching us from all sides as we passed, hundreds of them, antiques, propped up on every bare surface, cloth legs dangling over bookshelves, phalanxes of dwarf beings, mute and coldly watching. Jeschrist! Reaching out their stubby fingers to touch us. The old witch still alive in them, regarding her fat daughter with myriad disapproval. You could nearly hear the susurrus of dry, chiding papier-mache and porcelain lips. I gripped my elbows and coiled into myself, wondering what any of this had to do with me and why I hadn't waited in the truck.

Mom sat up in bed, propped on pillows, her bony arms resting on the counterpane, scarcely any flesh covering them at all...or her cheeks. Brother Zack flipped on an overhead as we entered and the austere room was filled with light, bare but for a dresser and coat rack and rattan chair in one corner. I got the feeling he had been cleaning up; three black trash bags lined up like pudgy brothers along a wall. A huge porcelain-headed cloth doll sat atop the dresser, cheeks apple-red, mouth puckered in an obscene kiss as if about to perform oral sex, long-lashed doll's eyes goggling. Mother of all dolls! Stout nearly, with pudgy knees and feet. Zack said it was Mom's favorite doll, which seemed remarkable given her disapproval of her daughter's girth. But no explaining such things, the metaphysics of family relationships, the ties and secret longings that bind us, the wish to forgive, the seeming impossibility of it.

A nightgown strap had slipped down one of Mom's sharp shoulders, and Margie pushed it up again. She smoothed the sheet up under her chin. "There...there, that's better."

Carlie could not go near her mother. Seeing her lying there in gaunt abjection, straw-dry hair scattered, cheeks sunken into her mouth, eyes wide but pupils angled downward as if she were trying to peer into herself, Carlie gripped her belly and spun away, shouted at Zack, "My God! She stinks. What's the matter with you? Can't you smell her?"

"She's maybe a little riper than she was last night when I went to bed," he said indifferently.

"You sick bastard!"

Margie gripped her friend's shoulders, but Carlie shook her off, cringing away from hands that had touched her dead mother. Not that I blamed her. What smelled was not just the old witch's decomposing flesh but the longed-for love and forgiveness that had died with her. Dead love stinks to holy hell.

Carlie went to open a window, the hardwood floor creaking beneath her. A shaft of light slid into the room at an angle when she opened curtains; dust motes floated and danced in a thick wedge of it, got me wondering if a corpse releases molecules of flesh into the air—isn't that what causes smell, microscopic particles of a substance?—to float and dance and creep up our nostrils. Not a pleasant thought. Zack touched Carlie's arm to warn her against opening the sash. "Flies," he said.

"Oh, for God's sake. Would you call the undertaker... please!" Reminded me of Carlie in her cooking mode: no nonsense, *Will you get the hell out of my kitchen!* She stepped forward, as if she would go to her mom after all, but Margie planted a palm against her chest and shook her head, no!

So we escaped the place, and Zack called the funeral home on his cell from the front porch. (Odd, they had service up here when so many places didn't.) We could breathe again out there in the cool, damp, mossy air of an Oregon morning.

"She wants to be cremated," he said, hanging up, "her ashes scattered up in the orchard."

"I can't do that," Carlie said.

"What? Too fat to climb the hill?" His snorting laugh again. "I've seen Mom's will, Sis, and I better warn you. I get the furniture, you get the dolls and appliances. I get the land, you get the house. Now that's one shitty joke, right? Mom's final 'Fuck you both.' Can you believe it? I'm over here twice a week, I take her shopping, I service the car, I drive her to the doctor, I prune the fucking apple trees, right? What do you do, Sis? You cook and grow fatter. You expand. You break her heart."

"Shuddup...please. Would you...please?"

"What do I get for it?" He seemed to ask me. "Huh? Work your tail off for somebody and what do you get? Do they appreciate it? Oh," he said, "right! I get her bank account, what smidgen she has in there, and puny IRA account, I get that. BFD! Whoooeee."

"Don't you care at all, Zack? Mom lying in there?"

"I about wore it out, you know. Like the smell! Hang around long enough and you don't smell it anymore. Hey–Clarence, is it?–you wanna help me here for a minute?"

So we went back to the bedroom and carried Mom out to the porch fireman style: one arm supporting her back, the other under her skinny buttocks. She was light as a cardboard box, unnaturally cold. Me protesting I didn't think it was such a good idea, but Zack insistent, bullying even, *What, couldn't I handle a whiff of runny cheese?* The smell, I'm here to tell, clung to my skin and made my hair crawl. We set her up in a wicker rocker on the screened porch under the women's incredulous gaze, and Zack slipped some clean socks on her feet. "Her toes were stiff as a board last night," he said, "but they've loosened up good. You got a problem, Carlie? Hey, she loved sitting out here; she used to say she could spend eternity sitting on this porch."

It seemed Carlie would not respond, a hand covering

her eyes.

Zack had asked about conditions down south as we carried Mom out: fires, civil unrest, shortages, and all. "You got to be crazy to stay down there," he told us now. "You got to have a death wish or maybe believe you're safe behind all that blubber. Up here, no problems. Tell you what, Mom, Carlie's going to have to get *her house* off *my land* pronto, so I can subdivide and make some money here. Whaddaya think, hon?"

"You're an asshole," Carlie mumbled without looking up.

"So we'll buy the lot beneath the house from you, and you can subdivide the rest." Margie wasn't asking but telling. "I'm sure you'd like that, Mom." She smiled at that corpse, sitting there amicably among us, as if the old gal could hear her. "Wouldn't you?"

"Who are you, the fuckinay husband?" Zack howled laughter. "Whoooooeee, damn!"

"He won't sell," Carlie whispered. "Not to me he won't. No way."

"You got that right."

"I can start loading things," I told Carlie. "You want me to, I could start."

"Could you load the hutch and grandfather clock first, Lawrence?" she said, snapping out of her funk. "Then the walnut gateleg dining table and chairs. Mom promised me those for Chez Amie," she told her brother.

"The hell she did! Dolls and appliances, period!"

"Didn't you do, mother?" The tears coming again.

Incredibly, Mom answered: sitting there, dead, slumped into herself, beginning to stink. All of us gawping. She spoke in a scratchy, high-pitched voice, weak from age and frailty:

"Of course I didn't. Yuck, I hate fatties. My daughter is awfully fat. She's obese, really. She makes me ill. She let herself go. Well, I've tried. She knows I disapprove. I've told her I can't hold a fatso in my heart. She disgusts me. She makes me sick. She used to be such a pretty girl. Now she's a fat homosexual." Then you realized it was brother Zack, projecting his voice as a ventriloquist will, lips barely moving. "Whatever do they do to each other, these lesbians? Why, they can't even make babies together."

Mirth boiling in him, making his belly heave. I thought I would get out of the chair and whump a fist atop his head and deflate the giggling shitbag–if Margie didn't beat me to it. Flat pissed off. But we were chastened by Carlie's expression. She regarded her mother as if the old gal had truly spoken, was still alive and spouting the old familiar family line.

On the radio, I knew, they would be reporting the latest casualty figures from *The Forever War*. Yesterday, as we drove north, they reported the capture of an entire platoon of Marines in revenge for their destruction of a southern village. They would gouge out their eyes and cut off their tongues, the announcer said, while they were still alive. Once, they had censored such disturbing facts, but they no longer bothered.

"Couldn't you   try, dear?   For me! Lose a weensy twenty pounds. I would be so pleased, so proud of you, honey. For every twenty pounds you lose, I promise you one of my antiques. How's about? Like I used to promise you chocolate cake if you earned high marks at school. I had no idea you'd become a fatso—all that chocolate cake—I am just sick about it. It's my own fault, I know. I accept responsibility. Ohhhh Gawd! Still, you will do this for me if you love me. I know you won't do it for yourself. However, I don't imagine what I did to make you a homosexual. You must bear responsibility for that yourself."

"That's about enough," I said.

"You think that's enough do you, Clarence?" He had snake-lanky arms; he could do serious damage, might take me. He knew it. It's the thin mean ones you got to watch out for.

"Yes," Margie barked. "In about two shakes I'm going to come over and wrap your testicles around your throat and strangle you."

"Wheeewy." Zack wasn't laughing anymore; he stared at her, abashed and edgy.

"What's the point?" I muttered. "Why rub it in?"

"All right then," Carlie announced. "Mom wants to be cremated and she will be cremated."

She stood and dusted her hands together, as I've seen her do a hundred times baking in the kitchen at Chez Amie, went over and fussed hands about her mom, as she does putting finishing touches to supper plates, buttoned the nightgown collar up to the old gal's neck. Then snatched her up out of the chair and heaved her over a shoulder like a sack of meal. Strong. Fatties often are, sumo wrestlers and all. We stood to watch her carry Mom back into the house, thinking she'd simply had enough of the old gal's sermons (I can tell you about that myself) and wanted to put her back to bed, maybe sit a minute and make peace with her.

But She Lay Her Down In The Living Room
amongst mumbling, wide-eyed dolls and antiques, her boxes of—so Margie told me—doll clothes, thousands of complete outfits, and old almanacs from the former owner of the farm, which looked into the tides and phases of the moon and best time for planting and when the blackberries were expected to ripen and how cold the winter would be...might even mention Armageddon in there, but couldn't have imagined *The Forever War* and the mess we've gotten ourselves into, because, in those days, it was assumed things would pretty much go on as they always had. Carlie lay the old witch out on the

couch, scooting a space for her, and stood smiling down. We thought it best to give her a little space. Zack had someone to call—no doubt the developer who hoped to get his hands on the place (amazing they were still building houses up here). So I saw my chance and edged up to Margie on the divan, wanting—I might say *needing*—safe harbor...and another feel of her tits and whiff of her fruity perfume (or maybe it was her own natural smell). She politely repeated, no, she wasn't into guys. "Especially now. If I were, Lawr, you'd be at top of my list." Nonetheless, we were kissing when Carlie appeared in the doorway, red faced and flustered, surrounded by smoke, shooing her hands at us to get out, vamoose, frowning at her girlfriend. You know, I thought I had smelled smoke lingering into Margie's spicy, baked-apple aroma as we kissed.

"Out!" Carlie cried. "Mom's being cremated—along with my inheritance." She clutched a box of strike-anywhere wooden matches in her hand.

Flames belched out the door behind her, sending her leaping forward half gracefully. I caught a glimpse of the blaze, as I stepped back after shooing the women outside. Good God! that hellfire—consuming dolls and roaring through boxes and clinging to walls before dripping off—would have gotten the Haney sisters (and our arsonist) orgasmic, might even have gotten my father off. It moved the old girl, too. Her muscles contracted in the heat, and she sat up on the couch to peer at me a moment before dropping back down again, dead center of all that anger, beyond pain but not fury or awe, understanding at that moment, I'm here to tell, that her daughter is damned good at braising all types of meat.

I caught Brother Zack's wrists as he attempted to push past me into the house with a fire extinguisher, weeping and moaning about his antiques, his tear-streaked face betraying a resemblance to his sister's—several sizes smaller. Not half so strong as I imagined he would be. I dragged him out into the yard, had to keep an eye on him for a time. He was inconsolable, insisting his sister had no right to treat the old gal that way. Carlie actually smiling.

"You wanted her cremated," she said.

Studying her, I tried to fathom the satisfaction she seemed to be feeling, hoping to share in it. Wondering if you feel peace for good after torching the world around you, avenging old wrongs, or if the feeling is transitory. Wondering if we are all going to find out soon...and, if we do, if it will be worth it.

Some Months Later

I delivered a load of wood out to Margie and Carlie's place. Not Chez Amie but their house. As usual, they gave me the key to the gate, which I would drop off at the restaurant after I'd gotten their firewood delivered and stacked—citrus this time, though it broke their hearts to be burning up fruit trees. I went inside the house as I never do. Curiosity, I suppose. Couldn't say what I was looking for: sex toys on the bed table, a blowup of Hillary Clinton nude? Just a look! Sorry, girls, don't mean you any harm. I found a beautifully equipped kitchen, something of a cathedral with high stained-glass clerestories. One serious kitchen, I'm here to tell: brass-bottomed pans, dozens of stainless-steel knives in a long rack, chopping blocks and blenders everywhere, maybe ten thousand dollars worth of gas range with a soapstone grill. They had separate bedrooms. Surprised me a little.

What surprised me more, sitting there upright on the oak dresser in what must've been Carlie's room, was that plump cloth doll, mother of all dolls, that had reigned alone in her mother's bedroom. But charred, its ceramic face darkened and cracked from the inside on the left, with a crackling of tiny fissures, so it appeared to have aged instantly against the bright, childish features of its other half. A leg and arm one side were black and shriveled; the fire had breathed against its clothes and worried them some, pulled them taut against its body and browned them as a hot steam iron will, but, miraculously, the cloth torso hadn't caught fire. The doll remained plump and unrepentant. Even through hellfire it had refused to diet, remaining true to itself.

Fire is a fickle force and works by its own logic—much like the logic which guides our behavior with those who are closest to us. Did Carlie run back inside to rescue that doll when we weren't looking? Not likely. Did she bring it out under her coat unnoticed after setting the blaze? Then how would it have become charred? Did her brother Zack find it in the rubble, trying to dig his land out from underneath, and send it to her? Possibly. Or was it there waiting for her when she arrived home? There all along, perhaps. Was what I had seen in her mother's bedroom in Oregon merely a ghost trace of some earlier conflagration, some older injury? An injury so important that we must enshrine it, sleep beside it, construct our lives around it, look daily into its distorted face, set the world ablaze when we fear that we will not keep faith with it.

Tommy's New Brain

For years now Tommy Whitehead has been collecting people's used PCs and storing them in a shed behind his dad's gas station. Here lately, he has pulled the CPUs out of them and hooked them up in series somehow, as you would car batteries. "What I'm doing," he tells me the other day, "is synapsing them together, using the model of a human brain—all those interlaced neurons with long dendrites making multiple connections. The more you wire together the more power they generate, dude. I figure that's the key to artificial intelligence—if we ever plan to get up to human capacity."

"You're trying to match human capacity? That's a bit of a stretch, isn't it?"

Tommy was studying the physiology of the brain down at State before they cancelled classes. I guess he's putting what he learned to practical use. Damn smart kid, Tommy, if a little scary. He shrugs. "Takes a lot of patience making the interconnections—chip to chip, you know. But doable."

"I'm a Luddite through and through myself, a skeptic. I don't much trust hi-tech, artificial brains and all," I tell him. "Why not learn to use the ones we have first?"

He laughs. "You and the Haney sisters." Granny laughs with him—sitting back in a corner of the shed in the dark, sucking her gums and cackling, like the Whitehead family pet. Startles me.

"No, the Haney sisters think technology is evil. I just feel it's overrated, causes as much trouble as it prevents. It's half the reason we're in the current mess."

"I thought that's the war." He grins. "Global warming and all that." He shakes a wrench at me. "You'll see, dude!"

"I wouldn't let the Jesusers know about this. They're likely to burn the place down."

I don't think about it again until our lights begin to dim in the evenings; there are rumors that we might lose our power altogether—like over in those places where we are fighting *The Forever War*. Thing is, you lose it and you don't get it back again. Come to find out it's Tommy's new brain impacting our power: every time he fires his contraption up he about puts Sluggards Creek in the dark. So we send a delegation to talk to him: Sinclair, Benson, Laney Silverstein, Hector Dario (representing the end-of-days crew), and me. Hector's a mistake, but Laney insists the Jesus crew must be included. We are standing outside

the shed, surrounding the boy and granny in her wheelchair like a council of elders. Tommy looks consternated,
as if his brow puzzled up some days before and froze that
way, lines set in flesh like riffles on a pudding. "I can't
figure it out," he says. Laney telling him it's not that we
don't believe in progress, "and youthful enterprise, Tom.
We surely do!"

"I want to go home now," Granny interrupts.

"You are home, Grandma W. You live here with Dad
and me now."

"I do not," she barks. "You liar."

"You realize you are screwing up everyone in town's
electricity?" I say.

"What I hear, it's the whole damn region affected,"
Benson says.

"What happens, I fire it up and it just buzzes along
a minute, lights winking on in all units, like a million twinkling fireflies–wink-wink-wink–glowing like
brighter and brighter for a few seconds. Then it like hits
a wall, dude. I hear insulation sizzling, there's this burnt
smell, so I shut her down quick, scared she will go up in
flames. Kafoof!" Throwing his hands in the air to demonstrate.

"Vanity! All is vanity." Hector Dario's brow is fur-
rowed in righteous outrage. "Beware the pride of intellect
which goeth before a fall."

"Yes, sir," granny says, grinning, her top dentures in

crooked, "my husband so loves his moustache."

Tommy pats her shoulder in approval, as if she's uttered some profound truth.

"We know the routine, Hector," Benson says. "An active mind is an evil mind and all that crap! Clear on back to Galileo. But I doubt your Jesus was as much of an idiot as you people make him out to be."

Hector draws up. "I didn't come here to be insulted."

Tommy's dad, Glen Whitehead, strolls across patchy ground from the gas station. "You got the city council over here now, Tommy? Come to condemn your damn gizmo?" A gruff man, Glen, lanky and perpetually scowling, his cheeks stubbled, a deep cleft in his chin. Since his wife died three years ago, he lives in the gas station and mechanic's shop, like his home life died along with her, leaving Tommy to fend for himself...and grandma. "You know what that is in there—" jabbing a thumb at the shed "–that's my boy's brain, 'cause he don't have one in his head. Maybe you come over to piss some Jesus water on it, Hector?"

We are all embarrassed but for Laney. For a time, after his wife died, Glen dated her. Didn't work out. She takes him aside and speaks low to him, tapping his chest with a hand. Glen seems to become even more upset as she explains our mission to him, and Tommy appears about to flee, throwing abashed glances at his dad.

"Won't you stay to dinner?" Granny asks. "Well, it's

not like my home in Palo Alto."

Sinclair, the techie in our crew, nuclear physicist in the old days, wants to see "Tommy's contraption," so we follow him inside the shed which has been converted to a white-walled lab, a row of florescent lights along the high sheet metal ceiling. Tommy Whitehead's super processor takes up much of the room, like a cyclotron or great artificial brain turned inside out, colored wires bristling everywhere, shiny, naked circuit boards exposed, thousands of white plastic connectors like artificial myelin sheath covering neurons...six feet high and thirty long. Those many CPUs fused together in a single unit. Sinclair and Benson whistle, Hector Dario mumbles a prayer, reluctant to go inside at all. "It looks dangerous," Laney cries, following us in.

"That's exactly what it is," Glen Whitehead says. "Got the whole town turned against us. What kind of genius is that? You ask me, that boy's a smart moron."

"Moron!" Granny claps her hands.

Tommy ignores his dad, talking animatedly as he leads Sinclair around his "brain," pointing out features, Sinclair regarding him with the shy, admiring smile a graduate student might bestow on a favorite professor. "Weird thing is," Tommy says, "the amperage at this end terminal was amplified by a factor of five-thousand from the input cable when I tested her last night. Freaky deak, dude."

"Five-thousand!" Sinclair exclaims. "Good Lord! that's dangerous, Tom. You shouldn't be in the same room with this."

"What'd I tell you! A moron. So smart he's stupid. Can't zip up his own pants."

Granny collars Hector Dario and wants to know if she can wear his shirt to dinner. "Such a lovely shirt." While I hear Sinclair tell Tommy, soto voce so his father won't hear, "My God, if any gas fumes leaked in here—"

"Well, goodness!" Laney cries. "We have fires enough already."

"You're saying it's a fire hazard?" Glen Whitehead demands in alarm.

"Jesusfuckingchrist!" Benson says.

"You think it's funny smearing our Lord's name in filth?" demands Hector Dario. "It makes me about sick, people." Hector looks like a pentecostal owl with the light of LEDs hopping off his glasses. Granny grabs his shirt sleeve and rubs it between her fingers, cooing. Laney laughs so vigorously she must clutch her belly. We stare at her, haven't heard Laney laugh since her caretaker, John Sylvio, killed himself.

"We're discussing here, Hector," snaps Benson, "something important. Two thousand years of practice and you geeks haven't learned squat."

"Would you take it easy, Benson," I say. "Hector's disturbed, like the rest of us–superbrains and power surges and fire danger and all. Takes some getting used to."

"Thank you, Lawrence. Still, I know where the Lord's presence isn't wanted." He turns a malignant smile on Benson. "I forgive you, brother Benson. Myself, I prefer not to, but the good Lord commands it: Bless them that curse you and spitefully use you." Hector exits like a sullen teenager, trailed by Granny in her wheelchair. "Are you going to the meeting?" she cries. "I want my shirt!" Hector unbuttons and yanks shirttails out of his pants and tosses it back in her lap–following another of the Lord's commands, no doubt–and exits in his ribbed wifebeater. Right then I know there will be trouble.

Tommy saying you could probably power all of North America if you hooked a power line into an actual human brain and drained the amplification off the output end. Sinclair nods. "Circuit amplification is a known phenomenon in physics."

"Listen to 'em! Two geniuses!" Glen Whitehead scowls. "They say Albert Einstein was a screwup, too. Couldn't even shave properly."

"Your son is a prodigy. I realize that can be threatening," Sinclair says.

Glen points after Hector. "You wanna fuck off outta here, professor. Class is over."

We all agree, given the drain on our power supply and fire danger, Tommy must stop firing up his brain, except for closely supervised periods in the early a.m. The

boy is crestfallen, looks like he will cry; the shield of genius melted, revealing the kid beneath. His father nearly
gloating over his son's disappointment. Granny pulls
Hector Dario's striped shirt crookedly over her sweater,
after repeatedly sniffing the armpits, hands smoothing
the fabric, troubled by the tension between her son and
grandson, mouth yanking grotesquely aside in a kind of
tic. "Moron...moron," she laments. Laney's smile a blessing that would give anyone hope. "It's going to be fine,"
she promises the Whiteheads. "You'll see." But I doubt
it: Hector and his friends will be back, and Glen mutters
about destroying that "fool's brain."

§

So I tell Cora I am giving Laney Silverstein a lift
down to Glen Whitehead's garage to pick up her Taurus,
which Glen has tuned up. "I think she needs moral support going over there. She and Glen dated a while, you
know. I don't think it ended well."

"Before you dated her or after?" Cora's hands hiss over
damp clay; she doesn't look up from the pot she is turning
on the wheel.

"I never dated Laney. You know that. True, I considered it before meeting you."

"What I know is you are giving Laney a lot of moral
support lately."

"Oh, for shitsake, Cora. She needs support after Johnny Sylvio's death. You know that. Laney's a good friend. End of story."

"What kind of friend, I'm asking. Maybe you want to see which end Glen got his end in. Huh?" Looking up at me with a nasty smirk.

"That's disgusting. I'm surprised at you."

"*That's disgusting,*" she quacks back. "Grow up, Lawr!"

"Okay! Yes, I considered dating Laney. Yes, I find her attractive. Okay? Yes, okay, she turns me on...used to. But it's like the attraction you feel for a mountain you never expect to climb. Cold and distant. Are you happy now?"

"I guess you're stuck down in the flats with me?"

I'm out the door. Flat pissed off. Maybe should be flattered by her jealousy. But it's like brush fires in the mountains; you never know how far it will spread. Simple truth is when I met Cora all my fantasies melted in that caldron. No contest. But I'll be damned if I'm going to tell her that now. I nearly confess her suspicions to Laney, but don't.

Glen slides out from under a pickup on a trolley and lies squinting up at us, his face streaked with oil and grime. "You bring your boyfriend along to chaperone?"

Laney blushes. "Lawrence was kind enough to give me a ride."

He taps the huge spanner he grips in a fist against

the tire of Laney's Ford Taurus in the stall beside him. "You're wasting your money and my time. Three months from now there won't be any gas to fuel this hog. Supplier says I just bought my last shipment."

"Well, that's awful, Glen. What will you do?"

"Close up shop...like everyone else. Twelve-eighty-five a gallon, low test."

"You could switch to bike repairs," I say, pissed off at his insinuation; I will tolerate Cora's suspicions, but not Glen Whitehead's.

"Tell you what, you can give Laney a ride on your bike next time." He boosts up to a squat, supporting his weight on his fists like a chimpanzee, pushes to his feet with a moan. "Or maybe she can ride you over bareback."

We are stunned. You don't talk that way about a woman like Laney S, not even with Glen's filthy mouth. What in hell has gotten into everybody?

"I will need my keys," Laney snaps.

"Have you looked at me recently?" he demands, raking hands down his torso. "I smell, I don't bathe regular, I don't eat good, I don't sleep good, I don't have no fun... since Chippy died. I don't even go in my own damned house no more. Why would I? Mom and my boy lives out in the shed with his damn brain anymore. She can't put two sentences together no more besides. Brain dead. What kind of conversation can you have?" As he speaks, he edges toward tears, his son Tommy rising in his face.

He steps forward and raps a blunt, oil-stained finger against my chest. "That woman there, I don't blame her none for not wanting to date me. Not one bit. What do you know? You don't live in fear you're gonna end up like Granny. I can already hear the bees leaving the hive in my head, flying away!"

"Goddamn, Glen," I manage, "I didn't know—"

"That woman there—" poking me again "—I woulda loved her good. Promised Chippy I would. She coulda used a man after Johnny Sylvio died, and I coulda used a woman's hand in my boy's life. But, no! Katey bar the door." He laughs—not at himself exactly.

Laney touches his arm. "I'm sorry, Glen. Truly, I am."

"Yeh sure, you bet." He cocks back that spanner, large enough to crack a skull. For a horrid moment I fear I will have to wrestle it away from him—if I can. Snaps it off his shoulder and sends it through a grimy window across the garage. "Whoops." He grins. "Better repair that. Keep me outta trouble."

Laney leans in the passenger window of my pickup as I prepare to leave, her face strained and haunted. "I do wish it had worked out. For Tommy's sake. And Chippy's. But, my God, Lawrence, the smell! I could not sit next to him. I don't know how she lived with it." She was blushing, ashamed of herself. "He's a good man, really. He collects all the anger the rest of us are afraid to feel and uses it up. It's a hard job."

§

Tommy calls me early one morning. I grab the handset and automatically say "hello" before realizing it's the first time the phone has rung in three months. "How did you get the phone to work?" I ask, knowing who it is before he speaks.

"Johnny Sylvio's got inside my supercomputer," Tommy whispers. "I just talked to him." Voice trembling.

"Johnny Sylvio is dead," I whisper back.

Cora props up on the pillow, mouthing, *John Sylvio? Is it Laney?*

"Yeh, SEEPU is alivening itself, dude. And Johnny must've alivened with it."

"SEEPU? What the hell are you talking about, Tom?"

"My superbrain. That's what Granny and me call it. Granny talks to it, and it's talking back." He wants me to come over, afraid to be there alone with his Frankenstein monster.

"I'm asleep. Why not get your dad in there if you need company? Or Granny?"

"Granny's no good. She thinks SEEPU is a fancy slot machine. My dad's threatening to smash up the whole kit and caboodle–after he heard I might blow up the gas station, dude."

"What a lot of nonsense," Cora says when I explain it

to her. "Is everyone going nuts or what? A livening itself, for goodness sake!"

The shed is black dark when I arrive, but for flickers of low incandescence rolling in combers across that living, humming beast, like luminous algae afloat on tropical waves. "You've got her running without impacting the power. How'd you do it?"

"Using a six volt car battery to power her, dude. I had too much juice going in. You got to think human brain–low voltage organic." Standing in the green glow of a console, LEDs pulsing along with the brain, Tom looks eerie, miniature Phillips head screwdriver piercing his nose septum, hair stuck up in an accidental silver Mohawk, looking the part of a scientific prodigy stepped out of a sci-fi comic, even his T-shirt futuristic, though not spun of metallic fiber as it appears to be, just filthy with oil and metal filings worked into the weave–the Bob Marley logo almost wholly effaced. "It's Johnny Sylvio. Definite," he says. "No mistaking his voice, dude."

"Look, Tom, first you offer to power up North America, then you tell me your CPU is resurrecting the dead. What can I say? You're beginning to worry me."

"Resurrection is the next logical step." He shrugs. "Think about it."

"Johnny Sylvio? Johnny was about as anti-hi-tech as they come. He epitomized lo-tech."

"Yeh, but super mechanical; he could fix anything.

He probably heard me down here cussing this thing out and decided to cross back over to help me out. Remember his lists of instructions? He left me one." Tom goes around one side and fiddles with a bank of printers until a piece of paper flies out. Appears to be a bulleted list, the print ghostly vague:

>> *Dont wurry nun....peeple gonna....*

>> *About that vultage situashun....then whut you....*

"I can't make it out at all. Spelling's about as bad as Johnny's was."

"It is Johnny! You'll see when he starts talking, dude." He runs around to the console and tweaks this and that, turns dials. The brain begins to slow, motors whirring deep inside, combers of light dimming, shakes something terrible, the whole building shakes with it, then, with a great tremble and commotion, it comes back up to speed. "There!" Tommy cries. "You hear him?"

All I hear is an odd, barely audible chatter–along with Granny's hoarse croak, so close I half jump out of my skin. "Lots of earthquakes in Japan. This one's a real doozie." She sits in a puddle on the floor–not, I hope, of her own making.

"Shouldn't Granny be in bed?" I ask.

But Tommy is beside himself, arms wide, dashing from side to side of the monster. "What are you doing inside my brain, dude? Y'r supposed to be freaking dead."

"I am dead," Granny says, "I just don't know it yet."

"Tommy...there's no one there. I can't make out a word."

He stops before me, his look of incredulity giving over to a revelation of disappointment and outrage (worries me that Granny's occasional bouts of fury might run in the family) as he perceives the gulf between his genius and my mediocrity—how I can't hear what he hears or see what he sees or know what he knows—and realizes how abjectly alone he is in this. I wish to comfort him, assure him I can hear. His face bunches toward frustrated tears.

What I do hear is a commotion of voices outside, like a gathering close of migratory geese, the sound swelling, assaulting the air. "What in hell is that?"

"The Jesus crew, dude. Hector, Myrna and them. They think I'm satanic." He giggles, relieved that, at least, I can hear something.

Stepping out of that tin shed into the first wan daylight, we are accosted by swaying, fist-waving chanters, like angry Christmas carolers or right-to-lifers around an abortion clinic. Hector Dario and his family, Myrna and Melinda Haney, Floria Davis (Noodles on a leash tied to her ankle) and her sister Evangeline, Idaho Butch, and Sippy Kroener, others of the parishioners down at Truth Tabernacle Church...out-of-towners from Haneysville. Encircling the place, holding hands and chanting. I'm afraid they will rush forward and trash Tommy's new brain and us in the bargain. *Thou shalt not fashion graven images,* they chant. While Tommy laughs and does a little jig and seems to be thoroughly enjoying himself. *Thou shalt not deny the Lord.* "It's alive," Tommy taunts them, "it's breathing, dude, it's thinking, it's smarter than God." I seize his arm. "Shut up!" Dumb kid! Can't he see these people mean business? *Beware the sin of pride.*

I warn Tommy it would be a bad idea to let on that his brain is resurrecting the dead. Not realizing that a columnist from *The Haneysville Daily News* already has. Of course, there's no newsprint these days, but *The News* manages to print a few column inches on old recycled shopping bags. (Though, as Cora says, "Who needs news anymore?" We know *The Forever War* is going on forever, the president's still president–after cancelling elections– the rich are getting richer, and the glaciers are melting.) Last night, columnist Cal Pierson reported that boy wonder Tommy Whitehead has constructed a super computer in a mechanic's shed behind his dad's gas station in Sluggards Creek, with computing power equivalent to a nine year old child's brain, and this superbrain has become a medium to communicate with the dead. Writing in his "Nowadays" column:

> *Tommy has no explanation for his super CPU's ability as a medium. "Except," he says,"that my machine is super-sensitive to electronic stimuli,*

dude. Maybe dead people leave electron traces behind, and it picks up on them. So imagine a human brain turned inside out and exposed to the air; it might pick up on all kinds of weird signals that is under the radar for a brain shielded by a skull."

Cal's column was printed on the back of napkins, text-messaged through the few cell phones still able to pick up a signal, left in public restroom stalls printed on individual sheets of TP. Doubtless, it helped to bring the Jesusers out.

Myrna Haney steps forward and seizes my arm. "I know you are not a Godly man, our Lawrence, but I always thought you were a good man. Now I see I was mistaken." Myrna has a habit of coming into your face and speaking rapidly, spittle bombarding your lips. "That *brain* is a blasphemy, an instrument of Satan. Yesterday, Sissy Jenson passed by and heard devils shrieking inside the shed."

"That's just Granny." Tommy laughs. "She had a pissed-off day yesterday."

"Besides," I say, "Sissy hears devils wherever she goes." Poor Sissy fried her brain on LSD years ago, before finding Jesus. She once saw Buddha sitting inside her refrigerator.

"The blood of Jesus or the blood of man, you must choose, our Lawrence. Sissy has made her choice. I suppose you have, too."

"Tommy's brain has nothing to do with Satan. It doesn't speak to the dead either. Trust me, that's a lot of rot. I think Tommy hopes to be the next Bill Gates or Steve Jobs, hopes to take artificial intelligence to the next level. You and I might not like it, but there's nothing evil about it."

Glen Whitehead emerges from the trailer beside the station, shouting at the protestors to get the hell off his property. "Goddamn stinking Jesus idiots. You, too, boy! You and your damned nonsense, y'r as bad as they are, bringing those nutjobs over here."

"It's blasphemy!" Hector Dario barks at me. "That monstrosity is fashioned in the image of man–like you said yourself–and man is fashioned in the image of God."

"Hardly, I think."

"The Book forbids it!" Furious, Hector makes strange signs in the air between us. "'Thou shalt make no graven image. Thou shalt not bow down to them, nor serve them.'"

Granny is scooting about in her wheelchair, waving hands at protestors, telling them to shoo, the meeting is over. Glen Whitehead has Tommy backed against the metal shed, he jabs a finger toward the humming brain inside. When his son tries to protest, Glen firms a huge mechanic's hand over his mouth. The boy sputters.

"Now look what you people have done," I whisper.

Hector Dario accosts the arguing men in full-on preaching mode, smelling blood. "'Turn you not unto idols, nor make to yourselves gods.' Deuteronomy 16:22. 'Neither shalt you set up any image which the Lord thy God hateth.' That in there is what it's talking about, boy."

"I hardly think the book refers to computers," I say. "There weren't many computers around in Moses' day."

"The pride of vanity has many faces." Hector is smug.

"I heard Jesus in there, too, dude." Tommy manages, looking ridiculous with his head pressed against the wall and mouth squeezed half shut.

"Tell the preacher to shuddup," Glen barks. "I'm talking to my son here."

"Burn them down!" shouts a protestor, holding up a sign proclaiming THEY SHALL KNOW HELLFIRE. Others take it up: "BURN THEM DOWN!"

Scares hell out of me, I'm here to tell, about where all this is headed–angry, vagrant energy moving in combers across the crowd, like flickers playing across the surface of Tommy's brain. Intuitive as any good family pet, Granny picks up on the ambient fear and anger. The protestor waving the "hellfire" sign screams out and slaps back at Granny's dentures, which have sprung free of her mouth and are clamped on his buttocks. Father and son turn to cheer. "Anyone lights a match, I start busting heads,"

Glen warns. "I want you turkeys off my place. Now!"

"Look folks," I insist, "why don't you let me talk to Tommy before you do anything rash. No need to start a war over this."

§

What do I hope for exactly? To get him to quit his project? Hardly. I enlist Laney Silverstein's help, picking her up that day in my pickup, troubled by the attraction I feel for her. Does she feel it, too? Can she know that Cora and I have decided not to marry...not yet? Seems hardly the time for exchanging vows. Laney is an attractive woman, stately almost, classy, her hair gone prematurely silver. Imagine a cross between Princess Di and Meryl Streep and you have it. I tell her of Hector's threat to demolish that shed to get at the computer, Glen's promise to throw the components into Sterner Gulch. "I'm afraid Tommy would go ballistic. No telling."

"I'm very fond of that boy," she says.

"So Cappy hoped you would marry Glen after she died?"

Laney laughs a small, swallowed hiccup. "Hopeless. Imagine! Glen and me!"

"His greasy, prying hands." Just slips out of me. I blush at the indiscretion; Laney looks out the window. These crazy times make you say stupid things.

The protestors are still there, keeping their distance. Hector sits in his patrol car across the road keeping an eye on things. No doubt he's told the dispatcher in Haneysville that they have "a situation that bears watching in Sluggards Creek." The "hellfire" signs have been replaced by others reading: THINK FAITHFUL and, of course, THE MIND IS THE DEVIL'S PLAY PEN.

We suggest Tommy will have to shut down his project for a time, until folks cool off. "You know, Tom, maybe they have a point. The last thing we need is a superbrain modeled in our own image, given the mess we've gotten ourselves into."

I've never seen Tommy looking as much like his dad, out-jutting chin, hair slicked back almost in the close-cropped, thinning DA that Glen wears, regarding us with arms folded across his chest. "It's a free country, dude," he protests. "Anyways, I'm near a breakthrough. My brain spoke it's first full sentence yesterday. Far cool, huh?"

"Spoke?" Laney asks.

"Yeh. Didn't really speak exactly. It gave this little quiver, then all the printers clicked on at once and spewed out pages all with the same line on them." He seizes one off a small stack and shows us:

Peanut butter is full discountable tomorrow

"Why, it's nonsense," Laney says.

"Sounds like Granny," I say. The old Gal right there in her chair, making those peculiar, side-twisted, open-mouthed grimaces of hers and sniffing the air like an animal. Remembering her dentures sunk into that man's ass, I back away, but she pursues me to stay within biting range.

"SEEPU isn't fully educated yet, dude; she's still learning the basics. She will learn to speak more profound thoughts. Your old caretaker, Johnny Sylvio, has been helping me out a lot."

"Whatever are you talking about?" Laney is scandalized.

"He alivened inside SEEPU's brain. I already told Lawrence. He's been advising me how to tweak it—from the inside, you know. John mastered cybernetics in maybe two weeks. The dude can't spell for shit, but he's like super smart."

"This is totally inappropriate, Tommy. John Sylvio is dead by his own hand. You shouldn't be taunting the unfortunate dead this way. I know your mother would agree. Perhaps Hector, Myrna, and your father have a point, you have unleashed an evil."

"I didn't ask Johnny in there. He just appeared, dude. I think it makes him happy to be helping out."

"Don't you dare! Tommy, I want you to shut that monster off right now."

Tommy and I exchange a look, surprised and intimidated by her anger. We've never seen Laney angry before. It's flat impressive.

"That's not fair," Tommy squawks. He can stand up to the Lord's angry minions, to his father, the entire town. But he's defenseless before his dead mother's friend.

"I warned you about this rebirthing business, Tom," I say. "You mix technology and mysticism and people get upset. I warned you!"

"It's going to kill Johnny again if I shut it off," he tells us, near panic.

Laney steps past him and makes straight for the control console and—as if she knows precisely what she is about—begins flipping off toggle switches, shutting the contraption down, while Tommy dances around her, jiggling hands in the air, and Granny circles behind, looking for a good angle to sink in her teeth. "SEEPU," he cries. "I might never get her started again."

"Of course you won't," Laney barks. "We are going to disassemble it." At that, Laney throws open the double doors and invites fresh air and light and chanting protestors inside the shed. Hector Dario and Myrna lead the attack. Folks tear off CPUs by main force and heave them onto a growing pile outside, rip out wiring, stomp circuit panels underfoot, furiously smiling, telling us what a great victory it is for The Lord, mouths blood red and joyful. Poor Tommy walks in furious circles outside, hands gripping his head, while his father stands grinning beside that growing mound of wire-hairy CPUs, slapping Jesusers on the back, telling them it is the first sensible thing they've done. "Call me a believer!"

"I built it for us," Tommy cries out at him, "for you, for our family. Not for Granny; it's too late for her, dude. I built it for you, Dad—a substitute brain for when you're gonna need it. 'Cause it's strong in the family." Hanging his thin, weepy face in Laney's, tears dripping off the miniature Phillips head screwdriver piercing his nose, and Granny weeps with him. "My dad always said he'd get Granny's brain rot some day. So I built him a new brain. Like an artificial leg, dude."

Laney stares at him, abashed, shocked really. Admonished.

Glen Whitehead pulls protestors outside, knocking components out of their hands. "Leave it!" he barks, silhouetted against the shed doorway in the semidark, regarding his son. "Well, goddamn. Don't that beat all? You hear that, people, my son built me a spare brain."

"I was gonna tell you," Tommy says, "when I got all the bugs worked out."

"Bugs...yeah!" Glen taps his head and grins at the boy, who grins back, a bit miserably, as does Granny. For an instant you can see the family resemblance. Then Glen steps forward and hugs the boy's head roughly against his chest. "I believe your mother would approve," he says softly. "I believe she'd be proud of you. Yeh, she'd like that a lot."

"Me, too," Laney snuffles, gone weepy herself. "I'm

sorry, Tom. Can you forgive me?"

Outside, protestors prod the pile of electronic components with their shoes, not sure what to do next, not looking at each other, all the outrage drained out of them. Myrna firms the wires she has begun to pull away back into place. Outside, she pats Tommy's back, her lips forming reluctant apology. Tommy's brain, what remains of it, barely embryonic, a small distraught pile of computer parts. Dense gray smoke from fires in the foothills lies like a fogbank on the horizon. When the sun sets, it will stain the western sky fiery red, the rich, rusty color of blood passed down from one generation to the next, connecting us all.

SPOOKS

Fred The Goat Man, as people called him, sat up in bed, his bare back against cold wood of the cabin wall. He smelled vaguely of goat, but Tia had come to love the smell, associating it with all things manly. Besides, she could not tell where the smell of goat gave over to the musk of Freddy himself. No doubt it was the same with her and the smell of crab. "It's weird how history comes full circle," Fred said. "We had Nam, now we got this current mess. We had floods in the seventies, water up to our asses, now we got nothing but rain."

It beat tirelessly against the shake roof, rattled window panes, knocked at cabin walls, a music Tia generally loved, but which had become tiresome after endless weeks of it. Mildew crept up cabin walls near the front door where paneling never fully dried; moss insinuated over the surface of anything left outside, coated the branches of trees so that everything looked fuzzy.

"It's like ten million trolls knocking to get in."

Freddy laughed. "I'd want to get in, too—you lying naked in here."

"You are in." Tia pulled the blanket up to her chin. Cold enough in the cabin that breath hung ghost-like in the air. Spook spirits, she thought. Why all this moisture should conjure up memories best left alone, she could not say. It seemed to do so for Freddy, too. Maybe the spirits of things past always hang in a vapor around us, but we don't notice them until they precipitate and slosh at our feet.

"It's so cruddy damp in here you could wring out the air," Tia said.

"Damn! Where'd they get you?" Freddy's eyes caught yellow light of the kerosene lamp, drifted over photos she had mounted on the ceiling—sixties flower children with unruly hair, John and Yoko full-frontally nude, dolphins leaping high out of the water, Richard Nixon giving the peace sign, and, quixotically, the world's foremost mountains: Everest, Annapurna, Lotse, Kilimanjaro, Whitney. *Life*—some philosopher said (she couldn't remember who)—*is about reaching the loftiest peaks and the lowest depths.* She believed that.

"Is Lorna milking this morning?" she asked. Sometimes Freddy dropped into moody silences, as if he had drifted back into some hurt or trouble which he kept to himself. War ghosts! He could fall away into days of moody silence, unavailable to her. She hated that. She licked his biceps, loved to lick his lean muscles. Even the cheeks of his face and butt rock hard. Was Lorna just an employee or was he sleeping with her, too? Hippy girl with long gray-blond hair, an oh-so-sweet face, hairy legs, and strong milking hands, too obviously naked under the baggy cotton dresses she wore. Freddy complained of it: "That girl's indecent when she milks. I warned her. But, damn! She flat pulls it!" At least she had to wear long underwear in this cold.

"Woops," he said, "milking time. Gotta go."

Four-thirty a.m. Not light out for two more hours— three in this rainy gloom. Some life. But he loved it. She stretched extravagantly. "I have another whole hour."

He was silhouetted against the lantern, looking down at her. She imagined him buck-naked going in to milk his goats, resting his face against their warm flanks. The image delighted her. She might suggest it—if not for Lorna. "Crabber," he teased. "Damn! Never thought I'd fall for a crabber."

"Goat Man!" She stuck out her tongue. "The cycles of the moon," she said while he slipped on jeans and boots, balancing on one foot, then the other, "zodiac and menstruation and hibernation and the seasons...more circles. All of nature circles back on itself."

"You still on that? Menstruation, hibernation, and the stars, that's some crew. Rain, too—used to be. Now it don't recycle no more; we got mud up to the *katookis*. The goats about had enough."

"Me, too," she said. "And the sixties! We've come full-circle there, too. Come back home to the sixties."

He regarded her quizzically and shook his head; his face, in the soft lantern glow, like a boy's face surprised into manhood—firmer, tempered by sorrow, dimpled chin and perpetual beard stubble. "Wasn't no home to me," he said. "No, ma'am. They about lit me up over there."

"Over fifty years ago. Can you believe it? How old's that make us, lover?"

"Makes me older than dirt. You weren't born yet. What in hell do you know about the damn sixties, girl? It's all just a dream to you."

"I do know. I've lived in the sixties all my life."

He was gone—out into the endless rain. His laughter left on the air behind, suspended inside a comic book balloon. Back home he would slosh through ankle-deep mud to the goat shed, light the big hurricane lantern which threw his long shadow against a wall, as he slapped the ass of one of his girls, prompting her up onto the milking stand, bleating joyfully—Tina or Woolsey or Moonlight or Frisco...twenty-six of them. She could hear the ping of yellow-rich milk into the scrubbed stainless-steel bucket over which his strong hands worked. Chiseled of stone, those hands, yet remarkably gentle. "Maybe it's his hands," she told the girls at work, who seemed fascinated by her attraction to a man who smelled of goats and was over thirty years her senior, a reclusive misanthrope, ill-tempered, quick to anger, rumored to have killed a man once in a bar fight in Ft. Bragg, holed up on twenty acres with his goats. "Freddy has genius hands." She sighed thinking of them and envied those goats. Besides, she might tell them but didn't, Fred's the most virile of men–seventy-one going on forty–he can ball all night, then rise before dawn and work a sixteen hour day without blinking. *Yeah, but he's crazy,* the girls would reply. *Makes two of us,* she might tell them.

Occasionally, she went to help him milk before her shift at the plant in Noyo Harbor. Not much use. She liked to think that pulling fragrant white Dungeness crab meat out of crab claws all day had given her strong hands, but they cramped up after two goats, with that pulling, wringing motion on the teats. "Hand exhaustion," she told him once. "It hurts."

He laughed, then went moody. "Try standing up all day with your arms raised."

He'd spent six months in a North Vietnamese prison camp before the peace accord was signed. Wouldn't talk about it. There were other sorrows, too, vague, shadowy mental ghouls which dogged him and occasionally howled in the night; she would sense him inwardly grimacing, hands over ears, though remaining stoical on the outside. "Who is Tina named after?" she once asked of the big brown Nubian with a white star between her eyes, his favorite goat.

"There will always be a 'Tina,'" he said merely. "This one dies, there'll be another."

And she knew it was time to stay quiet.

She also went over to keep an eye on Lorna, making sure she didn't feel too much at home in Fred's good graces, with her Jesus talk and God willings, all that damn sweetness. You could run Lorna down in a crosswalk and the girl would bless you for it. She would squat before the milking stand, skirt gathered between her knees, strong hands working dark teats, humming a hymn, while Tia watched, fascinated, trying to convince herself that Fred could not possibly be attracted to a girl with hairy calves and cherubic cheeks, knowing he couldn't help but be, docile as she was, so much like one of his "girls." Would there soon be a goat named "Lorna"? What about "Tia"?

At six a.m., Tia got dressed, sore and exhausted from their all-nighter. She would be asleep on her feet all day, ready to drop over onto the conveyor belt. Up front, light spilled out of the big house into the gloom, smoke didn't rise from the chimney but lay over flat in the rain and wind. Her daughter, Tangerine, would be asleep in the trundle bed before the big stone hearth. Tia must get her up for school, drop her off at the bus stop on her way to work, pick her up at school after work (it was a good shift that way).

"C'mon in, hon," Louise called, motioning to a pot of coffee on a trivet. Louise was coffee wealthy at a time when most people couldn't get the stuff. Before the troubles began, she had run the Coast Coffee Company in town and still had a back room full of coffee beans in burlap bags. Officially, she was Tia's landlord. Tia went first to rouse her daughter, hugging her close, rocking her awake. Tangerine smelled of shampoo and cozy sleep. "You didn't have to bathe her," she chided Louise.

"I love to bathe her. Don't we, hon? I get to tickle her toes."

Tangerine spasmed at the memory, curling up in Tia's arms. "When will it stop raining, Mommy?" she asked.

"I wish to hell I knew." Patting Tangerine's fanny, sending her to the bathroom.

The women sat before the huge fireplace, feet on the hearth, the blaze warming their cheeks, adding red highlights to the bun of black hair atop Louise's head. Always a happy little game to guess what ornament would adorn Louise's bun in the morning: a redtail hawk or sea gull feather, a pair of shiny white chopsticks, turtle shell comb. This morning it was bare. "Oh," she smiled, touching the bun, "I'm not dressed." Almost no gray, though Louise was pushing seventy. "I can't believe you two... wow! Nonstop for hours. Really something. Well, it's none of my business...still!"

"We're that obvious?"

"You are both pretty good shouters. I'm afraid your little cabin is going to jump off its foundation one of these days." Louise laughed.

"Another all-nighter." Tia burped a laugh. "Gawd, I can hardly walk."

"Lucky you. He must take Viagra-double-plus—wherever he'd find it."

"It's just Freddy."

"Goat Man. I guess. I had a fellah like that once, my sailor Sammy. Fantastic."

"People warn me I should watch out for him. I shouldn't trust him."

"People say a lot of things. Nosy little turds! What does anyone know of anyone else, really? Oh, they think they do! They're just jealous. Hey, I'm jealous, too! But I get Tangerine for the evening. We played Old Maid, then she went straight to bed."

"Thanks so much, Lou. I always feel guilty."

"For needing some pleasure in life? I thought you didn't believe in guilt."

"I don't, but it's sneaky. Like what do you get out of it, okay? Some cracked crab meat from time to time."

"Oh, horse piss! And you know it. I get the pleasure of her company, the pleasure of your pleasure. And if you want to send Goat Man over here when you're finished, that's okay, too. Trouble is, you're never finished."

They both laughed.

"No more double shifts, anyhow. I'm just scared they will lay us off soon. It's slow."

"Are they running out of crab, too?" Louise was alarmed, as always when it came to natural disaster, what she called *our slow holocaust.*

"Crabbers think there's too many dead fish on the bottom, they're not attracted to their baits anymore. Some think it's too murky, with all the mud and debris flooding out of the rivers. Nobody really knows. It's not for lack of rich people to eat crab."

"That's sure. What will you do?"

"Help Freddy or harvest shrooms."

"Why not? We could start a business."

§

People said the big house was haunted. Years back, just after turn of the century, it was a lodge frequented by tourists on excursions from San Francisco. They would hike to the headlands or into the pygmy forest or take horseback rides into the redwoods. Legend had it that the lodge burned down one night when a guest knocked over a kerosene lantern. The proprietor's wife, a young beauty eight months pregnant, burned up in the fire. Now she walked the property looking for her dead baby. Mrs. Sinclair, a quarter mile down Oliver Creek Road, had seen her. "Gave me such a fright I couldn't talk for a month." So had Bearclaw, who lived in the tiny cabin at edge of Louise's property. "She's like super-beautiful, like awesome. She looks like a hippie girl with like straight red hair down to her waist, like wearing a beaded white wedding gown with all these pleats. Her eyes like melt you down to your soul, super-sad cow's eyes or something." But Bearclaw took so many drugs you couldn't be sure she hadn't just seen her own reflection in the mirror.

"I seen her once," Freddy said, "only just her back walking away. Long red hair and this fancy white dress what glows in the dark. Spooky-dook. People say you won't see her until she approves having you for a neighbor."

"Bearclaw?" Tia asked. "She's one dicey neighbor, you ask me. Always coming in my cabin to steal food and grass—if I have any. The Woman In White has never shown herself to me, so I guess she doesn't approve."

"Oh, Bearclaw's okay. She's a fruitcake, but harmless. Kind of proves your theory about the sixties coming 'round again. Only she thinks it never left."

So had he slept with Bearclaw, too? More hauntings. These woods, with their vagrant fogs and wide, cathedral-like naves under the redwoods, far-off moan of fog horns in the night, and sudden chills, were prone to them. "Everyone up here is haunted by something," Louise said. "That's why we came here." Louise told you right off what haunted her. "My nephew, who I raised up as my own son after his mom died of cancer, was murdered by our military over there. They sent him into battle without proper equipment." She led local protests against *The Forever War* until people lost interest. "A soul rent by tragedy needs to heal, just as the body does. It won't heal just anywhere," Louise said. "You need to go to one of the earth's chakras where nature can work its magic. Like here in the redwoods."

But could it work its magic anymore, with the incessant rain, fog horns moaning not just at night but constantly, tubercular fogs haunting aisles between the big trees, frogs popping out of drains, Fred's goats getting hoof rot, Bearclaw lying under a sleeping bag in her cold, damp, unhealthy shack, too depressed to get out of bed, no dry firewood to burn, Little River swollen as broad as the Columbia...all of it? The days of sunshine angling down through lacy redwood boughs behind her cabin, tiny trillium and day lilies gaily mixed with maidenhair ferns across the forest floor, morning air freshly scrubbed seemed gone forever–those lovely days when they still had sun.

"Do you miss him terribly?" Tia asked of Louise's adopted son.

"Half my memories are still too painful to remember all these years later." Laugh lines at her mouth tautened by grief. "Freddy's, too. He used to speak to me about his panics. He'd be right back in battle again, could hear the dustoffs, as he calls them, circling above the LZ with guns blazing, poor Fred hunkered down in the jungle, waiting to carry some poor screaming wounded boy out to the medevac. One night he broke out through his bedroom window to escape the house. My hauntings are nothing to his. Maybe he's gotten over them now. Do you think?"

"Panics maybe. Now he has quiet attacks...hauntings."

"What about you, dear? What brings you here? You've never told me."

"It's not about memories," Tia said, "but the ones I won't have. You could say I've lost what I'm never going to find, Tangerine either." It was at least partly true.

Louise nodded solemnly. "You mean the mess we're in?"

"Although I'm not really sure you can lose what you never had," Tia said.

"Sure. You can lose hope. That's the worst loss of all."

"I was losing it. Living in L.A., a baby girl, and scared about where we were headed, scared they were going to use a dirty bomb or we'd run out of water or the riots would spread. People getting weird. I wanted a brighter future for my baby, a guy I could trust."

"Ahhh, so there's a guy involved? I thought so."

Tia ignored her question. "Somebody told me about up here!" She shrugged.

"All those years ago, Jeff and I used to talk about coming here, used to plan—" Louise gripped her eyes with thumb and forefinger and waved it off. "Healing takes a long time."

"What they say about the Lady In White, I believe it. Being cheated of the life you will never have—or your baby—could haunt you right up out of the ground."

"Well, I've not seen her," Louise said, "and she supposedly lives in this house. I guess I still have some healing to do. She's attracted to calm souls."

Once, you couldn't stay down for long on the coast: just take a walk in the redwoods or go out and stand on the headlands, which shook with waves freight-training into rocks at their base. The danger was you could go to sleep here, hopes and memories mixed together in a thick mist which washed over your senses and numbed you. People were swallowed up in it and lost.

§

Sometimes Freddy just showed up, knocking at her door, and she must tell him, "Not tonight, lover." He never stayed to dinner. "I'm not a sit-down eater." So she had never broken bread with him—except for snacks of goats' cheese and soda crackers he brought over for all night stands. It made her uneasy not to sit down at table with him. I will not, she promised herself, be one of those loose mamas who beds my daughter down in the room where I entertain my man. That's bullshit. Fred threw

Tangerine long-eyed, resentful looks at such times. Tia wished he would warm to her. "Think of her as one of your goats," she told him, "something to protect."

"I prefer not to."

Although he did name a gentle orange-brown Nubian with black socks and ears after Tangerine. "Matches her coloring," he said.

He went home, on these occasions, to his goats and shortwave radio, fascinated by inclement weather reports from around the globe and news of social unrest, but changing stations when news of *The Forever War* came on. What people did not understand about Fred was that he despised violence and wished only to avoid it.

Occasionally, Sunday mornings after milking, he came to have coffee with Louise and Tia, bringing a warm bottle of goat's milk with a crust of cream atop. "Put that on the girl's cereal, you want her to be smart." He motioned roughly at Tangerine, who sat talking to herself at the kitchen table, dabbling at thickening oatmeal with her big spoon.

"I don't like goat's milk, Goat Man," Tangerine called to them.

"He's Uncle Freddy to you, young lady," Tia scolded.

"Naw, it don't bother me none," he said. "Besides, I am the goat man."

"Goat Man...Goat Man..." Tangerine grinning so impishly she brought a guffaw from Louise. "Are you my mommy's boyfriend, Mr. Goat Man?"

"I guess you better ask her."

"Freddy's a very dear friend, okay?" Tia changed the subject. "I heard knocking again last night two sides of the cabin. Didn't we, honey babe? High up, so it can't be a skunk."

"Wooh-wooh-wooh." Fred spooked fingers at her, the hint of a smile like a thin new moon in his eyes.

"Truly, Freddy. Tap-tap, tap-tap...regular, like somebody trying to get in. Scary."

"We did," Tangerine cried, "honest!" She had paved the table around her with oatmeal cement.

"Maybe it was me," Fred said. Tangerine appeared beside his chair, climbed over the arm and dropped into Fred's lap; he didn't protest.

"I went outside to look, but I didn't see anything."

"Was that smart?" Louise asked. "Anyone could be wandering about these woods."

"What's really weird is when I was outside the cabin I heard the knocking inside."

"You mean in the walls?" Fred curious now. He lifted Tangerine off his lap and placed her gingerly on her feet. "Rats, might be."

"Not rats. It's The Woman In White. She's not ready to show herself to me yet, but she wants me to know she's there. Maybe came to warn me about something."

"About me maybe." Fred grinned.

"I think she wants to know if she can trust me. I don't think she means us any harm."

"Hell!" Fred laughed. "Why's a ghost need to trust anybody? It's us has to trust them. And good luck." He'd gone suddenly moody.

"I believe if you accept them they go away. They're looking for acknowledgment. Right now she's testing me, seeing if I will accept her. I'm trying."

"That's bullshit," Fred snapped, as if he knew something about the subject. "They go away when they're good and ready. Period. Isn't a damn nothing you got to say about it."

"Well, I dunno," Louise said. "I think Tia's right. We have to learn to accept our ghosts."

"I heard enough." Fred stood quickly up, then dropped to a knee on the floor and gripped Tangerine's shoulders in his big hands, so that she cried out and Tia asked what he thought he was doing. "Mix you a little honey in that goat cream and mix that in your mush; it'll go down real easy." He took her hand and led her to the kitchen and did just that, beating the concoction nearly to the consistency of whipped cream. Tangerine lit up on tasting it. "It's tasty," she cried, and dug into her oatmeal. Fred stuck his head back in the main room. "It's some things you can't never accept!" He turned on a heel and was gone.

"Now, he's pissed off." Tia sighed. "I won't see him

for weeks."

"Oh hell! I didn't mean to upset him, hon."

"You didn't upset him. It's his spooks, whatever happened in the war...and after. Some chick named Tina. It's like he's in a rut, you know: Tina and Tia. You never know what's going to set him off. Anything...nothing. All those cruddy spooks!"

"Yeh, they'll get you."

"I thought you said we came up here to escape them."

"It doesn't mean they cooperate."

Much of that week The Woman In White came knocking. She started down low by the cabin door and worked her way up to the rafters on the far side of the cabin, tapped lightly at the windows, which spooked Tangerine out most. "Do you think she wants to steal me," she asked the darkness one night, her voice so small in the corner that Tia got right out of bed and went to her. Funny what kids pick up from adult conversations: surely she'd overheard something about The Woman In White being bereft and in search of her lost unborn.

"Don't be silly. She's saying hello. It's kind of like a test, sweetheart, a spelling test or arithmetic; if we get the right answer she will reward us with a real sit down visit. I think so, anyway."

"What's the right answer?"

"I don't know yet." Tia was on her knees on the cold floor, her head snuggled beside her daughter's on the pillow.

It amazed her that, while the rest of the world reeked of sour dampness, her daughter smelled like freshly-baked bread. "It's like a quiz, a learning test. I'm going to leave the kerosene lamp on so you won't be scared."

Shortly after she lit it, a puff of errant wind blew it out, did so again when she relit it. An invading breeze? As the knocking might be some aberrant physics of red-wood shakes swollen with moisture to the point of agony or a night bird pecking for insects or raindrops organized in thumping clusters. Or some ugliness that wanted in, that slow holocaust in the world beyond creeping up on their sanctuary on the north coast. In that moment, she was back on that rickety fire escape in L.A., while Syd raged through the apartment inside, kicking over furniture, cursing her and threatening to kick her ass. She stood stock still, her back hugging the brick wall, clutching baby Tangerine to breast, terrified she would start crying. The slightest movement would get the fire escape creaking agony on loose bolts anchoring it to the wall. She hummed softly over her daughter (though her heaving chest betrayed her). Any moment he might come through the window with his pistol. One of these days, he would find some excuse—the thermostat set too high or no beer in the fridge—and would execute her. Maybe Tangy, too.

Tia tried to stay calm. On the third night, she heard a slither-whisper high overhead; photos and clippings she had mounted to the ceiling began to rain down on her; one hit the bed table with the unmistakable whock of heavy paper landing on edge, a staple bounced off her forehead. Tia seized the flashlight from the bed table; in its beam she watched staples pull slowly and deliberately out of the collage she had stapled to wood paneling, as if invisible pliers extracted them. She couldn't believe her eyes. The heavy picture of Mt. Kilimanjaro (where it is said to rain almost incessantly on lower slopes), mounted on heavy cardstock, pulled free corner by corner and plunged in a zigzagging swoop to clunk against Tia's head. My God! A poltergeist! She had a poltergeist.

She gathered Tangerine up in her arms and fled to the big house, calling upstairs as she went in, "We're haunted, Louise. Come look! We have a poltergeist!" Not thinking until too late that she would give poor Lou the fright of her life, barging in that way middle of the night. Louise appeared at the upstairs balcony, struggling into her robe, hair akimbo, looking tired and frightened. "What is it, dear?" Relieved to hear it was only a ghost. Sadly, by the time they ran back to the cabin, barefoot through mud, the poltergeist had concluded its work. Pictures and staples lay scattered everywhere. For an instant Louise regarded her friend dubiously.

"You actually saw them?"

"Staples pulling out one by one, I watched." Tia picked up a staple, expecting it to be hot or preternaturally cold. It was just a staple. She handed it to Louise.

"Did you see it, too, darling?" Lou asked Tangerine.

"No." Tangerine was hugging her mother's waist.

"Not that I doubt you," Louise said. "It's just, you know, peculiar. Why would it—"

"It's The Lady In White, she wants me out. Don't you see? I believe she's jealous. She died too young and she feels cheated. I feel sorry for her. Still...!"

"Yes, it is odd—" Louise squatted on the floor to inspect the fallen pictures. "Why, the staples have pulled completely free, none left in the paper at all. Typically, there would be."

"There isn't anything typical about it. So you really don't believe me?"

"Of course I do. But, you know, knocking, lamps blown out, pictures pulled out of the wall, it's very odd."

"How else can she express herself?"

"I suppose so. Do you think she's gone?" Louise's eyes walling white as they traversed the room.

Tia dropped suddenly on her daughter's bed and pulled Tangerine onto her lap. "I think I know what this is about. It's not about a young mother burning up in a guest lodge...not only. It's about something else."

Louise sat down beside her. She looked fatigued and old, hair hung down in scraps over her ears, much grayer than you realized it was when swept up in a bun; she looked naked without her hawk feathers, her breasts sagged inside the nightgown, wrinkles deeply incised above her lips. "What is it about?" she asked. "Not about Freddy, is it?"

"Not about Freddy, no." Tia about to tell Lou about her waking nightmares—Syd stalking through the apartment, waving his gun, that time he'd broken her arm—but at that instant the kerosene lamp whooshed out. There was an actual whisper, as of breath exhaled. No apparent draft in the room. "Come in," Louise spoke in the darkness. "You're welcome here. Isn't she, Tia?"

"Some things aren't welcome," Tia insisted. "You must agree to leave them outside."

§

Because when the world comes unglued people come unglued with it, because even the most public tragedy is always personal—no helping it—because nothing happens in a vacuum, because Tia had not shared all her spooks with her ghost coast friends, who struggled to deal with their own—Freddy, Lou, the gals at work—because she understood a principle that remained operative even in this parlous time when everyone was in peril: people avoid those who suffer misfortune, fearing it will rub off on them. Had The Woman In White not perished in that fire but survived, her baby dead, her body covered in hideous burns, she would be a pariah rather than an object of fascination, avoided by neighbors and friends who could not bear her misfortune. Maybe this is human nature, maybe forgivable, but then Mother Nature might be forgiven the nonstop rain, too; it was perfectly natural. Nonetheless, people had come to despise it. So Tia kept her secret misfortune to herself.

Had The Woman In White come to warn her that Syd had discovered where she was? Was he on his way to make good on a promise he hadn't been able to fulfill in L.A. before Tia fled? Was he on the coast? And that tragic lady wished to alert her to it? Or was this ghost rain simply washing spooks out of hiding? The Woman In White risen from her grave on ground water that had fully saturated the earth and turned every low place marshy, reawakened artesian springs, swelled rivers to torrents that reached the ridge tops and washed everything within reach out to sea. There were reports of entire cemeteries washing out, coffins bobbing along swollen creeks. It was not easy to sort reality from dream in such surreal weather. Maybe everyone suffered their private ghosts more acutely at such times. Then, too, maybe The Woman In White had not come with a warning but simply to pay a visit. Tia couldn't be sure.

Lorna stopped by one evening at dusk. She sat in a wicker chair, her long dress dripping water on the floor, her hair a soggy orange mop. It seemed for a time she wouldn't speak but just sit there dripping. Tia made her a cup of chamomile tea; Lorna cradled it in both hands as if coveting the cup's warmth, letting the steam rise up into her down-turned face. The way she looked in the lantern light reminded Tia of a van Gogh painting, "The Potato Eaters, " raw-faced peasants seated around a table. Surely she had come by for some reason. Perhaps a warning of her own.

"How's Freddy?" Tia asked. "How are the goats?"

Lorna looked up then, transformed from sodden and taciturn to angelic, pinched cheeks and agate-bright eyes. "That's what I wanted to tell you—"

"Is Freddy all right?"

Lorna shook her head, then nodded "yes," as if she couldn't decide. "I'm praying for him. Tina got real sick, pneumonia or something, and no more antibiotics, so we're milking and he like sits there muttering like he does...war stuff, so he yells, 'Watch out, get out of it! Get to the LZ!' or something, looking at me like crazy, and he runs outside into the rain."

"When did this happen?"

"This morning. So I like want to finish milking, you know, and go home, God willing, 'cause he scares me when he's like that. So I ask Jesus to give my fingers like the strength to hurry up and finish, and all of the sudden he comes back, like he has a rifle or something and he's ducking behind stalls looking around, bent over and sneaking from one to another, then he sees me and he like stands up straight and he's pointing the gun at me and I'm really scared, you know, praying real hard—" She cut off and sipped the tea, looking vaguely about.

"That's all, Lorna?"

"What? No. There's more." Nodding and looking at Tia, her eyes half-mad.

"You want to tell me?" Tia asked gently.

"So he's like walking...with the gun, you know, pointed or something right at me, and his eyes are just like okay...crazy. 'It's me,' I say, 'me, Lorna,' 'cause I don't think he knows who I am, really. 'God willing,' I say, 'please don't kill me,' I say. He has like the barrel, you know, grinding into my head or something, and I feel like the Lord has forsaken me, I want to think, want to be calm, I want to pray, I want to prepare myself in the proper way, I want to believe...but like I can't, that's the awful part. I forsook Jesus at that very moment."

"Nonsense, Lorna. You were scared is all. I'm scared just to hear you tell it."

"Then all of the sudden he swings away and there is this really loud blast right in my ear and I think he killed me or something. I'm still like wondering if he did right now, my ears are still like ringing, I feel weird... but then I realize he shot Tina—God forbid!—he must've seen like a movement in her stall or something and he swung around and shot her...bam! Then he walks over and shoots her again...in the head."

"Ohhh Gawd. Not Tina. Oh shit. How is he? How is Fred now?"

"See like that's what is so weird: like he's in a dream and the gunshot woke him up or something. He puts the gun up and stoops down on a knee and puts his ear against Tina's chest, then just hugs her and lets go a big sob, stands up like and dusts off his hands, 'So that's done,' he says, just all like Freddy again. He's okay. Just, what you call it, temporary insanity or something, devil possession, evil spirits. Satan entered his body then he left again. This tea is like really good."

"You can't go back over there, you realize, Lorna."

Lorna shook her head profoundly, then nodded again. "I was just there. He's fine. But I wanted to tell you: he's really hurting over Tina, he needs God's blessing right now and the blessing of his friends, we need to pray for him."

Tia nodded. Strange how the very thing that made you sympathize with a person could also make you fear them. Spooks. Posttraumatic stress. She understood it all too well. Understood, too, that a violent man is a man to be avoided.

She felt afraid of Freddy for the first time, absolutely spooked. Perhaps it was true what they said about his violent nature. For the first time, she locked her cabin door at night. She suffered terror spells in those days following, dreamed of standing on a rickety fire escape that pulled free of the wall and yawned out over the street, and she couldn't tell whether it was Syd or Freddy stomping through the apartment, firing off shots. She woke in violent sweats, the sheet soaked beneath her. Tia dreamed that The Woman In White was sleeping with Fred, the unborn who had burned up in the fire was Freddy's daughter, and he was 140 years old. The Woman had an iconic face much like Lorna's, the heavenly face of a Byzantine Virgin Mary. When she came in lovemaking, she cried out, "God be praised" or "Bless our union or something." Though she was beautiful, she smelled of mildew, goats and sweat (they bathed rarely back then); like Lorna, she didn't shave her legs. Watching those two go at it from the foot of the bed, Tia saw that the bottoms of their bare feet were filthy, and she had a weird, unnatural desire to wash them with a rag.

"Some dreams need cleaning up," she told Louise over coffee next morning.

"Oh, I know." Lou looked vaguely off. "I have a recurrent dream of riding in that half-track with Jeffrey when it hits the land mine, and I must clean up the mess after, reattach the limbs of platoon members on their rightful owners...and I can't sort them out. Just awful."

"My God!" Tia stared at her, regretting she'd mentioned dreams at all.

Lou waved a dismissive hand. "It's her again? More knocking, dear?"

"Worse! She's invaded my dreams. I'd prefer to keep her on the outside. No telling what mischief she will cause in my head."

"Oh, horse piss," Louise said. "You might talk to her, ask her what she wants."

"I know what she wants. At first, I thought she wanted Freddy and my daughter, but she's spooking him, too. She wants to steal our peace of mind, wants to turn loose the past on us and spook us good. We have to watch out for her."

"I hate to burst your bubble, but I think she wants to come inside is all. I think she's miserable out in the rain and cold. Who wouldn't be? Even the dead are popping up out of the soggy ground, sick of this rain. She used to be content to walk in the moonlight before it started raining nonstop; she didn't bother us back then."

"She knows she can come inside any time she likes if she'll behave herself and not pull shenanigans, tear things off walls, not bring the grotty past along with her. It's not just me she's after. Fred shot Tina yesterday."

"Oh, no. He loved that goat."

"Love is no protection. It makes us an easier target. He's doing PTSD again. Badly. I'd like to be there for him now, but not—" She stared ahead into the fire, wet wood smoldering more than burning, stinking of wet ashes.

"Not what, dear? You said...*But not*...What?"

"Not, you know, as someone I left behind in L.A. I

can't go back there. Not him! Not as a ghost. Just Freddy."

"Is there something you need to tell me?" Lou asked.

"I don't know if I'd put it that way."

"Listen, missy—" Lou reached across table to tap Tia's wrist with a finger "–there are things you learn in hoary old age. One of them is that we are all on this ark together. Isolation is horse piss, we're none of us isolated, what affects one affects us all. This weather insanity teaches us that. If something's weighing on you, you may need another pair of arms to help lift it off."

Tia nodded. "You think maybe *she*'s come to help me do the lifting, The Woman In White? She doesn't want other ghosts invading her space and she's out to chase them off? Why won't she show herself?"

"It doesn't work like that. You must invite her in. Think of her as yourself just after you escaped L.A.– scared, lonely, wanting safe harbor, needing healing."

"How do you know so much about ghosts?"

"We've had a lot of practice. Freddy's had decades, for crap's sake, surrounded by his Nubian spooks."

Tia regarded her friend, the warm brown eyes haloed by what Tangerine called her "flying saucers"–luminous coronas surrounding the irises like Saturn's rings. "Do you suppose *he* started that fire, *he* meant to burn her up in that lodge, her and her baby? Her husband did, I mean. And she knows I will understand? I will believe a man capable of that?"

Louise looked at her a long time without answering. She got up to get the coffee pot, asked very quietly, "More, dear?" Then sat again and sipped out of her own cup, looked out the high clerestory windows at a sky that was the color of the dark ocean during a storm, incredible that any light leaked through the dense humidity. "It looks like it sucked up all the oceans on earth," she said at last, "and the creatures in them. Soon it will be raining whales and fishes." Then her eyes flashed over to regard Tia, her saucers lit up, ready to take flight. "I know *he* didn't do that to you, whoever *he* is. Something else maybe, not that."

"What do you know about it?" Tia snapped. "He would have if I'd given him a chance. He was crazy enough, mean enough. But I got out of there."

"Is Tangerine his child?"

"No! She's mine!"

Louise nodded. "He won't find you here," she promised. "Some day maybe you'll tell me about it."

§

That night Fred came knocking. At first, Tia thought it was The Woman In White. But then he called from outside, "I shot my favorite goat yesterday. I killed my best friend."

Tia scrambled out of bed, gathered her sleepy daugh-

ter up in her arms and tiptoed to the window at rear of
the cabin, firming a hand over Tangerine's mouth when
she whimpered, as she'd done years ago when she heard
Syd outside the apartment door, drunk and belligerent,
trying to fit his key in the lock, and climbed out that
window onto the fire escape. Rain plashed brassily into
standing water outside as if they were surrounded by
a lake. The window frame swollen shut so she couldn't
open it. "It's just Freddy," Tangy whispered. "It's wet outside, Mama." Freddy pounded on the cabin door. "Open
up! It's wetter than duck piss out here." Just Freddy.
Nothing more.

　　"Goat Man!" Tangerine cried, when Tia opened the
door.

　　"No more," he said, standing forlorn in a rain slicker,
water pouring off the rim of his cowboy hat so his face
was hidden behind a veil that cascaded down over his
shoulders. "Ain't 'Goat Man' no more. I become 'Ghost
Man' now." He looked bereft, laugh lines at his eyes deeply eroded. Seeing him this way, Tia couldn't help think
that the old axiom had been stood on its head with the
topsy-turvy weather. Instead of repulsed, she was attracted by his misery, as her own near admission that she was
haunted by a violent past had melted Lou's heart earlier.
No doubt if The Woman In White appeared disfigured
before them they would find her more attractive than if
she possessed legendary beauty.

"It was an accident," Fred said, then shook his head. "Wasn't no accident. Poor gal was suffering something terrible, she needed to be put out of her misery; I told myself I couldn't do it, but then I blacked out and done it. Woke up and she was dead. It's over and done now. They took what they wanted from me and went away."

"Your spooks did?" she asked.

"They pulled that trigger. Still..." He unzipped the tent-like rain slicker and pulled out an M-16 rifle.

Tia leapt back, seizing Tangerine and turning away from Fred to shield her.

"Look...look here!" He placed the gun on the floor. "It's okay. I couldn't never hurt you or the girl. What you take me for? Still, I don't want it on my place. I want you to hide it somewheres for me. It ain't loaded or nothing, just a damn dead hunka iron."

Tia had turned back around to face him. Just Freddy, forlorn and heartbroken, as if all the grief of a grief-haunted life had him cornered, his eyes beseeching and frightened.

"Afraid I might shoot more of my girls. I black out again that way, I might. There's some spooks just want to pull things off the wall and scare you, others has a bigger appetite. They'll eat everything you love if you let them. Hide it." He zipped the slicker up again and turned away to the door. But Tia lay a hand on his shoulder and asked him to stay.

"They aren't going to eat me," she insisted.

She wanted Fred's touch, wanted to share his pain, so took her daughter up front and asked if Lou could baby-sit. His strong hands moved over her body, as she imagined they did over goat Tina, petting her, thanking her, asking forgiveness. Mostly they lay together. He had little vigor; maybe true that he wasn't Goat Man anymore—not for a time. He took from her and was grateful. "Your hippies is gone," he said when finally he noticed the empty ceiling. When The Woman In White began knocking on cabin walls, Fred knocked back, laughing, enjoying the game. He pursued her around the cabin to the door, looking sprightly and goatish, his firm white butt contrasting his dark arms and neck, hair clinging tight as a pelt to his skull. Throwing Tia a glance of mock alarm when something scrabbled at the door. Springing away when the door opened with a long, requisite creak. "Holy shit!" he cried. "What's that?" Then gathered his wits. "Well, close the door if you're coming in. It's cold outside." The door closed. Fred stood straight up and stared, then hurriedly stepped into his pants, keeping his back turned to where he imagined the intruder to be. "Time for me to go home to my goats," he muttered.

"I thought you would spend the night." Tia scarcely aware she had spoken, staring at this numen, this guest from another time and plane. Not that she actually saw her, certainly not the beautiful woman in a long white flowing dress that Bearclaw and neighbors described, with red hair to her waist. Just a vague disturbance of the air, though you could follow her progress about the room, a shadow moving across shadows.

"I ain't used to screwing with company in the room," Fred said, "especially if it's company I can't see. Besides," he said, "I had enough of haunts for a while."

Oh, yes, we are used to it, Tia was thinking: we always have company in the room when we make love, our ghosts. Though we've never admitted it. And this, perhaps, was no personal spook, rather communal, one they all shared in common. Not very spooky, really, even calming. Seemingly not to Fred; he was out the door into the wet night.

"Don't take it personally," Tia said when he'd gone. "He's had a rough time. Maybe guys aren't comfortable in your presence. I'm glad you finally came inside. You can sleep on the cot tonight. Tangerine is up front at Lou's, but you likely already knew that."

Remarkably, at that moment, instead of feeling haunted, frightened, any of what you were supposed to feel in a ghostly presence, Tia felt liberated. She felt blessed—as Lorna would say—honored that The Woman In White should pay her a visit, that she had found the right answer. She felt strangely freed from her L.A. spooks, *him*, all the fears and dangers she had left behind in the city.

"I am going to have a lot of questions for you," she

said. "Not now...eventually. I think we have a lot in common. Actually, I think you have much in common with all of us. Tomorrow morning I'll take you up front to meet Lou...if you want. I think you're going to like her. Freddy, too, eventually. And if you have any pull at all with The Powers That Be," she said before falling off to sleep, "I wonder if you might suggest that they turn off the spigot for a while. Good Lord, anyway! It's making everyone crazy."

Her sleep was as deep and sound as it usually was not on those active nights when Fred came to visit, the sleep as erotic and fulfilling as sex. She woke with no shadow of suggestion that The Woman In White had been there. But didn't wake to sunshine as she dreamed she would, rather to a downpour so thunderous that she dreamed near waking that she was asleep on a subway platform. She stripped and ran outside to shower in the rain, sudsing herself up, nearly enjoying the rain's caress, despite the cold. Just finishing her rinse off when the rain stopped flat as if someone had turned off the tap. For a moment there was absolute silence. No distant moan of fog horns...nothing. Then the pitter-patter of water dripping from branches and eaves, the first twittering of birds.

By the time she went up front for her daughter, the cloud cover had begun to fray and come apart, rays of sunshine broke through, ghostly at first, ethereal, then solid and magnificent pathways of light. Louise ran out of the big house with Tangerine, both cheering, their arms thrown in the air, Tangerine bleating, "Wow-wow-wow, it stopped." Jays and nutcrackers and crows answered her, emerging all at once from wherever birds hide in stormy weather, raising their songs of joyful exorcism.

FLY-BITTEN

Lately, we have been plagued by flies, not just common house flies but carrion flies, fat-bodied, metallic bluebottles and viridescent greenbottles, typically associated with death. They crawl into our eyes and mouths and darken the walls of houses. Nearby mountains shimmer under their assault. Disgusting little beasts, a hungry, demonic intelligence behind their honeycomb eyes. "Waiting for us to die," Cora says, believing them forerunners of an alien invasion. "Why shouldn't space invaders be intelligent insects rather than hulking monsters with octopus arms and exposed brains?"

I ask Sinclair what he makes of them. "They thrive on corpses, don't they, Jack? Where are all the corpses?"

"They're after the Earth's corpse," he says, "species die-off and environmental holocaust."

The idea chills me: flies born from the Earth's corpse! But I tell him that's a lot of hooey.

Myrna Haney says they're a sign that The Beast reigns on earth, the end of days is at hand–Beelzebub, Lord of the Flies, and all. Myrna typical. The Jesus crowd is near ecstatic over their advent, anyway, having long awaited them.

My own theory: it's one of those mass hatches, like locusts or cicadas, that come once every so many years. Most of us haven't lived here long enough to remember the last fly hatch, and natives are too loopy to remember (this is California, after all). It's like the Passover plagues in Exodus. How could captive Jews new to Egypt know that such plagues were not providential but a local manifestation of nature's periodic extravagance? We don't need gods and space aliens to explain such wonders.

Along with the flies has come a more troubling plague. People have begun avoiding each other. Few folks showed up at our last Sluggards Creek community dinner, and those who did were sour and argumentative. Cora believes it's due to fires burning in the mountains, floods up north, economic woes, and *The Forever War*. "In hard times we avoid each other," she says, "since other people remind us of our own troubles."

"That's ridiculous. We should find comfort in one another during tough times."

Her lips turn out, rebukingly purple. "Grow up, Lawr! Don't be a simp."

"If it's grown-up to be meanspirited, then I prefer to remain a child."

"That should be easy." She winks unpleasantly.

Soon it becomes obvious that Cora is avoiding me. I come out with cups of morning coffee—not coffee, we have no coffee, but roast manzanita berries which I steep in hot water—and she at once excuses herself to go out to her pottery shed. "Okay, I'll come out with you," I say.

"No, Lawr. I have a lot of work to do today."

I might ask why, given cancelled craft shows and nobody buying pots anymore. Instead, I sit alone out back under the chinaberry trees sipping my ersatz coffee—well, not outside exactly, given the damned flies, but under the screened-in grape arbor. Is Cora tired of me? Am I tired of her? Are we all fed up with each other, the human condition? Are we going misanthropic, given the mess we've made of things? What rot! I decide to do something nice for Cora, take her to dinner at Chez Amie. See if I can lay my hands on some real coffee.

I drive down to Benson's QuikMart. There's a sign scrawled with a felt-tip pen across plate glass windows: WHATEVER YOU WANT, WE DON'T HAVE IT!

I chuckle going in. "That's one damn poor advertisement for a quikmart, Benson."

"What the hell do you want?" he demands.

I step back in alarm. "Hey...it's me! Your old friend Lawrence! Remember me? I brought you a load of firewood last week. What's the matter with everyone?"

"That was last week," he says gruffly. "This is now. Get used to it."

"Anyway, you got lots of stuff in here. Canned goods—pears in nectar, cream of okra soup, refried beans." I read labels on the shelves. "Got any coffee stashed away somewhere, maybe?"

"Hah! No coffee, no cigarettes, no beer, no Coke, no corn chips. That's fifty percent of my business gone! No lottery tickets neither."

"A shame we lost the lottery. Real shame."

He comes around the counter wielding a fly swatter and sets to smacking me about the head and shoulders. I duck away, covering my face. "What inna hell, Benson?"

"Damn fool! You brought bluebottles in with you. They'll get at my lunch meat."

"What lunch meat?" I retreat down an aisle, pointing at the empty butcher case in back, and get out of there. Benson, for crissake! Most civic-minded man I know. Used to be! What's up?

So I'm exiting the parking lot—in a huff—when old Juan Alverro passes in his dilapidated Ford pickup, a hand on his horn, shaking a fist at me. "What the hell, you old fool? I didn't even begin to cut you off." I pull onto the empty road behind him; Juan screeches over on the shoulder and leaps out of his cab, cursing in Spanglish and throwing rocks at me. One clatters about in my pickup bed as I floorboard past. Imagine it! Soft-spoken Juan Alverro, most inoffensive of men, always first to volunteer for a search party when a hiker goes missing in the mountains, heaving rocks at passing cars. Amazing! You might expect anonymous hostility down in the flatlands and cities, road rage and such, but up here in Sluggards Creek we all know each other.

I stop at Chez Amie, fearing that if Carlie and Margie have caught this madness we are in deep shit. Most kind-hearted people I know, those two. Always taking in strays—cats, dogs, run-away girls (reuniting them with their families). "Hearts of cheesecake," Cora says. Come to think of it, they missed our last community dinner. Odd. I go in the back door, as always, past dish-washing sinks, and stick my head in the kitchen, not knowing how I will be received. "Knock, knock," I say. Greeted by a huge pot of soup stock simmering on the stove. But no sign of the girls. I hear feet scamper in the dining area beyond swinging doors, and I'm alarmed. Carlie and Margie are too heavy on their feet to scamper. An intruder? I seize a meat cleaver off its rack and tiptoe inside, sensing trouble, not knowing what I may do.

Clean morning light slides through casement windows and falls across white tablecloths (flyspecked by the shadows of flies crawling on window panes) and sparkles along long, faceted stems of water glasses, shellacs warm wooden surfaces of antique tables and cane chairs. A red-cheeked, cherubic Frans Hals girl smiles from a print on one wall, her cat eyes reminiscent of Carlie's, narrow and watchful. Something bumps in the cloakroom up front. I throw the door open to those two cowering in pith helmets in separate corners. "What are you doing?" I cry. "It's me! Lawrence! Don't tell me you two have caught this avoider's disease, too?"

Margie shrieks and points at the meat cleaver. "Gawd! He's going to chop us up!"

"Ohhhh Gawwwwdddd," Carlie cries.

I drop it clattering to the floor. "Me? Nonsense! Sorry, girls...I only thought..."

"You only thought?" Carlie demands. "Well, we thought..."

"Yeh, we did...we definitely thought..."

"What I mean...the way people are...afraid something...you know..."

"Does someone want to complete a thought here?" Margie stands stiffly up, hands in the small of her back.

"Not sure what I thought...just...weird as people are behaving—"

"Look who's talking. Meat cleavers?" Margie demands. "My God, Lawr!"

"Sorry. Just trying to be protective."

"We thought you were someone else," Carlie says. "We heard the back door open, and we...it doesn't matter. Whassup, Lawr? Glad to see you." Smiling hugely, like the girl in the print, cheeks red as watermelon pickles.

"You two are your normal affable selves then? Thank God. Everyone else in town snapped my head off today—

Benson, Juan Alverro. Cora won't even talk to me any-more."

"No, not Cora—of all people. I didn't think it would get to Cora."

"Didn't think!" Carlie agrees.

"What would get to her?" I follow them back to the kitchen, air a thick broth of garlic and leeks. Carlie stirs her soup stock. "What is it, anyhow?"

"Everyone's cancelled for Thanksgiving dinner," Margie says. "They don't want to be out in public now. We had turkeys, too."

"That's not the half of it," Carlie says.

"Not the half. Teenage boys are shooting up our sign, shouting filth as they drive past. Mouth garbage that doesn't bear repeating. It's drive-by homophobia."

"Doesn't bear!" Carlie nods. "Not only boys either, grown men. Ugly."

"Disgusting drivel about fat dykes, godless homosex-uals, and hog sloppers," Margie says.

"Oh, for goodness sake!" Carlie snaps at her.

I tell them I get the picture. I intuited something was wrong when I grabbed that cleaver. "What's got into peo-ple, anyway? Why all the piss and fury?"

Margie shrugs. "It's a hate epidemic. People looking to blame someone for the mess we're in."

"Like an illness, you mean?" I stare at her.

"You bet. Illness of the heart and soul—moral cancer."

"You two haven't got it. How come? Me neither...I don't think. Hope not. Except for that cleaver—"

"You don't!" they both cry at once.

"I'm afraid Cora does. Makes me sick, I'm here to tell."

"Not Cora...of all people." Sweat drips off of Carlie's chin into the soup stock—one of her secret ingredients? "Margo calls it bluebottle fever: a fly bites you and you get it. We haven't been bitten yet...hopefully won't be."

"We're taking precautions," Margie says.

I realize then that mosquito netting drapes off of pith helmets to cover their faces; I thought their features were simply blurred, as flies blur everything lately. Few flies in the kitchen. I slap my sleeves and pants' legs, recalling Benson's alarm over flies crawling on me. "Good God! Any cure?" Thinking of Cora, wondering if her hostility might be contagious.

"It's like bubonic plague," Margie says dourly. "It has to run its course. The flies hatch and pour out of your mouth."

Awful image. Imagine Benson, Juan Alverro, my Cora with gaudy fat flies clattering out of their mouths, carrying away bits of tissue, larva fattened on victims' innards before they pupate. No wonder people are ill-tempered. If Cora did a somersault would I hear their papery pupal casings tumbling and chafing against each other in her belly? Good Lord!

"How long's it take to run its course?"

"How should I know, Lawr, for goodness sake? This is all new to us."

"Not new," Carlie says. "It's the same old same old. Sometimes things are just so good that we don't notice. Once times go sour, here it comes right back at us again."

Margie and I gape, amazed to hear Carlie talk this way. She's no cynic; she believes in homemade bread, fresh garlic and sundried tomatoes. "Maybe," I say, "but I don't want to believe it. Just a bad day everyone's having...bad week. Can't say why everyone is having it at once. Collective unconscious type thing, I guess, like a mass psychic larval hatch."

The girls sit me down with a slice of cheesecake before I leave, just to show me there is still love in this world–in rich, cheesy spoonfuls. At Chez Amie, you might believe the world is not on short rations, there is no *Forever War*, and no epidemic of misanthropy.

§

Cora is not in her pottery shed next morning, not in the screened grape arbor, nor the house, nowhere in the yard. I have brought her out a cup of manzanita tea, but she has disappeared. The dogs pace about in circles in the yard, snapping at flies. I find Cora's note pinned to the front door: "Out settling scores. I'll settle with you when I get home, buster." What the hell? What scores? Cora doesn't nurse grudges. Her philosophy: *Let it go! It's nothing we can't handle.* Some time later, her yellow jeep comes barreling up the drive, throwing dust. A pair of hiking boots bounce on her hip as she approaches the house, hung by shoelaces from her belt, sprigs of greenery tucked under on the other side, a car antenna bent into a horseshoe hangs around her neck. She is a scowling Sioux warrior returned from battle, scalps tied at her waist—in the regulation khaki shorts she wears regardless of weather. "Trophies," she snaps, pushing rudely past me into the house. "I'm getting to you, buster." She thumps my chest.

"What did I do?"

"Quit your whining. You sound like Hector Dario and that lot." Raising the aerial overhead in a victory salute—busted off of Hector's Hummer, I realize, his pride and joy. Hector claims his car alone of all the vehicles in Sluggards Creek "knows the Lord," plastered with decals announcing it.

"Oh no! What do you have against Hector?"

"*What do I have against Hector?*" she nanners. "I'm sick of his holier-than-thou crap. So are you, hypocrite." She rattles foliage against her hip and smiles satisfaction. "This is from Laney Silverstein's lilac bush in the front yard. I chopped it down."

"You chopped it down? Ohhh, no. What on earth do

you have against Laney?"

"For starters, how about her constant flirting with you. The bitch thinks she's queen of the hop; she makes me sick." Cora laughs caustically. "She stood there on her front porch gawping at me, flies buzzing into her mouth. Hah! Felt great!" She stretches gleefully.

I am beyond incredulous, heartsick. Hate epidemic indeed! "And the boots?" I manage.

"I snatched them off Margie and Carlie's porch. Oh, not to worry, I'm taking them back...after I fill them with cement. Whooo-eee!" She sinks down on hinges of her knees, squeaking laughter. Maybe she's learned that I smooched with Margie on that trip to Oregon months back, but Cora and I weren't together at the time, for goodness sake. "What are you looking at?" she demands. "You going to defend those fat dykes, too?"

"Those *fat dykes* are our friends." I throw a hand at her. "I don't know you, don't know any of you anymore. I believe you've been fly-bit and lost your wits. You don't seem to know it."

"Quit your kvetching and grow up!" Cora snaps.

Occurs to me I'd better clean up after her: replace Hector's aerial and find Laney another lilac bush (can't imagine where) and retrieve those boots before cement hardens. Cora will be furious at my interference. She's fiercely independent, will not abide trespass on her sovereignty. Such actions will surely precipitate a crisis. But not to act would be indefensibly cowardly and unneigh-borly and would make me an accomplice. I am at a loss. Maybe we don't need to be fly-bitten, we can contract the meanness out of convenience or cowardice. Conflicted, I decide to mull it over a bit.

§

Hoping to avoid the perils both of acting and not, I decide to act anonymously. Parking down the road from Laney Silverstein's rancho, I approach cautiously with my tools–maybe 1:30 a.m., lights out in the house but the dim porch light on. Cora cut down the lilac bushes with an axe, leaving stumps ragged. I quietly saw off ravaged tops to achieve a clean, flat surface, slit the stumps with a buckknife, and plant leafy twigs in the slits (Laney hasn't hauled off foliage, as she hasn't removed Johnny Sylvio's trailer from the place, wanting to keep it as a memorial to her dead caretaker); I bind split trunks with twine and paint them with roofer's tar for a tidy, disease-resistant graft. Attach a note: *Greetings from an anonymous friend.*

I stand in the yard a moment, watching moonlight wink across the silver hull of Johnny's trailer, hoping he might approve of my handiwork–master of domestic repair. Surely, Johnny would avoid being fly-bitten. Car headlights suddenly appear in the drive, shining through the low wrought iron gate, as if the car has been waiting there all along. I hit belly on the grass behind a huge yucca, striking my hands against its fleshy, spine-tipped leaves as I go down and piercing my palms, nearly cry out in pain. A police radio crackles, and I realize it is Hector Dario's cruiser, just as his spotlight sweeps across Laney's house toward my hiding place, bumps over the lawn and illuminates yucca fronds, casting the plant's grotesque shadow against the house behind me. Has Hector seen me? Will he arrest me for Cora's "pranks"? (I will confess, of course, not wanting her to be implicated.) If he has been fly-bitten, what justice will his hostility exact, given that his beloved, born-again Hummer was vandalized? Will he charge me with wanton destruction of property, public nuisance...hate crimes?

The light holds me captive; I hear Hector's halting voice on the radio. Doubtless, Laney has asked him to keep an eye on her place. Has she already busted Cora? His car door opens, I hear his feet crunch over gravel, imagine him climbing over the gate, how it will feel to have a cold gun barrel pressed into my forehead. I'm about to make a run for it–back toward Johnny's trailer and up the hill behind–when footsteps retreat. Hector's voice on the radio sounds close in the quiet night: "Base, this is One-Eleven. All quiet here. I'm coming in. Over." I watch his cruiser back down the drive, not believing my luck.

My wounded hands burn something fierce; toxins re-

leased by the yucca barbs ache up my arms. Flies attack
the wounds, rip into wounded flesh with their sharp little beaks. No helping it. I was planning to go by Hector's
next to replace the aerial–having removed the one from
my pickup, hoping it will fit his Hummer–but I've had
enough of Hector for one night. So I hightail it straight
over to Chez Amie, having liberated an old pair of hiking
boots from Cora's closet, same size as the ones she stole.
I've written a note to Margie and Carlie:

> *These are temporary loaners while*
> *we clean and oil your new boots.*
> *Thanks for the opportunity.*
> *– An admiring friend*

Because, damn it, I want to prove Cora wrong, her
philosophy wrong, anyhow, that humans are antisocial
by nature. I want Carlie and Margie to know there are
many of us in town who love them dearly–for who they
are! How I will square it from here, find Margie a new
pair of boots, I don't know yet. But, damn it, I will.

Takes only a minute to place boots and note on the
back porch. No one around. As I exit the lot with my
headlights cut, a car pulls in front of my truck to block
escape, like a ghost car, its own headlights out, tires
crunching over gravel. Spooky, I'm here to tell. I know it
is Hector before he speaks, before he shines a flashlight

in my face, from the jangle of hardware on his hips as he approaches my pickup. "Hands on the steering wheel," he barks, standing by my window. "I'm surprised to find *you* in a dirty business like this, Lawrence. It's like the book says: *Trouble shall be upon trouble and meanness upon meanness.*" (Hector likes to invent scripture, believing his position as spare time pastor at The Good News Tabernacle entitles him to do so.)

"What business is that, Heck? I brought Carlie and Margie a gift is all. Would you get the light out of my eyes, please?"

"No, sir, can't do her. Put your hands on the steering wheel where I can see them. Now!"

"For goodness sake, Heck, I don't plan to shoot you." Dumb thing to say, I realize at once. He grinds the gun barrel into my temple and my hands leap onto that wheel. "You don't need to do that, Heck. I'm pacified, I'm cooperative. Good and scared, really."

He speaks into the microphone clipped to his shoulder. "Base! This is One-Eleven. I'm at Chez Amie in S.C., got a perp in custody on suspicion of malicious mischief. Over."

I read you, Hector. Are you requesting backup?

"That would be a negative...at this time. Over and out. What we're going to do here," he tells me, "you are going to get out of the vehicle—real slow—and I'm going to put you in the back of the cruiser and search your truck."

"Search for what, Heck?"

"You better shut it. You are in deep doggy doo, Lawr. The Lord shall exact swift and mighty vengeance." There's glee in his tone.

I feel sick, like a man condemned to die, like an actor in someone else's movie. Not imagining how I've gotten into this mess. Protecting who? Not knowing why I shouldn't give it up and tell him the truth. Furious at flies buzzing at my ears, mouth, nose...every orifice, demanding entry. Unable to swat them. Heck stands me up out of the truck, turns me around, clamps on cuffs–tight! "Any firearms," he asks, "You got any knives in there, felt-tip markers or eckcetera?"

I don't reply. He pushes me into the backseat of the cruiser. Soon returns with the boots, buckknife and foldup saw; he whips the aerial which I'd hoped to mount on his Hummer against his palm. "I seen your truck parked over to Laney's," he says. "Funny—" sliding into the driver's seat, a screen of sturdy wire mesh between us "—I had the radio antenna tore off my GodMobile yesterday. Looks to me like you been spreading your mischief all through the neighborhood, Lawr. You about admit it ri'chere in your note! I knew you was stiff-necked, but I never took you for a boot-licking pervert, an abomination onto the Lord."

"For crap's sake, Heck. I took Margo's boots to clean and oil them, that's all."

He rakes my saw across wire mesh. "What else you plan to cut down? Huh?"

"You know me, Heck. Have known me for years. Malicious mischief isn't my thing."

"Maybe. But nobody's acting like theirselves here lately. I run Benson in for setting his own store afire last night. Didn't burn much. Besides, maybe you don't consider nothing wrong with shooting up a gay place of business. There's some wouldn't."

"I'm not one of them, believe me. Margie and Carlie are close friends." I ask him what kind of sentence I'm likely to get if convicted–which seems a foregone conclusion.

"Six months...used to would have. Now it's work in the POW camps, first time offenders such as yourself."

I'm stunned silent. Mind racing, looking for some way out. "Okay," I say, knowing I should hold my tongue, but nothing like panic to bring out the worst in us, "let me suggest something here—"

"You need to shuddup. I heard enough nonsense. I'm running you in."

He's right. I need to shut up, not speak what I am about to say. But I do. "Listen! Writing those slogans on the restaurant was ugly, maybe. Still, some good may come of it. Shooting the place up was insane. Still, it might serve as a wake-up call to the girls."

Hector doesn't quote scripture at me. He remains

quiet beyond the mesh, ears out-turned, supporting the cap, attentive and listening. "Go on! Speak your piece."

I barely choke it out: "Maybe they need to hear it, those two, living the evil lifestyle they do. There's some might say an unkindness visited on them is a blessing if it leads them to recant their sinful ways—maybe save their souls. Okay?"

"Tough love?" he answers after a time. "I never thought I'd hear you say it."

"Whoever wrote those nasty slogans—it wasn't me!— could be seen as a better friend to Margie and Carlie than those of us who passively support their lifestyle."

Words gum up my mouth as if it is filled with feces. Can't believe the shit I'm talking, can't stop myself. Worst of it is I sound sincere—even to myself. Shakes me up good, I'm here to tell. Betrayal, ugly and absolute. Kneeling at the altar of bigotry. Isn't about being fly-bitten or catching a nasty bug, it's about joining up—to save one's own skin or get ahead or get even. We might betray most anything: belief, friends, neighbors, family. Flies swarm over my face in that enclosed space as if I am putrefying. Hector turns around to regard me under the dome light.

"What I noticed: flies seek out the truth, they flock to it. You will hear people say those flies are devils. No, sir! They are angels of the Lord. You shall know the truth and the truth shall set you free." Locks on the back doors pop open (he'd removed the cuffs when he shoved me into the cruiser). "Get out," he says. "Go on home. Don't come back." Spearing a finger. "I got my eye on you, Lawrence Connery."

As I drive away, stunned that I have beaten the thing, I understand that I have given Hector moral cover, a balm for his guilt. For he wrote those slogans himself, I realize, and shot up Chez Amie—believing homosexuality is an abomination onto the Lord, often preaching as much in his sermons. Grateful that I have endorsed his warped brand of compassion, Hector—in brotherly homophobia—has let me go.

§

I sit unprotected on a lawn chair out back next morning, disregarding Margie's warning and letting flies feast on my bare arms and neck as I mull things over, gratified by their predations, knowing I deserve them. I have not slept all the short night, cannot bear my own smell, the sight of my face in the mirror, the tightness of skin over my cheeks and shoulders. I would gladly join the fly clan to molt and shed my maggoty old self, sprout wings and fly away. Let them feast on my guts, my liver and spleen. Mouth wide open, I gag on their hairy, vibrating little bodies. And discover a strange phenomenon, perhaps a new law in a natural order that has gone mad.

Whenever my thoughts turn to deflating the seriousness of Cora's trespasses–and my own–labeling them "pranks" or "minor indiscretions," no real harm done, flies thicken the air about me, swarm over my arms and teeth, and drill their proboscises into my flesh, just as they do when I decide that my woman and townmates are right to fear their fellow man. We have good cause to be paranoid and standoffish, given so many enemies–criminals and terrorists and devious, betraying friends and neighbors (am I not proof of it myself). Why pretend differently? Get real, Lawrence. Grow up! The world is an ugly, sordid place. Yes, flies hum joyfully.

But when I shake off such notions, like a dog shaking water off its coat, and recognize hatred as a state of morbid neurosis, spiritual depression and defeat, when I focus my thoughts on the warm company of friends–Carlie's cheesecake, Laney Silverstein's laugh, gravel in Johnny Sylvio's voice, the smell of Cora's hair...the serendipitous kindness of strangers–then flies scatter, skedaddle away and form a distant circle, sphere rather, three-dimensional with me at its center. Remarkable! A shimmering, buzzing, translucent dome which blurs my surroundings. When I embrace kind thoughts, I am anathema to the little beasts. They cower away, banished to the psychic outskirts and slums of despair. And I think: if kind thoughts can accomplish this, just imagine what kind acts will achieve!

I decide that I must do what paranoia forbids. Not

just act as though Cora and Benson and Juan Alverro and, yes, Hector and the drive-by shooters at Chez Amie, myself, and everyone else will do the right thing, I must fully believe we will, must count on it, must make it my conviction. Trust to people's essential humanity and good-heartedness and maybe they will begin to trust it themselves.

Listen, I am no Christian, I embrace no religious faith, but I recognize that Jesus's most radical teaching was to turn the other cheek. Imagine it! Imagine that instead of attacking our enemies when we are attacked in *The Forever War* we send them season's tickets to Yankees baseball or an Ultimate Bagels & Nova Gift Basket from Zabar's. Madness? Perhaps. Or perhaps a realization that the best way to neutralize an enemy is to befriend him.

The moment I consider this and stand up to leave the yard, determined to visit Cora out in her shed, the flies disappear, their obnoxious, incessant buzzing gone. "What I'd like to suggest," I say, entering her studio, "is I drive you over to Margie and Carlie's. We can return her boots, I will confess my betrayal and ask their forgiveness, you can, too. Okay? Then, if they can find it in their hearts, we'll all sit down and have a slice of Carlie's cheesecake. Then we'll dirve over to Laney's and see what more we can repair of that lilac bush."

She glowers. "You didn't hear me, Lawrence Connery? Weren't you listening at all yesterday?"

"The thing is," I say, "I made out a little with Margie, but it was only friendly affection. You and me were on the outs then, besides. All right? Hey, the concrete will crack and fall right out after a couple of good whacks, anyway. I don't know where we'll get Hector a new aerial." I chuckle. "But you'll do a better job of mounting it than I will." (Cora is mechanically adept.)

Her mouth hangs open—there'd be bluebottles flying in and out of it if any remained—she's too flabbergasted to speak. Or undecided about whether I have found a clever way to diss her. And Cora flat hates indecision.

"Have you noticed—" I smile "—no flies!" I throw the shed door open. None.

She is about to be furious, but notes my arms, my lips swollen with fly bites, and all the fury drains out of her. Gone. "What hap...hap...pened to you, Lawr?" she stammers.

I shrug. "They flew off. They've had all they want of us, I guess."

"Your arms, Lawr?" She points. "Your lips, your face?"

True, they are red and swollen, skin pocked with welts and tiny lacerations, fly-gnawed and pathetic. I show her my swollen hands. "Guess they had something of a love feast. Who knows, maybe a single bite is infectious, but get enough venom in your system and you build up resistance. It is a kind of disease, after all."

She takes me into the house, anyway, and rubs salve on my arms and face, talking excitedly about her plan for extracting those concrete cores whole from Margie's boots and using them in a sculptural piece which she will donate to Chez Amie. "I think they'll love it!" Clapping her hands, she rises and goes to the window. "Will you look at that! Juan Alverro just left a box of apples at foot of our drive, then drove away." She laughs. "Why on earth would he do that? Nutty, huh!"

"No," I say, "it's probably like any other epidemic: starts somewhere and there's no telling how far it will spread. But when it's spent itself...when it's done, it's done. Thank God for that."

HEAT WAVE

Some blame the greenhouse effect, others say it's the hole in the ozone layer spreading across the continent, and some believe we're sinking toward the molten core of the earth, having pumped all the oil and water out of the ground. The weatherman doesn't give his opinion, just warns us we're in for another scorcher: sixty-five straight days now over one-hundred-twenty degrees. A melt alert on the I-10: the fast lane liquefied between Palm Springs and Rancho Mirage. We hear how the AC conked out in an elder hospice in San Bernardino and with it the respiratory systems of three dozen old people. The federal government has just declared the first Regional Heat Disaster Advisory in history.

Diamond Valley Lake over in Hemet is depleted to crackled mud, and the Colorado River barely trickles over the line into Mexico; they say Mexican troops are amassed along the border to protect their "sovereign right to drinking water." Riverside County Sheriff Harvey Barbur has given his deputies shoot-to-kill orders for anyone seen out in the yard with a garden hose. So we sneak out nights to hide our hoses. I stow my neighbor's away for him, knowing Freddy won't do it himself. The fat fuck wakes us up at five a.m. screaming how someone stole his frigging hose. All over the Southland there's spontaneous combustion of compost heaps, inflatable rubber pools, and couches stuffed with poly foam, and the choir of St. Jude's Catholic Church in Indio burst into flames singing "Nearer My God To Thee" when the foam lining of their choir robes suddenly ignited. I won't go into accounts of kids parboiled in wader pools.

Organizers of the Democratic National Convention have changed the venue from L.A. to Seattle, not wanting a purple state delegation to burst into flames on TV. The Republican presidential candidate blames the epidemic of public nudity in the southwest "on eight years of moral laxity under the Democrats," while the Democratic frontrunner has challenged his opponent to a debate in Vegas. "So the public can see which of us sweats more profusely–in sympathy with the suffering voters of that great region." The Green Party nominee says we ain't seen nothing yet. "Nature is flat pissed off."

Myself, I blame it all on the devil, who's grown keen and lively in the heat. What a lot of people don't realize about the devil is he's more trickster coyote than fallen archangel. Like a car full of teenage boys on a hot summer night out to fuck with things for the sheer joy of fucking with them. Right now he's totally enjoying himself. Causing heat-crazed moms to kill their children and the control systems of jet liners to burst into flames as they approach LAX. No doubt the heat wave will decide the election in California. But will we vote Democratic because their candidate offered to share his sweat with us or for the Republican because she refuses to sweat or Green for threatening us with extinction?

I feel relieved to have lost my construction job. Can't imagine framing houses under a sun so intense at midday that it roasts grasshoppers. My girlfriend, who works in real estate in Palm Desert, hasn't sold zip in eight months. Her theory is the economic meltdown led to the heat wave. "Nature needs to feel secure, too, you know. Just like everybody else."

"So you're saying the recession caused the heat wave, right?" I ask.

"Like, duh! Obvious." Her blond hair, which usually cascades down in curly combers, hangs limp over her ears; I wonder if the heat has fried her bananas. Naw, it's just Angie. She never has let logic interfere with her thought process.

So I tell her my plan to buy a teardrop trailer and have Jake come out with his dozer and dig a hole in the sandy soil out back of our modular. "Bury her maybe twenty feet down and do a combo air and access shaft leading down to it. Natural AC down there. That's why the prairie settlers did underground sod shelters. Earth insulation!"

"Like yuck! There's all kinds of ants and spiders and snakes down there."

"We'll be deeper. They're in the top layers."

"And it's killer dark." She grips her elbows. "Like a grave or something."

"Yeah—" I grin at the prospect "–time doesn't exist down there. Won't matter if you sleep day or night. We won't even know which it is."

On TV, they are showing National Guardsmen in sweat-soaked uniforms confronting an angry mob in front of a National Weather Bureau facility in Orange County. Rioters are inspired by Rush Limbaugh's claim that the Feds dropped 500,000 tons of moisture-eating polymers (like those little polystyrene balls you find in potted plants at Home Depot) across the Southland in a cloud seeding program that went wrong; the polymers soaked moisture out of the ground and intensified our drought. I can hear Rush shouting from Freddy's radio next door: "The Feds are cooking our babies in their cribs, friends. Believe it!" I step out on the porch and shout, "Turn it down, you fat freak." Freddy launches back a string of invectives. Angie covers her ears. It's gotten better, anyway, since Freddy and I stopped shooting at each other.

"The best thing about this whole deal," I tell her, "we'll be leaving Fat Freddy topside. We can do sex during the day again." Anymore, Angie will only do sex in the dark; she's convinced Freddy watches us through bullet holes he's blasted in the aluminum walls of our modular. She wears nothing around the house but string bikinis, drives me freaking crazy. "He's probably got you focused in his binocs right now," I tell her.

She flips him off. "All you think about anymore is sex sex sex. You really need to get back to work, you know what!" To Angie if y'r working, y'r mentally healthy; y'r not working, y'r messed up. She gestures towards Freddy's place as exhibit number one. Fact is, there's a whole lots of Freddys out here: sand rats, dried up old tumbleweeds blown into fall-apart trailers, hyper-tan old lizards whose skin is spotted with basal cell tumors. Rush lovers all.

"Did you ever notice all the major religions started in hot climates?" I say. "The devil showed up for the competition, then stayed on for the sex. Because hot is just hotter."

She shakes her head and puzzles at me.

The city council of Gonewrong, Nevada, where temperatures in excess of one-hundred-eighty degrees have been recorded in local attics, have changed the town's name to Goneright, hoping to appease the Lord. Water drips hot and fetid from the tap, they suspend summer school so naked teachers won't have to teach roomfuls of naked kids, and people are shooting neighbors caught scooping water out of their swimming pools. Oregon State Troopers are positioned along the border to stop northward flight from California's heat zone. Meanwhile, a crackpot state assemblywoman from Indian Wells has proposed a bill favoring the use of nuclear weapons to defend California–citing the Oregon Troopers and Mexican troops amassed along our southern border. Hearing the news, Fat Freddy marches nude out of his trailer, hooting and slapping his huge belly, which jiggles like an upright bowl of vanilla pudding, his little baggage hanging on like an afterthought down there. Sadly Angie misses the show, else she would sign up for underground living on the spot!

Generally though, we've gone apolitical, subscribing to the politics of misery. Can't sleep in bed without developing nasty rashes, can't sleep sitting up. A pair of jeans will chafe the skin off your thighs in an hour. For the first time I actually feel sorry for Freddy, imagining how he must suffer under all that flesh. Though maybe it provides insulation. Freddy's way out ahead of us: living underground above ground. Stomping around naked, jiggling and blowing off steam. Rage is his air conditioning.

People have retreated to basements if they have one. We wrap wet sheets around ourselves and sit in front of the fan until we get a brownout, eat habanero peppers to open the pores. You'll see whole families sitting atop SUVs in lawn chairs, tooting down the freeway, hair crackling behind them in the dry wind. Anything for a breeze. Angie and I take turns blowing on each others' sweaty bodies. Her skin glows like some phosphorescent purple mineral in the heat. She says it's the coolness inside her shining forth. She's begun to make more sense lately. "You want to climb back in the womb," she tells me. "That's what this underground burrow thing is all about. Because your mother died when you were young and you still miss her." Kind of stuns me, but I insist, "You have to do something; you can't just sit out here and die. The way I figure it: hot air will sink down the shaft and meet the underground cool, and water drops will condense on the aluminum walls; there'll be a channel along the bottom to collect them. Perpetual slow rain in the desert. Am I a fucking genius or what?"

"Now you're really getting me hot, okay."

Maybe she's right: all I really wanna do anymore is sex. We crawl under the trailer—only place cool enough—and do it, feeling a trace of ghost refrigeration creeping up from below through the dirt against our bare backs. Away from Fat Freddy's spy eyes, away from outdoor hell. Afterwards, I tell her about my dream to save the planet in my own little way. "Do things small. Do things smart. Not saying I'm Al Gore or anything—"

Friends whose AC still works invite us over for a cool air party. It's the thing anymore! Like people in the

fifties inviting neighbors over to watch TV. In that gar-
bage-stink, fly-swarm hellzone, palm tree fronds sagging
down trunks in exhaustion, these parties sometimes
turn into orgies. Disaster always makes people horny.
Mostly though we just lie about naked and sleep. Too
heat-exhausted for sex. You've got to wonder how people
of the Indian Subcontinent invented the Kama Sutra,
hot as it was. Angie reads to me from a blog specializing
in "cool air orgies," which claims the mind's erogenous
zones are stimulated by heat. "That's why children pee in
the hot water of wading pools," she reads.

"Bullshit. Hot as it is, we'd be peeing constantly. I've
about stopped peeing. Conserving moisture. You know,
we wouldn't need cool air parties if we lived underground."

§

By the end, birds fall dead out of the sky mid-flight.
Crickets go dead quiet. The *L.A. Times* reports the first of
the mass extinctions and notes that cockroaches and ants
have become more active. We hear them gnawing at plates
in the kitchen. San Diego beaches record such high counts
of coliform bacteria that the entire populace is ordered inland off the coast. Nights, we hear the hordes shuffling
toward us on foot—along roads become like the La Brea
Tar Pits, chock full of overheated cars sunk up to the axle

in molten asphalt. We envision massive social unrest once they arrive, pitched battles between locals and coasters.

Oddly, the heat wave doesn't cross the border into Mexico. Temperatures of one-hundred-sixty degrees have been recorded in rugged ravines north of Tecate on the U.S. side, but Tecate townsfolk stroll the plaza in the evening cool, discussing the climatic disaster in *El Norte*, thanking God they live in Mexico, where they've learned to accept the climate and not attempt to bribe it with air conditioning and golf courses, thereby provoking the desert under their feet. "*!Mira!*" they cry, pointing north. "*Desastre del sol.*" What joy to be a Mexican "illegal" in the US, able to stroll back across the border at will, while gringos who attempt it are shot on sight.

We watch a sleep-walking weather forecaster predict hotter temperatures into October. Showing video footage of underground bunkers people have dug to escape the heat. "Look!" I cry, pumping my fists in the air. Fat Freddy stands naked out on our porch. "So what's to celebrate?" he asks. I run out and embrace the smarmy bastard.

"We're moving underground, Freddy! I tell you, it's the call of the future."

He and Angie stare dumbfounded at each other's naked bodies.

"I think I'm dying," Freddy says. "There's blood in my urine."

"Okay, that does it, people! I'm starting right now." It's my social duty to save Freddy from his obsessions. He's given up Rush and gotten into mass suicide chat lines on the web—sado-necro-porno sites with names like CYANO-SEX, BLOOD HIGHWAY, and WACO STYLE. Move over Jonestown. Dis-fuckin-gusting.

With Jake's dozer out of commission, I start digging by hand, nights when it cools off to one-fifteen. Freddy's no help and Angie's in denial. But the hordes are coming, dead pets lie baking in the sun on brown lawns, we're nearly out of water, remaining salt pines and eucalyptus crack open with explosive bolts midday, even the mesquite and cactus are dying, the crisp bodies of dead insects crackle underfoot. It's gotten damn near dire.

Maybe five feet down I hit gravel, sedimentary rock at ten feet—mudstone and sandstone. I drop chunks of it on the porch between Freddy and Angie, who've taken to sitting together bareass in the gimpy shade through blistering days. "See that!" I cry. "Proof positive that conditions were better here once. And can be again!"

"Yeah, in maybe two million years." Freddy grins, Angie giggles. They've grown close, those two. My mom used to say, "We're all bunkmates under the skin." Those two sure as hell are. Soulmates. Both have lost weight from heat trauma and love to discuss—in minute detail—what it has done to their bodies. Freddy hoists his bowling ball belly in both hands. "Used to be I couldn't even lift it." Angie hoists her breasts. "Me either. I was twice this big before. No shit! Twice!" Shaking their heads in wonder.

No hope of carving out a large enough cavern to drop a trailer into, so I burrow into the rock, a ten-by-ten cave, smoothing and polishing walls into which the cool of the surrounding earth seeps. It's like going into a walk-in freezer. Moisture condenses on the walls. I salvage huge commercial AC ducts from an abandoned building at edge of town and install them in the shaft leading down to the cocoon—my perpetual rain machine. My new plan: move the modular atop the shaft and cut a hole in its floor. Underground air will rise up the shaft and cool the trailer; condensing water will trickle down into collecting pans. We can crawl down there when we need to cool off, sleep down there, all three of us, like bears in a den. Will shelter there when hordes arrive from the coast. Though some say fierce Santa Anas roaring through the San Gorgonio Pass have halted their progress. Others say most have died of heat exhaustion. Now and again we catch a hellacious whiff of decomp drifting in from the west.

Angie begs me to fashion a hoist to lift Freddy up and down from the cocoon. "He's really a nice person when you get to know him. He only hates other people because he hates himself. And doesn't even hate himself anymore since we became friends."

"So you're friends now?" Shaking my head in amazement.

"Oh, get over yourself. I mean, it's not like we're doing oral or something. More like girlfriends killing time together."

"You and Fat Freddy? Rush Limbaugh and the whole number?"

"He doesn't like being called 'fat,' okay. Besides, he's over that. Going naked has changed his political outlook. He admires you a lot. He calls you, 'The man with a plan.'"

We jack up the modular and work an old trailer chassis under it, and Freddy helps me push it inch by inch over the shaft. Strong dude. "You can live with us," I tell him, "but you'll have to allow us our privacy." A red tide floods from Freddy's face down over his chest, genitals, legs. "Fine!" he says, "if you allow us ours." It's then I realize he and Angie are sleeping together. Funny, how you expect the hordes to arrive from the west; instead, they move into your house from next door.

Those two are quite happy with the new AC system and all. Me? I consider moving into Freddy's trailer. Seeing Angie sitting in Freddy's lap, toying with his dewlaps is more than I can handle. "You'll have to permit me access to water. After all, I devised and built the damn thing."

"Oh, get over yourself," Angie says.

It's cooling off anyhow. Meltdown over. Given all the San Diegans perished in the flight from the city and real estate prices dirt cheap, I consider moving over there. Maybe do renovation work. Freddy and Angie talk about starting a family. "Wouldn't it be adorable: a bunch of cuddly, roly-poly little Freddy juniors running about with their Ipods tuned to Rush Limbaugh?" Angie claps her hands. I realize she has begun to put on weight.

§

I meet a gal in Palm Desert who insists this has all been a trial run. "The Supreme One is testing to see how resilient we are. Like North Korea. He's smiling to himself."

"Who's The Supreme One?" I ask her.

She winks. "Wouldn't you like to know?"

Miranda has thick black hair that hangs to her waist, she dresses like a Gypsy, wears dozens of gold bangles that merrily clank and jangle on her arms. The moment I step inside her house to replace mirrors that have cracked in the heat, she tells me we'd better go ahead and get married while we still can. "What the hell!" I laugh. "I don't even know you."

"Sure you do," she says. "Do you really think Freddy and Angie didn't know each other? You think they weren't soulmates from the very beginning?"

"Beginning of what?" I sputter. "How do you know about those two, anyway?"

She winks and tweaks my nose. "Wouldn't you like to know?"

I'm not half way through installing the first mirror when I see her standing naked in it behind me—but for gold bracelets and tattoos adorning her breasts, a dense embroidery of flowers, beasts, symbols across her belly and thighs. We begin a cool air orgy like the fantasy orgies written up on blogs. Unfuckingreal. Bangles jangle on her arms. We yip, nip and howl like coyotes that once roamed the hills. Afterwards, we lay together grinning up at the ceiling of her bedroom, on which condensation collects as it did on the walls of my sandstone cave. "So you knew this was going to happen before you asked me over here, I guess?"

"Wouldn't you like to know?" She points to my visage tattooed over her left nipple.

We are married within a week. What choice really? Fate is fate.

Of course, Miranda's right. When it comes, the great quake severs us from the rest of the continent. Earthquake weather: sere dog days of autumn that wrinkle the earth's crust. It's like instructions have been penned along the dotted line of the Nevada/Arizona/California border: *fold and tear here.* California and Baja slide into the Pacific like a great iceberg calf and begin floating to-

wards Hawaii. California Nuevo finally become the free
and sovereign nation it was always meant to be. Gentled
by the Japanese current, we are island people basking in
island breezes. Cuba invites us to form an alliance, with
Australia and Japan! Big dreams. The ocean floods the
Mojave and laps at shores of the Sierra Nevada. We stand
at heights of Kings Canyon among the sequoia and look
out at water stretching off to our east. Wind surfing off
our "east bank" is some of the best in the world.

Angie and Freddy? I haven't the heart to find out, but
fear they were asleep down in the cocoon when the Pacific came flooding into the Great Basin. Their dreams of
a family undone. I'd never imagined I was digging them
a grave.

Luckily, Miranda and I were sleeping outside the
night of the earthquake, our wedding night. After the
dizzying rush westward into the trough of the San An-
dreas Fault—riding atop a tectonic plate that bobbed like
a Boogie Board—we felt waters moving deep underfoot,
heard them thundering toward us from the northeast.
Miranda grabbed my hand and we ran to her dad's old
cabin cruiser parked on a trailer beside the house, clam-
bered into it just as the first breakers rushed in, lifted and
carried us away.

Moored now in the flooded canyon at base of the old
Palm Springs Tramway, like an Adriatic inlet, blue-green
waters of the Great Baja Causeway separating us from the

continent (just a line far in the distance). We've reinvented ourselves as ferry boaters, running tourists back and forth between Nevada and California Nuevo. Miranda reads their fortunes, and I warn them that her fortunes always come true. Of course they don't believe me.

Sure, we have our problems: threats of invasion from the Feds, boat people arriving from the Pacific Northwest ("We could handle the rain," they say, "so long as we knew we could always drive down to California and dry off"), ecofreaks who'd long assumed that when disaster struck we wouldn't survive it and are depressed that we have. There's still work to be done: bodies to bury, swimming pools to fill in, portions of our eastern slope that are sloughing off into the sea. In the pre-Nuevo days we worked, too, but never so seriously. Truth is, we've grown up some. All peoples must have a past, must be able to point back to disaster and say: *See what we've lived through.* Limitless as we were, we needed to define our limits and limit ourselves to them. *Death of the California spirit*, some say. I say, bullshit. We're the fifth richest country in the world and rapidly expanding, floating east towards Japan. Who knows what wonders are yet to come.

Out There

A loud crack–more of a pop really–woke Dee from the morning sleep that was so delicious to her lately, since she often didn't nod off until just before dawn. She rushed outside in her gown (no one to see her, after all), knowing what it must be. Another pop as she went out the back door. "Bad," she cried, "awful bad!" Stumbling backward away from the house in bare feet, she watched one half of the huge salt pine split away from the main trunk and go down atop her roof with a slow groan. "Not the house. My God! Not my house!" Incredibly, the old two story structure held the weight of half that split trunk, thick as a barrel, which lay now across the roof peak, stout branches flopping down either side. It dented the roof and half obscured the south side of the house, left an ugly white scar where it had torn away from the tree. "Poor thing," Dee whispered, not knowing whether she meant the tree or her house.

A branch snapped in the mesquite thicket. Not a coyote; they moved silently. Just the tree. She knew it unlikely for a person to be way out here this time of night–any time, for that matter–believed she could hear the roof moan in cellulose agony, similar to the agony of the tree. Then, with a great whoosh and splintering of timbers, the tree broke through into the attic. Dee watched dust snake out that hole in her roof, opened her mouth to taste it as it floated down wind toward her, the recent past coating her tongue: *my fiftieth birthday, drinking days with Tripp Henry, moving out here to the desert...the Petersons dying here on the place, the time their boy set the house afire*...on back before the turn of the century (this one of the earliest homesteads in the Coachella), and eons before that–the taste of time itself, alkaline and chalky, older than God.

"I believe it's going to hold. I believe the frame is going to hold it. Hah! A tree in your attic, Delores. Can you beat that? What the hell! You've lived with worse." She did a jig around the yard, sat cross-legged in the dirt and plucked puncture weed spurs from pink soles of her feet. Nasty stuff. "You'd best get busy, Delores, and dig it up, after you seal off the attic. Get Lawr out to cut up that tree–if he'll come. Tripp Henry to fix the damn roof–if he'll come. Sure he will! Hold a bottle before Tripp's nose and he'd follow you to hell." Depressed her to think of having him back on the place. The hard-drinking days with Tripp had all but killed her, half-destroyed her liver, left flesh sagging on her bones. The D.T.'s! My God! Scorpions, giant fire ants, and tree rats with phosphorescent yellow eyes invaded her bedroom, psychopathic drifters commandeered back rooms of that huge house—she heard them muttering to themselves through the walls—and still invaded her dreams. No sir, a woman living alone in the desert doesn't court delirium.

She stopped cold. Told Tripp, "I want you out! I don't want you back. About time, too. My kids wanted me to stop drinking years ago." Tripp sped away in his old jeep, missed a turn in his pisshead fury and crashed the jeep in a dry wash. Thrown clear of the wreckage, he broke his collarbone and both legs, lay for two days in the summer heat at the mercy of biting flies and feasting ants before she found him, his lips so swollen she could barely dribble water through them. She fashioned a rough travois of a blanket and mesquite limbs and pulled him to her pickup, got all two-hundred-twenty pounds of him up into it, took him to the hospital in Indian Springs. They saved the old bastard's life. His jeep remained in that wash as a symbol of self-destructive bullheadedness.

Those months following were a hell of cold sweats and stomach cramps, peculiar jabbing headaches that tingled around her cranium, desolation of mind and soul. Walking out in the heat of the day into a bleak landscape of scrub chaparral and mesquite trees half-buried in sand, she could not imagine what she was doing living alone out here, no other human soul within miles. No sense that there was an outside world at all. It couldn't be good for you.

Then she got busy: repaired the old windmill and chicken coops, bought hens, grew a garden in thin, scrappy soil, scavenging whatever sad vegetables she could from gophers and ground squirrels, made herself a pleasant little nest one side of the house. One-hundred-ten degree heat connected her to the desertscape, fused her with it, as did the night sky with its multitude of chorusing stars. She sat out in a lawn chair nights and conversed with them. Maybe she lacked human companionship, but she had the cosmos.

And painting. Taking up where she'd left off years ago in San Francisco, painting thinly, since (given *the troubles*) there would be no more oil paint and brushes when her supply ran out. She fashioned pigments of red mudstone and dark silt from the wash, alkali white, palmetto extract, and a pale yellow-green tincture from ground up yucca fruit, pink from the parasitic worms that invaded their seeds; she extracted a pithy turpentine from creosote bush; she made do. Painted her own "Starry Night"–pasting zucchini seeds to the canvas for stars. Walls of the house chockablock with her works.

She had saved a bottle of vodka for medical emergency (several, truth to tell), stashed away a little of everything–gasoline, kerosene for her lamps, the larder full of bagged lentils, rice, flour and such, the big tank brimful of water. If vagrants, who occasionally wandered past, knew what all she hoarded there would be trouble. But the old Victorian looked derelict, sandblasted to bare gray wood by Santa Ana winds, windows boarded up. The trailer house parked beside it, where the previous owner had lived, in better condition, but Dee liked a house. The south gable forfeited now to half a tamarisk pine—about all that grew out here, with mesquite and squaw bush, cholla cactus, and damnable puncture weed, a few stately Washingtonia palms.

A sharp limb had broken through the ceiling of the parlor south side of the house, bringing splintered rafters and shattered plaster down over furniture and bookshelves, finally wedging between two floor joists that held up the whole shebang. She closed the door between it and the back half of the house. Done. Upstairs, she sealed off the hallway with plastic sheeting to keep birds and lizards out of her living quarters—could make out long scaly tamarisk needles hanging down in whiskbroom bundles through the barrier. Cozy. However, it occurred to her it might be dangerous to live in a house that had half a tree resting atop it. The carcass gave off an occasional pop, and once the house shifted under her feet as in an earthquake. One such rifle crack woke her after dawn one morning. Dee expected the house to collapse like a deck of cards: south side going down in a detonation of rubble, pulling the north half over atop it. Her inside. She heard voices downstairs in the kitchen. What in the holy hell! *That you, Tripp?* She just stopped herself from calling out. Marauders, no doubt–bands of itinerant gypsies that went from place to place scavenging and killing at will. She seized the 12-gauge from the bedroom corner, broke it across her knee, rammed shells home, and cocked it with a gratifying clunk. Tiptoed down the back stairs in her nightgown and flip-flops towards a man's hoarse, oddly-recognizable voice in the kitchen.

"Don't nobody lives here no more, I don't guess. She must of moved to the trailer."

"Looks like it is, Pop," a boy answered in a high-pitched girl's voice.

"You bet there is." She kicked open the door and stepped off the bottom step, gun barrel raised. "Y'r trespassing."

The man threw up his hands histrionically and backed away. "Take it easy there, lady! How we s'posed to know it's occupied? You got you a tree through your house." Grinning.

"We thought it was vacant," the boy insisted. "We wouldn't never of come inside a occupied house, ma'am, I swear it. Right, Pop? We saw the tree and we got curious."

"Never," the man agreed. "We don't got much, but we got our principles."

"I wonder you do. First among them is eating. I don't

have booze if that's what you want. I can spare you some food. I expect it's you two stealing my chickens; it's you I heard in the mesquite the night my tree fell. I believed I had a fox until I saw the chicken wire slit. A fox works its nose through a weak spot, a coon gets hold of a hen leg from below and drags it down through the slats, eats it alive, a human reaches in a hand and grabs its neck. That would be you two!"

"Like I say, we got our principles. Right, Lester?"

"Yessir. My mom's sick, she needed chicken soup real bad. Pop said you had you a lots of chickens anyhow."

The man gave the boy a sharp look. "That's a deadly weapon there, lady." He studied the shotgun. She thought him ugly: whip snake lean, beard black and scraggly, fierce, hungry little eyes set deep in sockets, his red lips, plump and concupiscent, contrasting cheeks that were hard high lumps, hair caught back in a ponytail. In some men this would be an affectation; in him it was a provocation. The boy his physical opposite: corners softened, hair a tangled nest; Dee had an urge to brush it out. Their skin never saw soap. The man stepped abruptly forward, seized the gun barrel in a fist and snatched it away from her. *God help me now.*

"That would'a blowed up in your face you pulled that trigger, ma'am." Pointing out to her how the barrel was clogged with rust and gunk. "Once in a while, lady, you got to clean a firearm."

"I believed I did pull it," she muttered. "Where are you from?" she asked the boy.

"Missouri...once upon. Most everywhere between. We been staying up the road in that mesquite canyon."

His father gave him another angry look. "We're traveling...when we can score gas. Camped up the road a few days until my wife is fit to move on."

Wasn't likely to impress them that they were trespassing. They'd been spying on her for days, she realized, sizing her up—glimpses of movement she'd seen in chaparral, a creepy-crawly feeling at back of her neck. "I don't doubt you've been filling your water jugs at my pump?"

"She wouldn't of shot, d'ya think?" the boy asked his father.

"I believe she would of." The man spit some bit of gristle from his mouth.

She sent them outside and went furtively into the larder to scoop cornmeal and pinto beans into paper bags for them, knowing they could overpower her and take it all if they wished. When she went out, the boy was making his way up the tree trunk, sure-footed as a monkey, bare feet clinging to rough bark. Dee afraid it would give way beneath him and he'd go down with it into the rubble, but the boy stood on the tree trunk, shifting his weight foot to foot, declaring it solid as a rock. The man, gone Solomonic, marveled that she should still be living in the house. Dee made them a breakfast of eggs and cornbread. The boy actually licked his plate clean of crumbs and egg yolk, declaring it the best damn breakfast he'd eaten since leaving home. "Thank you, ma'am. I'll wash dishes." Dee felt she had formed an unspoken pact with him. But hoped they would be gone at the cost of two chickens, breakfast, and a little food and water, knowing damn well they wouldn't.

"My boy and me can buck up that tree and get it off your roof for you, ma'am. Pay you back for the chickens," the man proposed. "We got a bow saw back at camp."

"Yeah," the boy cried.

She agreed, knowing it could be months before Lawr got out this way with his chainsaw.

§

Dee walked down the road to the intruders' camp with a pan of biscuits. Makeshift tents and canopies of black plastic sheeting cluttered about an old Dodge van tucked into a canyon behind a fringe of scrappy mesquite, two skinned rabbit carcasses dried in the sun, flies sizzling over them. A spit—for broiling chickens?—suspended over the fire ring. She had smelled their wood smoke but dismissed it for smoke drifting east from wildfires in the San Jacintos. Seeing a figure dodge around a corner of the house one moonlit night, she had decided it was ancestral spook spirits, vestiges of the old ones. You saw them out here. Could not be frightened of such and live in the desert. Coyotes either. She threw rocks at them when they came too close. The desert more alive with beings, living and dead, than most imagined.

As the wan, skinny mother and a daughter who might've been the boy's twin—except her hair shorn in a buzzcut, eyes dodgy, mistrustful little rodents–approached her, Dee had the distinct impression that they knew her face, while she had never seen them before. Spooky. The woman looked like a Dorothea Lange photo of gaunt dust-bowl women, pale and sickly, so that the courage nearly failed Dee to say what she'd come to say. The boy put on the enamelware kettle for tea, turning on her that complicitous grin. "Nothing against you people," she began, "but I moved out here to be on my own. I dislike neighbors. Solitude is more precious to me than gold."

"I'd think you got lonely," the woman said. "I can't be alone five minutes without I do."

Dee regarded her thin lips and sand-dry hair. "It's other people make me lonely. I was never so lonely in my life as when I was a wife and mother. Other people existed but I didn't. Out here I cast a healthy shadow."

"She's weird." The girl frowned. The children, it seemed to Dee, tokened a family schizophrenia. Altogether unsettling.

"The fellahs say you hired them to cut up a tree. We

sure do appreciate the work."

"I didn't hire them," Dee snapped, "they volunteered. I'd like you gone once they finish."

"Not much generous, are you?" the woman said.

"She's weird," the girl decided again.

The men started work in the cool of the next morning and progressed slowly, complaining of the hardness of the wood, how they must crawl along the main trunk on hands and knees to cut limbs with the bow saw. At noon Dee invited them in for a bowl of bean soup and biscuits.

"You sure do like biscuits, ma'am," the boy said. "Me, too!"

The father gripped a flat biscuit between thumb and forefinger. "Kinda paltry."

"No milk to mix in the batter," she said. "I make do."

They spent the next day bucking up limbs cut from the trunk; the boy stacked pieces in a neat row to one side of the house. That night was unseasonably cold for early May; father and son returned next morning, looking ragged and chilled to the bone. "My wife is got her cough back bad," the man said, as they sat drinking tea by the firepit. "That box canyon is a Frigidaire. I bet you're toasty warm in the house. Not a care in the world." His quick eyes coming to rest on the trailer. "You got you a stove in that trailer, too, I bet? And nobody living there."

"I prefer a house," she said.

"There's people got no place to sleep but the bare ground—two kids and a sick wife. Here you got you two houses for one person. That don't seem right. Does it, boy?"

The boy ducked his head and murmured, "No, sir. Mom's cough is got real bad again."

"It's a long walk from camp, besides. Can't get her done as quick."

"My dad's knee is acting up again, ma'am."

Dee looked back and forth between. Working like team ropers, those two. "You're saying you want to stay in my trailer? Is that what it is?"

"We wouldn't ask, ma'am. But might take you up on it if you're offering. Get the boy's mother up offn the cold ground."

Dee scandalized at what she was tacitly offering—if she was. She'd known their kind in San Francisco—passive aggressive sorts who never asked for a thing but morally bullied you into offering. "I've lived fifteen years out here without neighbors," she said, her voice thin and defeated.

"We'd be thankful." The man worked a horny thumbnail into a gap between his front teeth; no doubt this nail-gouging helped to wedge them apart. Now and again he spat something indeterminate in the dirt. Somehow he reminded her of Charlie Manson. "Just 'til we get her bucked up, ma'am." Smiling at her, those obscene red lips.

They took the morning off work to move in—rusting van, dried rabbits and all. Dee overheard the wife telling her husband it was the least the "old witch" could do, "given all the work you done around her place for her." She had a mind to turn them out...if they'd go!

The fellows started bucking up the main trunk that afternoon: great thuds shook the house as heavy rounds crashed into the attic, and Dee feared they would break through into the room below. That evening the woman knocked on her back door to borrow some flour; she smiled ingratiatingly, while her dark green eyes roamed the kitchen, taking inventory—"emerald green," some would say; "devious green," Dee thought. "The children like their rabbit breaded," she said. "Actually, ma'am, they prefer cornmeal—if it wouldn't be no trouble."

"You people all set in the trailer then?"

"Jus' like back home. Surprises me you don't live there yourself, nice as it is." She studied a painting Dee had done of a red scorpion, its tail raised to strike, her cheeks sucked in.

"I prefer a house. I'm glad you're comfortable. Still, as I say, once they finish the job, I'd like my privacy back... please!"

"I was hoping I might bother you for a shower tonight, ma'am. I kinda...y'know—" raising her elbow to mock sniff an armpit.

Dee waved a hand. "There's a tank with a spigot in back: cold water, but I'm used to it. We'll have to share the privy."

The woman regarded her with that bloodless, thin-lipped gaze "A woman your age living on her own out here, could be dangerous, what with desperados and such like wandering about anymore." Her eyes, the green of glass seen from an opaque edge, revealed nothing.

"Desperados? You mean vagabonds like you folks? What age do you take me for?"

By way of answer, the woman rose to examine one of Dee's paintings on the kitchen wall: a coyote skull with datura leaves garlanded over it, moved on to a "Starry Sky" festooned with pumpkinseeds, her filthy fingers traipsing over the surface so that Dee feared she would scrape them off...into the living room uninvited to examine other canvases hung studio style, covering nearly the total wall space, recent works done on boards and window panes, since she'd run out of canvas. Fog paintings: vague faces and quixotic ancestral beings suspended in obtuse surreality, floating by with bulging eyes–whether in San Francisco or here in the desert on rare misty nights, Dee couldn't say. Her "Out There" series: cholla cactuses sprouted from the gaping maws of rotted car tires, carcasses of huge black dung beetles on their backs, antennae legs stuck in the air, insect skeletons ensnared in orb spider webs strung between bleached, skeletal tree snags. Tahquitz, of course, who preyed on desert souls, striding along at dusk like a roadrunner on jointed stick legs. The woman couldn't keep her hands off–like a child who must palpate the work to see it; her lips moved as if she were discussing the work with herself. Dee disliked grubby hands on her work, but the woman's childish need to experience her paintings tactiley warmed Dee to her.

"I see you been busy," she said. "Alf told me you was an artist."

"I wouldn't call myself an 'artist.' I enjoy painting."

"It's the most depressing paintings I ever seen. I wonder you don't sit here and cry."

Dee smiled. "Melancholy, maybe...the sadness of being alive."

"It's all and everything dead in them."

"Well, y'r never very far from death in the desert. Truly, they make me happy."

The woman regarded her as her daughter might, head cocked to one side. "Half flour, half cornmeal, if you don't mind?" she said, as if making Dee an offer.

§

Years ago, after her kids were grown, Dee left her husband, George, and moved to San Francisco, excited about her new life as an artist. She spent a miserable year living in a close studio apartment, working as a temp, hating the pointless hustle-bustle of making plans and making money, making whoopee–when you could get it, usually regretting it when you did. Never actually making anything at all. Except sad colorless little still lifes. She felt like she was living inside a glass bubble that wasn't glass at all, nor even tissuey cellophane, not filled with air but toxic fumes–half car exhaust, half urban malevolence. Not that people were unkind or unfriendly; it was society itself that seemed hostile. Sure, there were blessed times when salt fog rolled in from the bay and coated streets and houses in a thick gouache of moisture. Noises were muffled, you could open your senses and taste the ocean. She took long night walks in Golden Gate Park, oblivious to danger. Some would have invited the kids down to fill the hole in their lives, but Dee needed to do this on her own. Besides, they had always disapproved of her drinking, would disapprove all the more now she was drinking alone. She sent them postcards with no return address. She would reunite with the children once she was established. She felt called to the desert–open space uninhabited by humans. Odd that San Francisco fog and damp should spark in her a desire for arid emptiness. Loneliness, yes, for the fog enclosed you in a bubble of self.

Someone once said that self is a small package and that we can only find happiness by transcending self through involvement with others. Whoever said it didn't know the desert. The isolated self, combined with huge empty space, all that night sky, becomes a great cathedral, the mind a yawning cosmos. Dee was never unhappy; she only felt lonely when other people came around.

She sat out beyond the garden in the sagebrush that evening to watch the sky, heedless of red ants and scorpions detouring around her sandaled feet, could hear the alien sound of a harmonica and a woman singing near the house—sixties songs: *Me and Bobby McGhee* and *Mr. Tambourine Man*. Appropriate to have that heady, volatile time roll around again. Back then, people had spun idle fantasies about how dire things would be in the future, but they had no idea...none at all! They could carry a tune, anyway, but Dee preferred the music of silence. *Not that I dislike people, but they almost always disappoint me... and me them! Even my own kids. When I finally got around to sending them a return address, they never got around to replying. People are disappointing. Besides, people mean booze. Vi and Ernie back home each evening at four p.m.: "Cocktail time!" We drank for hours, while stuffed-shirt George rattled his newspaper in the family room and fumed about dinner. "We're starving, Dee, for crissakes." One advantage to drinking alone is you don't have to cook meals for people. No one to stop you from falling in the bottle and drowning either. Tripp dove in with me.*

They didn't dare cut more of that tree, the man said,

given the steep angle at which it lay against the house. "We need a winch or block and tackle. Maybe I'll come up with something." A week later they were still in the trailer. Mom and daughter alternated borrowing food, the girl thrusting out an importunate bowl: "Mom needs some beans...please."

"I gave you beans yesterday."

They soon discovered that she preferred the boy's requests. He ferried her shy, apologetic glances and asked what he could do for her in return, helped her repair the chicken coop and expand the garden. They sat at kitchen table and talked of desert wonders: how you can tell time by how fast a lizard does push-ups and see the Earth's slow spinning in the stars' movement across the sky. She told him of monsters she'd seen: giant desert roaches and devil Tahquitz who ate men's souls.

"You seen him with your own two eyes?"

"I did. He passed back and forth before the house like a vulture, waiting for me to weaken, taller than any man and stick thin, with hyena's teeth and yellow eyes. Well, I had withdrawal sickness bad from kicking the booze, but I wasn't that sick for him to take me."

"He'd eat your soul? Wow! What else you seen?"

"I saw Willy Boy one evening, a renegade Indian who killed and raped for the fun of it."

"I'd 'a blowed his head off with y'r shotgun."

"You can't very well kill him if he's already dead, now

can you?"

He considered this. "My mom seen stuff. When she's bad sick enough, she seen stuff. I'm glad I don't."

She might have told him that she had often heard his father's hoarse, unmistakable voice through thin walls of her house back in drinking days—one of those vagabond spooks squatting in front rooms of her house—knew that voice when she heard him downstairs in the kitchen that first morning, become corporeal. Since then she'd heard him shouting at the boy, heard the boy's protests and the sound of blows. "Tell me, Lester, does your father hit you?"

"He wouldn't never, ma'am. I promise he wouldn't. Pop gets pissed off if I mess up is all."

"Will you come to me if he does?"

"Yes, ma'am. But he wouldn't."

Next morning, the man flew into a rage when the axe handle split while the boy was chopping wood. He spun the axe around his head, so that Dee, watching from the garden, feared he would plant it in his son's skull. Instead, he flung it into the thicket of dense mesquite, shouting, "Now see what you made me do, you little bastard. We'll never find the gawdamned thing." He hopped from foot to foot in his rage, tears streaming down his cheeks as Dee approached.

"You'll give yourself a heart attack, Alf. Don't worry, we'll find your axe head; I'm sure I have an extra handle about the place."

"Mind your own damn business, you old cunt." He seized the boy's arm and led him off into chaparral, and Dee feared she had only stoked his rage through her meddling. *Mind your own damn business! Well, isn't it...here on my own place? Isn't it?*

After a time the man reappeared without the boy. Had he beaten him bloody and left him lying out there under the hot sun? Dee ready to go looking for him when the mother emerged from the mesquite thicket with an arm about her son–filthy, his clothes sweat-soaked, face and arms scratched and bloody, whether from mesquite thorns or a beating or both Dee couldn't say. He could barely stand up. He had not found the axe head. Mom went into the outdoor shower with him, clothes and all, and washed his wounds. This softened her towards the woman. But Lester did not return to borrow food or visit Dee again.

§

When she could not make up her mind about a thing, Dee went to the canvas. Before going on the wagon, she had done a painting of a human skull on the desert floor with a broken vodka bottle stuck through it. Now she began a painting of a Charlie Manson look-alike beside an agave with an axe raised over his head, her sketchy Victorian in the background, split in two by a tree, but could not finish the picture, not knowing how it would end. She felt sorry for the boy and his mother, but how could she help them? They were not her family, she wasn't responsible for them, she hadn't wanted them here in the first place, hadn't invited them to stay. Besides, didn't the daughter tell a different story, one of familial complicity? One day, she quickly sketched in the remainder: the wife cowering on the ground before her husband, hands shielding her head, Lester to one side like the renegade Willy Boy, bowstring drawn, aiming an arrow at his father.

Dee cleaned and oiled the old shotgun and determined she would not permit the man to beat his son again. Such an irony that at a time when few could have children (the planet gripped by Depressed Fertility Syndrome) people like this should be blessed with them. Humans had collectively, if unconsciously, decided the earth was too hostile an environment to bring children into; sperm and ovum shriveled up in the reproductive organs as if exposed to intense heat. Itinerants like these, annealed as they were by tensions of the road perhaps, were more fertile than most.

Weeding in the garden one evening, Dee was tallying up the toll her "neighbors" had taken on tomatoes and zucchini, when Lester hissed at her from behind yucca spears outside the fence. "My dad would get after me good if he saw we was talking," he whispered. "I know it's wrong to go against my dad, but it's wrong if I don't say nothing either. My Dad says we ain't going to cut up that tree no more and ain't going to leave, neither one. If you don't like it, he says he intends to run you off the place. It don't seem right."

"Is that what he says? What about you? Are you all right?" she whispered back.

"Don't worry none about me. He gets at me too bad, I'll run off. Mom knows."

"Listen, Lester," she said, for a plan had hatched in her mind fully formed, as they will at moments of extreme stress, "you tell your mother I need to talk to her. She's superstitious, you say?"

"Terrible superstitious, ma'am. She seen spooks herself. She got a gift that way."

Dee built a fire that evening in the ring behind the house, which she rarely did, fearing embers might reach the mesquite forest; all combustible things out here forever on the verge of igniting spontaneously. The woman joined her, pink-cheeked in firelight; settling down suited her. So Dee felt half guilty for what she was about to do. "Listen, dear, I've seen Tahquitz again, sniffing like a coyote at your back door. I believe he wants your children. He always did covet the tender spirits."

"What's Tahquitz?" the woman asked. "Some kind of animal?"

"The Cahuillas believe he lives in a mountain cave

and comes down below to feed on human souls. I've seen him roaming the desert, grunting and half-mad from hunger and loneliness. He looks like a human hyena covered in spots, gaunt and hideous ugly. I about jumped out of my skin the first time I saw him."

"Now there's a load of horseshit." The man approached from the trailer in the semi-dark. "If he's so damn hungry, why don't he eat you then?"

"I suppose he dislikes the taste of old women. He wants the young. I warn you, dear, you best keep your children inside after dark. I'd leave here at once if I were you."

"Well, you ain't!" The man's spittle hit the fire with a hiss. But Mom's eyes were huge and watery in the firelight, her slack countenance suddenly infused with energy. "I heard rustling right outside our door last night. Didn't I do, Alf? I told him it's not fit for children here, much as I like the trailer. But he don't never listen to me."

"I'll tell you what, everyone goes lunatic out here. She's always dreaming up something or other." Winding a finger around an ear.

"I seen a woman walking through the sagebrush calling on her babies. Nobody heard her but me. He said it's you, but I know it ain't. D'you suppose this Tawk-witch ate her babies?"

"I'm sure of it," Dee said. "I've seen her, too. You know, I wanted you people off the place, but I've become fond of your son; I might even tolerate him for a neighbor. Tolerating him, I've learned to tolerate the rest of you."

The man stabbed viciously at the gap between his front incisors with a thumbnail. "I told that little bastard to stay clear of you. I warned him!"

"No, no, now...I've missed him these past weeks." Dee recalling how husband and wife had argued half violently after the axe incident, and she'd feared he would beat her, too. "What I'm saying is I've grown accustomed to you. Still, I think you should go for the children's sake. Kids disappear from our desert communities all the time. Sometimes they find their skeletons—always missing the skulls."

"He eats their heads offn them?"

"Besides which," the man said, "we haven't finished cutting up your tree. I haven't figured how to do her yet. Haven't found my axe head neither. We got our principles."

"Don't you worry about the tree. I can live with it."

"She still owes us for a week's work," the woman said, alarm supplanted by mercenary resolve. Turning to Dee: "We could take it in gas and food."

"Oh, could you? Listen, I will keep a fire burning and sit watch for him."

On nights following, Dee sat cross-legged before the fire, feeding it datura leaves and sage, which filled the air with thick, skunkish smoke, her face painted in mud that dried and cracked and pulled at her skin, hawk feathers in her hair; she cut quite a figure, chanting incantations and waggling fingers in the air. She heard them arguing inside: father and daughter insisting she was a nutjob, mother and son intrigued.

Dee rode her bike to Tripp Henry's early one morning, not imagining what condition she would find him in. Tripp's old Airstream a relic from another time, as were the Corvettes and Mustangs he'd once lovingly restored, tires rotting under them, paint fading. The place a desert junkyard: motor blocks slung from hoists, eviscerated flatbeds and car chassis, a hippy schoolbus with remnants of a teepee frame inexplicably perched atop it (had been for years), tar paper peeled off the shack that was once his shop. Date palms alone looked healthy. Tripp came stumbling outside when Dee called to him, looking like death warmed over, taller even than she remembered.

"Why, you old bastard, I'd think it would of killed you to quit drinking."

"Who quit?" Tripp worked a thumb in his ear and hawked to one side. "It's yucca root beer mostly anymore. Gawdamned awful stuff going down. Still, y'r welcome to join me."

"I'm not about to start again; about killed me to quit the first time. I've got a bottle of vodka for you, Tripp. I wanted you to repair my roof, but it will have to wait."

She explained the scheme to him and said there would be a second bottle when he finished. Tripp whooped laughter.

"Driving off neighbors...Oh yeah, I'm good at that."

§

Tahquitz hobbled through chaparral in the moonlight, firelight dancing over his pot-bellied body–thin and tall, stooped as he naturally was, bare chest and legs glazed with red clay, polka-dotted with white splotches, his bald head skull white, as were his ribs, coated in flour paste, eye sockets black. He cursed and slashed at the air with a machete. Dee fled the fireside and pounded on the trailer door, shrieking for them to let her in. The woman wouldn't open. Finally the man did, standing in the open doorway, looking out at the demon, dodging from shadow to firelight, hopping like a lame, demented rabbit and grunting.

"What the hell's that?"

"It's him," Dee said, "Tahquitz!" Fearing the canny fellow might see through the ruse or, worse, attack Tripp. The mother had squeezed back in a corner of the tiny living room, hugging the kids to her, near hysteria, begging them, please, to close the door. Perhaps Tripp overdid it: he leapt over the fire and nearly fell back into it, approached the trailer, slashing the air with one hand, rubbing his belly with the other, and groaning. Vodka drunk and fearless. The man slammed the door on him and threw the deadbolt. "Whoever the hell he is, I don't want him in here, scaring hell out of my wife and kids. You got you a lot of maniacs out here."

"I've never seen him so hungry."

"Big dude like that, why don't he knock down the door and come right in?"

"He won't enter a dwelling...never. It's ancient tradition. Anyone outside is fair game."

"She says we're safe in here, Starr," he told his wife, who wept inconsolably and painted her children's faces with kisses. "We're all right now."

Next morning they packed to go, and Dee let them fill the van with gas from the tank—precious little as there was left—and packed them a bag of dried food and garden produce. The man had suspicions about Tahquitz, but the woman wouldn't stay another day. While his parents packed, Dee told Les, "You'll always be welcome here—if you ever do decide to run away."

"I like it here a whole lots...except for your cannibal."

At that moment, Tripp stumbled down the back steps of the house in his boxer shorts, muttering. Flour paste peeling off his skull made him look leprous. Dee had been afraid of this. Last night the old lech tried to get into bed with her, but finally gave up and settled for the couch.

"Tawk-witch?" the boy asked, wide-eyed.

Dee shrugged. "He's an old wino friend of mine. Guess we got caught."

Lester held a finger to his lips and grinned; both waved Tripp back inside just as his parents emerged from the trailer. "Remember what I told you," Dee said. "I enjoy having you about the place. Never thought I'd hear myself say that."

Tripp emerged again while alkali dust still hung in the air from their departing van—the taste of time or melancholy or blessed isolation. "I better hang around a few days in case they come back," he grumbled.

"Oh no you don't, Tripp Henry. You're after more of my vodka."

"The hell! I'm soberer than a teatotaler this morning. Just looking out for you is all."

"I appreciate it, Tripp. But if they wanted to clean me out, they would have done it. I'm looking forward to being alone again."

"Gawdamned parasites," he said.

She sat out that night under a sky so lucid, so star-blessed that the mesquite trees and squaw bush cast shadows, the Milky Way a swash of painted light; how often she'd tried—how often failed—to capture that sky in her paintings. The house's silhouette seemed out of place: crushed in one side, remnants of that salt pine leaning toward it. "We are never safe," she spoke aloud, "never

beyond surprise. Any moment things can change entire-
ly. Any moment we may change our minds." Speaking as
if the boy lay beside her on the sandy earth, arms folded behind his head, gazing up at the stars. *D'you s'pose
they see us back, ma'am?* she heard him ask. *D'you s'pose
there's someplace out there where it all works out the way
it's s'posed to?*

In a Strong Wind

lizards scurry around to the lee side of a tree and cling hold for dear life. Poignant somehow, like humans clinging hold no matter what. But here lately the winds are erratic, coming from all directions at once as if they can't make up their mind, as fickle as Granny Whitehead, no doubt suffering from meteorological dementia. Lizards clinging hold of bark with their sharp little claws like climbers on a sheer rock face, snatched away with a pop, vacuumed into the maw of the wind. It's disconcerting watching a lizard whip off like that, head craned to one side, stubby legs spread-eagled. Just gone! So where do they end up–lizards and mockingbirds, errant crows, ground squirrels, lawn chairs, roof shingles, palm beards, the occasional trailer house ferried off on the wind? As *windpack* in gulleys that splay off our local foothills? I intend to go find out once the wind lets up. Dust devils wriggle and thrash off the Earth's skull like dreadlocks, suspended in a filthy sky, surfeited with objects large and small. Mini-twisters that won't touch down. Walky Talky insists they don't reach sufficient velocity to be called "tornadoes." Dry and parsimonious, they wring moisture from vegetation; the air crackles with static electricity, blink and it shocks your eyeballs. Much more of this and we will all mummify.

"What the hell are they then?" Benson asks. "Dry earth cyclones maybe?"

"I'd call them 'Santa Anas supersized.'"

"Nonsense...you and your *supersized!*" Cora reminds me that the last fast food disaster closed down in Haneysville two years ago–burgers so full of E. coli by then you couldn't even feed them to your dogs. "Why do you want to resurrect all that?"

"I don't."

I fear our time is coming. Once there were rows of canned venison lined up in mason jars on shelves of the dining room hutch–pink chunks of meat afloat in what looked to be amniotic fluid, canned prosperity. We're down to the last half dozen. I haven't bagged a deer in two years. Drought or dying forests or pestilential terrorist bands training in the mountains have about wiped them out. We'll have to go to rabbit soon. Or gopher.

Myrna Haney down at Yesterdays says the winds are a sign of "God's almighty wrath." "It's the rapture coming. The Lord is scouring away evil with his mighty breath."

"I never took the Lord for having such foul halitosis,"

I tell her. "Have you smelled the breeze lately? A mix of burning tires and putrefying flesh."

"Well, I never!" Myrna squares up. "Listen here, our Lawrence, I have known the heathen to insult the Lord, but I never heard anyone insult his pure breath."

I'm the single customer in Yesterdays (her sister Melinda's restaurant), but for Henry Staidley who sits drinking coffee all day long, as much a fixture as the counter stools. I eat a piece of Melinda's "Believer's Cobbler" (rhubarb, potato and carrot, garnished with orange rind). Myrna strokes her big chin with a hand strong as a woodcutter's, watching me eat; her emerald eyes, unflinching in that square, spinsterish face, are nearly sensual, aglow with believer's passion. A conundrum, those eyes. She and her sister live together, unmarried, celibate—let's suppose, though Myrna was a freelove hippie once. Plate glass windows up front ripple like canvas sails in the wind.

"Whooo-goodness! The Lord will have his comeuppance, our Lawrence."

"Why, because I said *he* has bad breath? Actually, you did. Myself, I figure his breath is ancient and moldy. Your cobbler's mighty good today, Myrna. I'd take me another slice, but you'll need it for other customers."

She laughs and scoops me out another bowlful. "What customers is that, our Lawrence? Besides Henry, we haven't had a dozen customers this week."

"Damn depressing. Nobody in Sluggards Creek with work or money to spend."

Corners of Henry Staidley's mouth downturn. "Doom and gloom...doom and gloom! You see what I'm saying?"

Behind the counter Myrna stands frozen like Lot's wife, staring ahead. "The Lord will destroy a heathen race," she warns, "like Sodom and Gomorrah. His will be done."

"You need to try this cobbler, Henry. It will make a believer of you."

"I already tried. And it didn't."

"No, sir—" I nod "–it wouldn't! You folks won't convert anymore of us in town, Myrna. You've found all the believers there are to be found in S.C. Truth is, believers are born not made. Same as nonbelievers. We may believe we have free will, but it's an illusion. We're hard-wired to be what we are. Our natural temperament always asserts itself in the end."

Those two stare at me. Henry guffaws. "Where inna hell'd that come from?" Myrna's mouth agape, each square tooth buffed as if it has emerged from a car wash. "Blasphemy," she barks. "What a depressing place this world would be if sinners had no hope of redemption in Jesus Christ just because they were born heathen. Why, it contradicts the gospel of Good News."

"I'm merely stating the obvious: people don't change much once their personalities form."

Myrna hisses like a cat and disappears through swinging double doors back into the kitchen.

BUT I AM WRONG IN MY ASSESSMENT

of human changeability, as I am about to learn. Human constancy may apply under normal conditions, but there's nothing normal about these times.

Once the wind dies down, I drive up the mountain. Windfalls of Jeffrey pine everywhere, dead trees lie across each other like pick-up-sticks. Entire hillsides denuded. Depressing. First the drought, then pine beetle infestation—needles turning orange and trees dying, thousands of acres of them. Now this devil wind. Drought alone the forests can withstand, but not the ceaseless heat and parching wind. They say pinyon pine over in Arizona are mostly gone, ponderosa in the Sierras. Plenty of firewood to cut, anyhow; I aim to do my bit in clearing away dead snags. With so much fuel littering foothills, we'll have hell to pay once fire season starts. Terrorists are lighting fires up in the Pacific Northwest—were, anyway, until the rains began. A blessing if they weren't washing topsoil out to sea. From a satellite in space, they say you can see an underwater berm extending from the mouth of the Columbia River four hundred miles into the Pacific. The salmon run wiped out. All the news isn't bad. Andrea Basil and Glen Whitehead have taken up. There's a miracle for you, those two always hated each other. Another development, maybe good news, maybe bad: June Gilliam has returned to Sluggards Creek—my daughter's former teacher, my former lover, teensy, blue-blushing Ms. Gilliam. Like I say, maybe good news, maybe bad.

Bad news is global, good news is local. However, it's also true that the worst of bad news is local, seeded from global misfortune. The winds are of that variety. This afternoon they whipped up to a fury. Our chinaberry trees thrashed about like the damned, flailing their arms as if hellfire consumed them; limbs gave way in a fiery crackling and plunged earthward or were whipped off in the gale. The sky thick with leaves and palm beards and the rats that make nests in them. The house shook. I told Cora we'd better get down to the basement, but that required we go outside to reach the cellar door in back. No going out into that wind. We huddled beneath the dining room window, Cora's voice riding over the windhowl: "The other half of Midge Talmadge's barn just flew over. There go her bluetick hounds!"

"The dogs—" I cried "—my God! Where are Jack and Misty?"

"I thought you locked them in the studio."

"I think I forgot."

"How could you forget?" She gripped my shirt with both hands, her tear-streaked face right up in mine. "Gone!" she shouted. "What've you done, Lawr? Nothing can survive out there."

"I'm going out to find them."

"You are doing no such thing. Are you out of your right mind?"

"Look, maybe they took shelter." I thought of those lizards shifting positions like mad dervishes. A dog might hunker down somewhere out of the gale, then the devious wind shift around to ferret it out. It slammed the north side of the house, then the south, then the east...sure to jiggle it loose from foundations. Nothing can withstand such pummeling. Suddenly, the sky was filled with blackbirds, like a flight of fighter jets skimming over at Mach 1 speed, flight of their lives. A flock of what appeared to be movie posters followed: Helen Mirren, Harrison Ford, Leonardo DiCaprio...tiny visages visible an instant and gone.

"There goes what's left of LA," I grumbled.

"Good riddance."

"Likely the Hummers are still there. Nothing can dislodge a Hummer."

A flight of shoes followed, laces tangled. Before you knew it we were balling on the frayed rug under the window. Nothing like danger to get you horny.

"I just saw—*Oh gawd! Lawr, that's the spot...right there!*—Ed Harris. I love him."

"Him...no? *Good god, baby...good fucking god in heaven.*"

"There goes the Third Street Promenade," she gasped,

"and Bergamot Station."

I came at that instant. Something to do with art, no doubt. She'd been coming all along. Women are global, men local. By any measure of common sense, gals should be running things. "Can we do that again?" she wanted to know. I went down on her. Nothing's more comforting than a woman's pubic hair—that global nest—Cora's thicket especially! Half made me forget leaving the dogs outside. Afterwards, we lay whimpering a time, not noticing the wind had stopped.

Finally, we got up and went outside. God's halitosic breath had subsided; over the landscape lay a smell of overripe bananas. Preternatural silence was disturbed by the pitter-patter raining down of objects levitated on the wind: dust and pebbles, twigs and animal scat—a parched dry downpour...the whines of our dogs.

We searched frantically for them in that garbage heap that had been our yard. The wind took our pump shed, chicken coop, the few branches remaining on chinaberry trees. Trunks stuck up from the litter like gnarled, pathetic spars. Incredibly, the barn and Cora's pottery shed stood intact. Possibly, those errant, multi-directional winds had collided and cancelled each other out. Or nature was picking favorites; Cora always was blessed that way. That same principle may have saved our dogs— whimpering, mewling like sheep now. Surely, Jack and Misty were hidden in heaps of smashed branches and tin roofing, shingles, dead cats, and tattered clothing mounded across yard and fields. We ran from pile to pile, calling their names, going down on hands and knees to look inside. Then realized that the whining came not from ground level but from above. We went from tree to tree, looking up into those truncated skeletons. No sign of them! Nor in the dark, swirling maelstrom overhead (Cora believed they were suspended in a dust devil). Clouds were breaking up and dispersing. I went up the ladder to check house and outbuilding roofs. Nothing.

Cora said they were inside a garbage mound and their howls were boomeranging into the sky. So we got to clearing away piles of driftgarbage. I got out the chainsaw and amassed cord rows of firewood behind the barn. We worked all afternoon into the night, lighting the yard with torches. Although we found many animal carcasses, we didn't find Jack and Misty. Exhausted, we collapsed on the screened front porch. I woke up inside Cora again—seemingly, we'd balled all night—too sore to hold my pecker to pee next morning, but psychically rested as if I'd slept a week.

"Tired blood therapy." Cora grinned.

"The dogs!" I cried. We rushed outside and got back to work.

Half wolf that she is, Misty leads the laments, raises her muzzle to the sky and fetches arias from her larynx, hitting trills that cover full octaves. *Help us!* She pleads.

Bring us water. "We're trying," I shout back. By late afternoon we have it cleared back to the brush line. No trace of them. "Maybe it's our own guilty consciences we're hearing," Cora decides. "We need to get Hector Dario up here to see if he can hear them."

Hector stands four-square in the yard, feet wide apart, hands ahip on his utility belt, ear cocked as if to say, *Bring it on.* He looks like the land-locked first mate of a ship that has set to sea without him. "You hear them?" Cora and I both ask. Heck firms his lips together, his chin jerks to one side. "Nope," he says, "can't hear nothing."

"You don't hear them howling?" Cora looks anxiously at me.

"No, ma'am. No dogs up here. I guess you lost 'em. Been windy enough."

"Then it's in our heads, you know. Just like we feared."

Heck looks back and forth between us. He considers us heathen, but not lunatic heathen. You can see it worries him. Terrorists, anarchists and wreckhappies are lunatic heathen—Abu Al Sharif and his lot. His eyes remain glued on us in the rearview as he drives off in his squad car.

I TRY TO RECALL EXACTLY WHAT HAPPENED

in those minutes preceding the storm. I was outside, making sure outbuilding doors were bolted and no lawn furniture lay about; I whispered a hopeless prayer for the few chinaberry limbs remaining on spindly trees, shook a fist at the occult sky–inky, light-swallowing opacity of the clouds–the dogs following in my footsteps, freaked out, I recall. "Okay, guys, I'll put you in the pottery shed. You'll be safe there." I started off to do just that when something distracted me (a sound in the woods perhaps, damned if I remember). I do remember a feeling of dread that we wouldn't get through this unscathed, remember closing and padlocking a door, hearing them whining inside.

"I'm afraid I may have Alzheimer's...early onset," I tell Cora. "My dad had it, you know...may have had it, anyhow."

"Your father died of a heart attack, Lawr. You don't need to worry about your heart, judging from your performance last night. Listen, I don't think it's the dogs or our consciences we are hearing. I think it's a warning: ghost barkers that want to alert us to some danger. Watching out for us."

"Watch ghosts? D'you think? They sound like it–kinda filtered and abstract." I don't really want to go there, what with my son Jeff in harm's way *over there* in the war (last I heard, anyhow), but then we are over here, too. Everybody in harm's way anymore, what with rising sea levels and crazed terrorists and anarchy and creature die-off and drug-resistant diseases. Their yarooing grows weaker. At times only one of us can hear it. I embrace the diminution, interpreting it to mean that danger is diminishing. Maybe Jeff is out of harm's way. Us, too...maybe.

When I stop by Benson's QuikMart to ask if I can supply him with canned venison (if I can find any deer to bag), he tells me that Gil Ridley shot his wife.

"Not yet, he hasn't," I'm astonished to hear myself say, "but it won't surprise me if he does."

"Remember old Gil and Amanda Ridley sitting in the back row at the movies, making out like teenagers at seventy-five," Benson says. "They left condoms up there. How we had to tell them to quit necking at town meetings?" He chuckles. "Radical. You never saw such lovebirds in your life. So he's going to just up and shoot her then? Like I'm telling you, people are getting different anymore."

"Mercy killing is different, Benson. The cancer has spread all over Amanda's body, she's in awful pain. Some might see it as a desperate act of love."

He frowns at me. "I'm saying it's all topsy-turvy anymore. Did you hear that Tommy Whitehead give up science and got saved? Him and Granny both."

"Nonsense. You might as well tell me the Sahara is frozen over and the North Pole gone arid."

Benson turns out his hands and laughs. "There you go."

Come to think of it, maybe Tommy always was something of a true believer—first in hi-tech, now in Jesus!

"Like this rain we're getting, I never seen rain in September," Benson says. "Nonstop. Like the Midwest." He slaps a newspaper on the counter. *Kansas City Star*, one of only three dailies in the country still producing copy. I run the newsprint between my fingers, marveling at its thinness, gritty ink dirtying my fingers. It's years since I last touched a newspaper. The *Star* reports wide-spread disaster across the Midwest: Missouri River become a great pulsing inland sea, what with the ceaseless rain, former dust bowl a bog, swarming with insects, crisscrossed by water spouts (what Walky Talky calls "whirly-twirlys"). Ever since that mega-tornado, with its roving vacuum cleaner mouth, five miles across, took out Oklahoma City, people have abandoned the cities and scattered across the countryside; then came flooding and they flocked back into derelict cities, living in squalid, abandoned buildings, or migrated west as in Tom Joad days and now occupy huge refugee camps across Colorado and Arizona. "Two Okie families just arrived in town," Benson says. "That's how I got the paper. There's this lady says she knows you. A real looker, walks with a limp."

"Knows me?" Could it be my daughter, Lilly, I wonder. Were our *watch ghosts* divining Lilly's return?

"Brought bad luck with her, anyway," Benson says. "She brought all this rain."

"Like we don't have enough bad luck as it is."

Rain sure enough, anyhow. Walky Talky sits glumly in his cabin and reports that a low pressure system extends from the Gulf of Alaska to Baja California–largest sustained low pressure trough since the Biblical flood–a gargantuan water pump emptying the South China sea and dumping its recycled contents on our heads.

Later that day, Tommy Whitehead comes peddling up the hill on his bicycle, water pouring off his rain slicker; I stalk out of the house to meet him. He has supplanted the tiny Phillips head screwdriver piercing his nose septum with a wooden crucifix. "You planning martyrdom, Tommy? What's up?" I snatch the sodden watch cap off his bald skull. "You gone born-again skinhead or what?"

"Bless you, brother Lawr," he mumbles.

"Save the phony blessings, Tom. Your dad's half sick over this Jesus nonsense. Tommy Whitehead getting religion is like Abu Al Sharif converting to Judaism."

"Jesus reconfigured my hard drive, dude. I come up here to bring you the good news." He looks like a hi-tech monk: bald skull slick with rainwater that drips off that crucifix down onto his ball-bearing chin. I have an inexplicable urge to slap him; I grip hold of his handlebars and glare. Not like me at all! Just then I see his soul-self, his Tommy essence, skitter away on an errant gust of wind, phantom limbs outspread like a lizard's. Tommy lost to us, mired in the sticky pablum that passes for conviction. Cora slogs down the muddy drive bare-foot toward us, cocking her head from side to side like a puzzled dog.

"Is that you, Tommy? Or Hector Dario's kid brother, maybe?"

"It's a blessing to see you, sister Cora." He produces a tiny Testament and begins reading from First Corinthians, "*If any man defile the temple of God, him shall God destroy...*"

"Save it!" Cora snaps. "Don't you dare come up here spouting rubbish. What happened to him?" she asks me. "Did Myrna and that lot make off with his brain?"

"Afraid so."

He mumbles something about feeling sorry for us.

"You need to get laid, Tom. There's your problem. I'll take you into L.A. one of these days. There's nothing here in S.C. but married women and churchy spinsters."

Tommy's eyes widen, he tilts his head as if he's heard the Lord's voice. "Your dogs, dude! I hear 'em whining. Don't sound so good. You got 'em down in the cellar or something?"

We hear them: a groaning yarrrooo. "The basement!" I cry, slugging a fist into my open palm. "That's right! I shut them in the basement. I remember now! Damn it all to hell."

"You idiot," Cora shouts. "You fucking idiot!" Can't say I disagree with her.

JACK SPRAWLS ACROSS THE TOP STEP

of the cellar stairs, looking half dead, a foreleg gnawed, perhaps by Misty, who lies below on the cement floor, too weak to lift her head; she moans as I carry her upstairs, emaciated, pounds lighter than when I locked them up down there two weeks ago. I carry her out to a spigot and drip water between her lips, knowing you can't rehydrate a dehydrated patient too quickly. Water trickles over Misty's tongue and down her throat, her eyes roll back. Tommy yelling, "Jack's alive. Praise the Lord. Whooooeee, dude!" A little of the old Tommy returning to us with our dog.

Cora forgives me long enough to minister to the dogs. We feed them a gruel of pulverized venison and rice, squirted down their gullets with a poultry baster. They smell awful, outer layers of skin putrefied. I figure they survived by licking condensed water drops that appear like grubs on an exposed pipe running along a basement wall, pulled things off storage shelves to get to rats' nests in back corners (clean rodent bones litter the cement floor). No doubt Jack gnawed on his own leg, desperately hungry (would walk with a limp from now on), and tore layers of veneer from the basement door, trying to chew his way out. There's a lesson here, a trope of our own slow degeneration: we humans will be cannibalizing ourselves soon, too.

It seems that neither Cora nor the dogs will forgive

me. Jack and Misty veer away from the cellar door each time I let them out the back, and Jack growls at me from back in his throat when I pet him. Nights, when I slip into bed beside Cora, she grumbles, "Forgot where you put them, you idiot!" One night she makes up a bed on the living room couch, and I'm thinking: that's it, end of our intimacy. Cora doesn't forgive easily. To her easy forgiveness betrays a weak character. I remind her, "Neither of us looked down there. You either! How could we not check the cellar, for crissake? Where'd we think their howls came from?"

"How could *you* forget where *you* put them? Do you have Alzheimer's already?"

She's right, of course. How could I? Odd thing is, the moment we find them it all comes back. I recall that I'd even thought about bringing them down a bowl of water as I locked the cellar door. Then a gust of wind whipped through chinaberry branches, and one let go with a heartbreaking crack, and I dashed for the house.

DO WE WILL TO FORGET?

Tommy's sad tale about June Gilliam, for instance, which I wanted to forget the moment he told us. I'd forgotten that Tommy was in Ms. Gilliam's class in grade school—my daughter Lilly's class. I've nearly forgotten what my daughter looks like, haven't seen my little girl since she and her mom left me fifteen years ago. She is a grown woman now. I once told Cora that I don't trust a man whose children want nothing to do with him–forgetting that I am such a man (though I don't see myself that way). I wanted nothing to do with my own father, so perhaps it runs in the family. What I remember is mostly inconsequential trivia: how I last saw those elderly love-birds Gil and Amanda Ridley making love in a road ditch, for instance, their furious coupling akin to Cora and my own during the storm, or that June Gilliam wore purple lipstick and black eyeliner the last time I saw her and smelled of nutmeg, or remember that my daughter, Little Lilly, was afraid of spiders, while my son Jeff caught and buttoned them up in his shirt pocket. Spider keeper. So did I will to forget locking our dogs in the cellar? Surely I love them unconditionally, as they love me. I wish them no harm. But then I love my children, too, and I wish them no harm. Yet somehow I hurt them.

I remember what Tommy came to tell us the day he rode his bike up the hill and cursed us from First Cor-inthians. We'd gotten the dogs hydrated and fed and bedded down and Cora glared at me. Tommy said his old schoolteacher, Ms. Gilliam, was back in town. "She wants to see you, Lawr dude. She's even shorter than she used to be. She lost both legs, the left one from the thigh down and her right one below the knee. She's got hi-tech robot legs now. Freaking amazing, dude. You can't hardly even tell it when she walks. Still, she can't get replacement batteries no more, so I got to work out a way to recharge her batteries." Me glued to his words. My June bug legless–beautiful, blue-blushing June Gilliam! Cora watching me like a hawk, like I wasn't in deep enough shit already. "She was working in the Twin Towers on nine-eleven," Tommy said.

"That's how she lost her legs?" Cora asked.

"No, dude, she survived that incident without a scratch, walked down eighty-four stories. She lost her right leg like on a bus in Israel on a pilgrimage after she found the Lord, where a kid with a pipe bomb was sitting two rows in front of her. She's like healing from that, okay, and the Lord enters her heart and tells her to go on a mission to Somalia and like that—"

"Somalia? What kind of an idiot is this person anyway?" Cora asking me.

"She's like at the airport in Mexico City, getting ready to fly to Africa, when Abu Al Sharif blows up the freaking north terminal. Remember that? She almost died that time. Like three different terrorist attacks in three different countries is gotta be a record. Walky thinks so, dude."

"At least!" Cora frowned. "A bit extravagant."

"I never figured June to be so unlucky."

"*Unlucky*?" they both cried at once.

"Myrna Haney says the Lord's grace is resting on her countenance."

"Naw, that's just June. She has this glow; she used to blush bright purple...well—" grinning at Cora "–under certain forms of exertion, you know."

"No, I don't know. But I guess you do."

"Forget it! I always thought it had to do with blood pressure, small as she is, like the blood rushed about her body too rapidly, abandoned her cheeks and left them cyanotic. But she's okay now, is she, Tommy?"

"Yeah, except for her legs. Still as hot as she used to be."

In truth, the thought of making love with June Gilliam again has got me tingling all over. Imagine June legless, just her torso splayed across a bed, more doll-like than ever, deliciously illicit. Surely she hasn't lost her sensual nature, Christer though she may be. I must see her again. Then at once realize *I must not.*

So what is it with people like Tommy Whitehead and June Gilliam—independent-minded nonbelievers by nature—becoming Jesusers? Can dire circumstances lead us to betray our own natures to become something we are not? Did this happen under the Nazis? Is it happening again now? If nature can lose its bearings, why can't we? Maybe the loss of her legs traumatized June into timidity. Later, Cora asks me flat out, anyhow, if I've slept with this Ms. Gilliam person.

"A fling...over fifteen years ago," I confess.

"I'll bet your wife, Lilly, didn't consider it a fling."

"Lilly was dead, remember? At least I thought so."

"That's convenient. So do you plan to sleep with her again?"

"Oh, for crissake, Cora!" The woman's ability to get into my head flat drives me crazy. Speaking of invasion of privacy! "Have you noticed—" I change the subject "–that you can hear the dogs mewling in the cellar if you put your ear to the floor? Their ghosts are still down there, maybe undecided about rejoining our pack. Or they wish to warn us about something. Watch ghosts! I'll leave a bowl of water down there for them."

Cora throws a dismissive hand. "You're as flighty as the weather lately, Lawr, you know what. Blustery one day, glum the next. No telling what you'll do next."

I stare at her, a little alarmed. "Really?"

I MEET JUNE GILLIAM QUITE BY ACCIDENT

one day as I help Margie and Carlie sandbag Chez Amie. An impromptu creek has formed out back and flooded the parking lot, dammed up against the rear porch, and threatens to flood the restaurant. "Creekside dining," I joke. "You should capitalize on that."

"Very funny," both gals chide me.

We manage to divert the creek into a new bed that bypasses Chez Amie.

"Come say hello to our new pastry chef," Margie chirps. "She says she knows you."

Just as Tommy said, June is even shorter now, scarcely reaches my nipples. "Why l-l-l-look here," she says. "If it isn't law-law-little Lilly's father, Law-Law-Lawrence Caw-Connery. If it isn't..."

"It is. How the hell are you, June? You haven't changed a bit."

"Afraw-fraid I have." She kicks a knee in the air to demonstrate: the foot lifts and hangs stiffly. "Lost my law-legs and found the Lord's blessing."

"Still, you haven't."

Carlie and Margie watch us, noting how June blushes satiny purple, how a blood vessel beats fervidly at her left temple, how rigidly I stand in a puddle of discomfort. "Unh-oh," Carlie mutters. June lurches to one side, catches the handle of a huge, steaming aluminum stock pot simmering on the stove and nearly pulls it over atop her as she plunges to the floor. I get a hand against the pot and shove it back on the burner before it empties its scalding contents over her. Greasy hot soup stock splashes us, and we giggle in that hebephrenic way people have of celebrating barely averted disaster as I help her up—June's hiccupping, contagious titter. "My law-law-leg," she stutters, "my d-d-damned staw-staw-sticky-jointed pros-thaw-thesis got staw-stuck. It hap-ap-pens." She slaps it with a hand, then darts forward and kisses me full on the lips.

"Unh-oh," Margie says. Everybody in Sluggards Creek

will soon hear of our reunion, including Cora. Damned incestuous zone, can't get away with nothing—as if I'm trying to! June's lips graze my ear; she asks soto voce if I know Jesus. I feel giddy, not sure what will happen next. June saying, "Gaw-gaw-goodness, Lawr. You're burned." She smears my fingers with cooking oil. Rain lashes high windows that flood the kitchen with light. Crazy weather: from drought-parched to swampy-wet over-night, out of character for SoCal. Maybe it isn't. Maybe SoCal's Jurassic temperament is reasserting itself, era of fern forests, dinosaurs and monsoonal downpours. Perhaps we all embody many temperaments which emerge at different times, so there can be no ultimate knowing ourselves. An unnerving thought.

I return to the restaurant at five p.m. to give June a lift to the Doolittle's abandoned trailer where she's stay-ing, so she won't have to walk home in the rain. A mere pretext. We both know what will happen next—seems fated, beyond our intention or control. We don't dare make love on the Doolittle's bed for fear that whatever ailment took them may be contagious (given the rapid evolution of microbes and unknown diseases afflicting us recently, exotic STDs). I spread a blanket over wood chips in my pickup bed under the canopy. Shall I report a scurrilous love-making scene? Something tender and nostalgic? Should I tell how the laughter coursing like blood through June's tiny body infects me with a joy disease the moment I enter her? Me rationalizing that, since I knew June Gilliam years before Cora, she possesses prior amatory rights. Besides, there's nothing wrong with rekindling an old flame, bringing a bit more warmth into this cold world, especially if you make it clear that you are emotionally engaged elsewhere. (Well, it's none of your business, really. Besides, nothing happens. Seems it will, but doesn't.)

We lie side by side, me nervous about her family inside the trailer. Possibly a husband? She seems unperturbed. The modular is derelict, windows broken out, front door hanging off a single hinge. June and I neck. I run fingers through her hair, its wiry thickness enlivening tactile memories as it coils prehensile around my fingers. She tastes of nutmeg and milk. June clings to me, and I wonder if she returned to Sluggards Creek hoping to take up where we left off years ago. Impossible. I must set her straight, tell her I'm involved elsewhere. Then I am running my fingers over the straps and metal fastenings of her prostheses, caressing one leg then the other. The devices are hard and unyielding, remind me of the armored bras and girdles of my youth that were so hard to remove, currents work over their ceramic surfaces. I wouldn't dare take off her artificial limbs, reveal her existential nakedness; the prospect scandalizes and excites me. She is a doll-woman with removable parts; I want her desperately. "Enough," I say, just as she does. Laughing, she seizes my hand. "You haven't chaw-chaw-changed, La-La-Lawrence Connery. Still as ha-ha-horny as ever."

"Nonsense." I sit up against the rear window, looking down at her, so tiny and vulnerable. "I've settled down...I have."

Laughter leaks from her nose, her delicate features gone vitreous, translucent, her brow glows with subdermal luminescence: fluorite purple. Gone suddenly serious: "My law-law-legs? Is it?"

"For crissake, no, June. You're very attractive. But I'm devoted to Clara...absolutely. Besides, we don't even know each other anymore. People change, you know."

"I saw-certainly have. I've faw-found the Lord. I wanted to wi-wi-witness to you today, Law-Lawrence. I wanted to share my hap-ap-api-ness with you."

"I'm committed elsewhere," I snap. More than just a little annoyed that I've brought her home to have her preach at me.

"Why do Maw-Myrna Haney and the others call you 'our Law-Law-Lawrence'?"

"Because they know I won't join them willingly, so they've volunteered me."

The modular in worse shape inside than out: great holes in the walls, wires protrude from outlets, rain leaks down through the roof in a maddening timpani pattering into containers scattered across the floor, it stinks of mildew. I am startled by movement in a corner, make out two children huddled together on a cot in the semi-dark, whining like Jack and Misty in the cellar. The scene reminds me of Marmalatoff's dank, squalid apartment in *Crime and Punishment*, ragged urchins scrapping for bread crusts on the filthy floor. Their glowing eyes follow me in the darkness. "You folks can't stay here," I whisper. "It's unfit for human habitation. We have a dry room in the barn. Of course, I'll have to ask Cora." My heart sinks. She will never agree to having June stay. Besides, if she did stay, I couldn't trust myself not to sneak out there middle of the night.

June makes a noise with her lips as if to "pssssssst" me away.

Timidly, later that evening, I ask Cora if we could make the spare room in the barn available to a single mom and her kids. "They can't remain in that trailer. The little girl has an awful cough; June's afraid it's TB."

"So you've seen her? You want to bring your legless ex-lover and her sick kids here?"

My face hot as an oven; I can't look at her. "Seen her? Not exactly...I didn't...well, I s'pose I did. Look at it this way: if she stays here, you can keep an eye on us."

"Absolutely not. It's out of the question, Lawr. You know it is."

I feel foolish and compromised, having as good as promised June she could stay. Maybe I should put my foot down. It's my place, after all. Maybe I like the idea of having two wives on the homestead, like a Mormon patriarch. Maybe I plan to start a new faith.

THE GHOST DOGS' WARNINGS SOON BEAR FRUIT.

It rains sixteen inches in twelve hours overnight, Sluggards Creek rises in a torrent, overflooding its canyon. No one has ever seen anything like it—not Juan Alverro, not Walky Talky.

"Remind me of them hurrincane, Katrina II and such," Walky says when I stop by to see if he is all right.

"How much more are we going to get?" I ask him.

He paces the room and broadcasts in his best stentor reporting voice:

Item:

The National Weather Service reports a tropical depression moving up the California coast from Baja California. Expect barometric lows of twenty-eight-point-three inches of mercury. According to the Institute For Biblical Meteorology that is below what was reported during the Noachic flood of 1,726 B.C.

"Oh c'mon, Walky! They didn't have barometers back then."

Item:

Expect severe coastal flooding and rains up to sixty

inches in the mountains and deserts. Expect the Salton Sea to swell and fill the Great Basin in a second Lake Lahontan. Expect the Colorado River to wash Arizona deep into Sonora, Mexico.

Expect California's inland valleys to flood and populations to migrate into foothills.

Expect ugly confrontations between locals and refugees. Expect scenes of pillage and rape.

"That's us!" I cry, "that's Sluggards Creek! Where inna hell do you get this stuff?"

"Gowan outside and see for yoreseff," he protests.

I go home and check my supply of ammo—30.06 and 9mm. All I can do to get up the drive, what with water coursing down in a muddy, churning torrent. It will slow the invading hordes down some, anyhow. I hardly know myself anymore, ready as I am to take up arms against the less fortunate. So much for my proclamation about unchanging human character.

I dream that my son Jeff walks up the drive toward the house weighed down with Army ordnance, a somber, haunted expression on his face. Running out to meet him, I reach out to shake his hand, and my boy walks right through me. "D'you think he died *over there?*" I ask Cora next morning. "That's what our ghost dogs have been trying to tell me?" She waggles her fingers as if to say, *I can't go there.*

I HAVE NOT BEEN TOTALLY HONEST

about that afternoon with June Gilliam, rain beating out a cheery tattoo on the camper shell, her eyes aglow, collecting ambient light, me fearing I was about to lose my footing and plunge into an alien self. Lying side by side with my ancient lover–seemingly ancient with her severed legs and my priapic desire filling the tiny space like a vapor, the primordial rain–I considered Cora, knew I couldn't in good conscience do this, but asked to see June's legs. She hoisted her skirt to show me those shiny ceramic prostheses with their well-sculpted muscles–one short, one long, with an artificial knee, steel piston visible through gaps either side–which clamped down over stumps, held in place by snap fasteners and straps I'd already traced with my fingers. She'd written "pass" on the left leg, "don't pass" on the right with a felt-tip pen. Inimitable June. I caressed ceramic calves with my palm; tiny arcs of static electricity danced along their surfaces and raised hairs on the back of my hand. June pressed my fingers into her panties, the moist crevice between her legs. "Thank you, Jesus," she whimpered. I shut my eyes, ready to convert.

We made love as fervidly as Cora and I had during that wind storm, while a strong odor of nutmeg and garlic rose around us. Me thinking: *I no longer recognize myself–locking Jack and Misty in the cellar, betraying Cora and my own loyal nature.* It's an epidemic: Tommy Whitehead renouncing scientific rationalism and embracing Jesus, Jack become alpha dog since the cellar incident, pushing Misty around. June pleading, "My children need a daddy, Lawr. Their father was a firefighter. He drowned in the Ohio floods, trying to rescue people." No longer stuttering; seems I have a calming affect on her. So this is what it's all about, not unholy lust but a righteous search for a daddy for her kids. I kneel naked on the pickup bed beside her and pray for forgiveness. "The flesh is weak," we moan together. "I don't believe in this nonsense," I protest. She touches her fingers to my lips. "Shhhhh, our Law-Lawrence. Now you do." Churchies will stoop mighty low to recruit a fellow.

I CRASH THROUGH THE DOOR OF YESTERDAYS RESTAURANT

next day and demand, "What do you people think you're doing?"

Of course Myrna knows about my tryst with June Gilliam. "June witnessed at fellowship last evening, our Lawrence. You best tell Cora before she hears of it from a stranger."

"Tell her what exactly? That I no longer know who I am? That I didn't intend to sleep with an old lover...then I did? That I declined to let June baptize me under the gutter downspout..then let her? That I'm *saved*, for crissake?

Can you fucking believe it?"

"God be praised, *our Lawrence.*" Myrna lays cold hands on me. Henry Staidley throws me an amused glance from his stool. "Do you remember our Lawrence sitting right here telling us the Lord cannot work a change in a person's life, Henry? We are what we are without hope of redemption. Do you remember it?"

"Hell yeah, I do."

"Those weren't my words exactly, Myrna. I merely said the obvious, that people's nature remains basically constant. Once it's formed, it doesn't change much."

"Wouldn't you know, *our Lawrence* himself offers the surest proof he is mistaken. I have never seen the Lord's grace work a mightier redemption in a man. It's a blessing."

I'm shaken. There can be no more terrible death than death of the self. Living death: Alzheimer's, Parkinson's, schizophrenia, amnesia, psychosis...acute, irrational change—any such dissolution of the solid self. I spear a finger. "You put June up to it, Myrna! You know my weakness." I slam out the door.

Back home, I slog up the drive through mud two feet deep, pickup tires throw back black coxcombs of sludge. A voice emerges through the perennial radio static: Emergency Broadcast Network, first broadcast in years, warning about nomads from the lowlands invading other regions, carrying drug-resistant forms of TB and malaria. So what inna hell can we do about it, anyway, shoot them? Old Juan Alverro says there's no point in such warnings. "Ain't nothing you can do about 'em but become chicken. If it's gonna happen, let it happen."

As I step out of the truck, Jack and Misty charge from the house to greet me. I bend at the knees, preparing for Jack's big paws to hit my chest; I will bear hug him while he licks my face, cheered by their constancy and loyalty. But something in Jack's demeanor gives me pause—fierce hard little eyes, tongue not lolling from his mouth but pulled in tight, canines gleaming. His mouth opens wide as he lunges for my throat. I leap back into the cab—too late! Jack's teeth grip my biceps, Misty gets hold of my left calf and shakes it. I slam the door closed on paws and muzzles: loud yelps, including my own. No choice. They want blood.

"Damn it, guys! It's me! Your old pal. What's got into you two?"

I sit a time while rain lashes down at a forty-five degree angle. Find a rag in the glove compartment and firm it against my shoulder, watch grubs of blood wriggle through the weave of my shirt. The dogs slam against the truck door, claw at the window. Rain slicks back fur on their heads, they look like hideous leopard seals with huge teeth. I don't recognize them, nor they me. The collective personality change extends even to dogs, it seems. "Look, guys—" I crack open the window "—I'm sorry I

locked you in the basement. Okay? I'm sorry we no longer give you Goody Bone treats. Hey, the factory closed."
Jack gives a horrific snarl and hurls himself at the window crack, trying to force his muzzle through. He leaps
onto the hood of the truck, can't get his footing on rain-
slick metal. Thank God! Smacks against the windshield
with all his might, his teeth gnash at glass inches from
my face. He wants me.

My shoulder throbs. I'm sobbing, actually. Call it
self-pity. When your own dogs turn on you, the world
is a truly abject place. The rain washes down in combers
from the twilight-dark sky; instant rivers boil down can-
yons, carrying in their bloated guts flotsam torn loose
by the wind, flooding valleys below. Cora has thrown
my belongings onto a sodden heap in the front yard–including pages of the novel I started years ago, inkless
pulp now. She wouldn't do this; it's altogether out of character for her. Cora is strong-willed but never cruel; she
respects others' property, including their selfhood. The
changeability disease has taken her, too. Maybe Myrna is
right: God wants to teach me a lesson. Rot. He wouldn't
go to such lengths to teach one nonbeliever a lesson. Let's
hope he has better things to do.

Maybe this is another strain of the fly-bite disease
that afflicted us months ago. Or maybe this new afflic-
tion has its roots in unnatural causes, as the monsoonal
downpours do–rising CO_2 levels, methane, and the rest.

Maybe quiet panic has altered our character: anxiety about approaching hordes from valleys to the west that will soon invade our hillbilly utopia to escape the flooding, commandeer our houses, steal our food stashes, and slit our throats. Anxiety about the weather. And so many other things. Fear disease!

Seeing that Cora has thrown my hunting rifle and 9mm pistol onto that pile, I imagine marching into the house, a firearm in each hand, blasting away, taking out Cora and the dogs (those *hostiles* occupying my place). Good practice for what is to come. Shocked and disgusted by this vision, I throw open the pickup door to the pouring rain—and my dogs.

Water hisses and sizzles against my face, as if I have hellfire burning inside me, steam fills the cab. Jesus! Cool water quenches the blaze, my skin cools. I lean back against the headrest, mouth open wide, and gulp down rainwater. Jack stands on the running board, head level with mine, his meaty breath washes my face, dark, watchful eyes inches away. He does not lunge. He cocks his head side to side as if puzzled at who I am. His eyes close. Occurs to me the rain may be a blessing: it fills our creeks and cisterns, has ended the hellish drought and doused fires in the mountains (temporarily at least), has cleansed the planet. Oh joy. My clothes on that pile in the yard will be freshly washed; I need merely hold them up to rinse off the mud. I will march inside and beg Cora's forgiveness for sleeping with June Gilliam. (Surely she's heard about it. Why else that mound in the yard?) I will formally ask Jack and Misty to forgive me. If they decide to attack me on the way in, so be it!

THE TRUTH IS–DID I TELL YOU?–I DID NOT SLEEP WITH JUNE GILLIAM.

Nearly did, was about to enter her, knelt over her foreshortened body, pants around my ankles, but seeing her lying there, not so much a doll as a mermaid, legless and lovely, pale as a halibut in the gloom, translucent skin aglow from light leaking through windows of the pickup shell, I felt something snap in me, like an over-strained muscle. I seized her hands. "I can't do this. Want to awfully...but can't." June slapped me. Then offered me baptismal waters.

Jack whining and licking my bloody shoulder. Misty licking my calf. We limp to the house together, three old pals. Cora waits inside for us. Yes! But I pause first at that pile of my sodden, steaming possessions. Occurs to me that I am a spineless sucker not to stand up to her and offer a warm room to a needy widow. Cora was foolish enough to leave live shells lying about. I ram one home in the chamber of the ought-six and throw the bolt. Jack and Misty slink away from me. I shout and heave the gun, butt over barrel. It slams against the studio and dis-charges. Scares hell out of me. Madness. Actions alone count, I remind myself, not thoughts or fantasies. Cora meets me at the door. "I'm sorry about your novel," she says, teary-voiced.

I shrug. "Didn't know what I was doing anyhow."

"We need to make love," she suggests.

Definitely. I will confess about June afterward.

"This time the dogs are staying inside with us," she insists.

I nod. "Only actions count, you know. Thoughts and temptations don't mean a thing. If we act for evil, we are evil. If we act for good, we are good. Simple."

She smiles puzzlement and acceptance. She knows my heady flights of enthusiasm. It's a comfort to have someone know me for who I am. I pull her close and kiss her passionately. Feeling whole again, unbaptized, restored to my old constancy—my old failed, pagan self. I lick the faint moustache on Cora's upper lip and thank Eros for it. I'm thinking that, if they come, we will assimilate the migrating valley hordes into our community, welcome them. If they're here come spring, we will co-operate with them on large-scale agricultural projects to feed ourselves.

Jack and Misty pace the floor, heads cocked. Misty turns her muzzle skyward and howls. We freeze right up. Those ghost dogs are yelping in the basement again—another warning, no doubt. "Something more is on the way," I whisper. "More trouble coming."

"There's always something more on the way. Sometimes good, sometimes bad. That's the nature of things. Maybe they want to remind us of that."

When I tell her about June Gilliam, how much I desired her, Cora merely shrugs.

"Maybe you felt sorry for her. Or she you."

I'm dumfounded. The Cora I know would likely slug me. Maybe change really has infected us–for good and bad.

"Listen! Let her use the room in the barn, her and her kids," she says. "I don't mind. She's had her share of trouble, she could use some kindness. I got excited about the prospect of having kids around again. I've missed having children in town, I've missed their laughter."

I don't want to go there. It's a longstanding disagreement in our relationship, the children question. But I nod and smile, glad that we've restored peace.

SOMETIMES THE RAIN SUDDENLY STOPS.

You go for a walk along a soggy dirt road, excited by a ray of sunlight breaking through clouds, inhaling ozone, feeling euphoric. It's a transient feeling, of course. Such existential joy is always transient. All can never be well in the world for long. That feeling is so powerful and inspiring that it can get you through many a dark day. Snails cover the muddy ground; it is parthenogenesis:

no trace of them during the drought, but here they have suddenly regenerated by the thousands. I take care not to step on them. Still, I hear one occasionally pop beneath my boots. "Forgive me, Old Snail," I mutter, in the grip of a temporary darsana, for I have often plucked snails off garden leafage by the dozen and destroyed them for eating my crops and felt not a dollop of guilt in doing so. Perhaps our own best nature is fleeting, too. Perhaps, like that transient joy, it must be. But we will never stop aspiring to it.

FEVER

The rains had stopped and it had turned beastly hot on the Mendocino Coast. Starfish and mussels retreated from the rocks at low tide to avoid being fried by the sun, denying residents their last remaining source of natural food on the coast—except for those foolhardy souls willing to dive for mussels (strictly forbidden, of course). If a wave caught a diver wrong it sent him rolling over barnacle-encrusted rocks that flayed him alive. The more delicate ferns—maidenheads and five-fingered—that had proliferated in the endless rains turned brown and died. It would be a while still before redwood foliage went sere, since tree roots extended deep into the aquifer.

Tia wrote daily to Jay Connery, although there was nowhere to post her letters, and they would likely never reach him *over there* anyway. She had read that the Pomo Indians once whispered messages on the wind which carried them to a loved one. But there was not a breath of wind. Fred came by to see her soon after she arrived home. She placed a palm against his chest as he came in the cabin door and tried to explain: "Listen, Freddy—"

"Listen what? Gawdamn it! I'm about to burst at the seams here, honey gal."

No way to tell him "no" unless she ended their friendship altogether. Fred did nothing by halves, certainly not sex. Theoretically, it was impossible for a man to have multiple orgasms, but Fred didn't go by such scruples; that night he broke all records.

When Tia sent Tangerine up front to stay with Aunty Lou, her daughter looked at her curiously. Louise would surely think it odd for Tia to take up with Fred again so soon after her southland love affair. *I thought you and Jay were an item.* What response to give her? *Hey, I tried.* How explain that Fred The Goat Man was a force of nature, as sure as the ceaseless rain and devastating heat to follow? Tia's little cabin rocking with their ardor. Finally, they lay in a puddle of sweat. "Jes'christ!" Fred declared. "Much more of this and we'll all curl up and die—" meaning the heat not the sex. "My girls is suffering something fierce. I'm afraid they'll go dry on me." Tia had forgotten how strongly Freddy smelled of goat. Stank, really! Put your nose against his skin and you smelled Frolic and Moonlight.

"Tell you what—" Tia rolled onto her back "–I met this guy down south who says he used to know you in the sixties. Lawrence Connery. Do you remember him?"

Fred worked the name over his tongue. "Can't say as I do."

"You really didn't get along, he says. Your goats used to eat his garden."

"Him!" Fred guffawed. "Damn bleep long hair, lived down to Mitchell Creek Road."

"Bleep" was vintage Fredspeak, reserved for those whom he held in lowest regard. She didn't tell him that Lawr believed he had been killed over in Vietnam.

"Oh, he's not so bad," she said. "Super nice guy; people truly respect him."

"Yeh, I bet."

"His son is an Army Ranger. He just went back *over there*," she said quietly, knowing how Fred would feel about it. She had promised herself not to mention Jay, and here he was on her tongue already. Perhaps acknowledging Jay was the toll she must pay for sleeping with Fred, who gripped her chin now and pulled her face around to regard her in the candlelight–his goatish instincts. Seemingly, he decided there was nothing to worry about.

"Bleep creep raised some mighty tasty cabbages. The girls loved them. I'll tell you what, though, I sympathize with him, sending his boy *over there*. Shouldn't nobody be going *over there*. Bleeping politicians didn't learn a damn nothing from Nam."

"How's Lorna?" she asked to change the subject.

Fred squared his back against the cabin wall. "That's

what I come to talk about."

"Oh, you came to talk then? I didn't realize—"

"Well, y'know, one thing leads to another." Distract-
edly, he petted her breast; soon he would be scratching
her cleavage, as if between horn nubs of one of his "girls."
"Lorna got real sick. Can't hold food down, gets the shiv-
ers, there's some days she's too weak to stand up."

Tia thought of Lorna sitting across room in her long
peasant's dress, dripping water onto the floor, agate bright
eyes and cherubic cheeks. Maybe the heat made her ill,
tallowy pale as she was. Likely to melt in such heat.

"What I come to ask, could you help me milk the
girls next few days? I can't have Lorna around a milking
operation."

"I'm hopeless at milking, Freddy. You know that."

"Anybody can strip meat out of crab claws can milk a
goat. Just takes some practice."

"I do need work. I was planning to look for a job this
morning."

"Won't find none," Fred said smugly. "Fisheries
closed, logging, crafts." He stood at the window, first
light dancing in a nimbus on his bare shoulders, sagging
biceps covered with tattoos: *Semper Fi, Dakseang Survivor, Goat Power,* unselfconsciously declaring his *Just do
it* faith.

"I'll come over after I get Tangerine."

Later when Tia went to retrieve her daughter, Louise

asked, "Have fun last night?" More rebuke than irony in her tone. Not like her. Lou appeared to change her mind about a great horned owl feather she had stuck in her hair and withdrew a glossy black raven's feather from a vase full of feathers on the hearth; hands shaking, she replaced the owl feather with it. An announcement.

"If you'd prefer not to babysit Tangerine, I can take her down to Bearclaw," Tia said.

"That's not it and you know it. We had a good time playing Scrabble. I believe your daughter was a Scrabble virgin before last night. Now she's a threat. It's just...I can't keep up!" Lou held up a hand and gripped her belly, beads of sweat popping out on her forehead.

"Are you all right, Lou?"

Louise sat down and nodded. "Something didn't agree with me. Listen, I thought you were in love with that boy down south. You could have fooled me. I believe you thought so, too. Maybe I'm more conservative than I know I am."

"Jay is *over there* for God knows how long, and I'm over here. How's that work? Do you expect me to give up sex?"

"Women have done it for centuries."

"I'm not one of them, okay? Maybe I'm not cut out to be an Army widow. Maybe I never agreed to that sacrifice, okay? Just try saying 'no' to Freddy some time. It's a commitment."

"That's right! It's a commitment." Lou held up a hand, breathing hard.

"Are you ill, Lou?" It worried Tia that her daughter had spent the night with her.

With some difficulty, Lou got up from the chair she'd sunk into, grimacing, then sank down again. She had thrown a shawl over her shoulders. "Is it cool in here?"

"My God, no! It's hot. Stuffy. Ninety degrees already at seven a.m. Don't judge me, Lou. If you are my friend, you won't judge me. Fred or no Fred."

"I'm surprised, dear, that's all. Just trying to keep up. She's watching...is all—" whispering "–your daughter is watching your example. Last night she asked what had become of Jay. Listen..." Lou trailed off.

Tia realized she wasn't going to stay for coffee, wasn't going to continue a friendship that required self-repudiation. Then she understood what this was about. "Where's my daughter?" she asked curtly. "Where did you put Tangerine?"

"Same place as always. Where else?" Lou made a sweeping gesture, a kind of grand rebuke. "Listen, about coffee, I'm feeling poorly this morning. I have the shakes; I believe it's flu."

"You, too? I hope Tangerine doesn't get it."

"Well, I hope so, too. Goodness!" Lou actually clutching her belly.

Tia went to the trundle bed beside the cold hearth,

kissed her daughter on the forehead, tried to scoop her up in her arms–she'd grown too heavy–managed to boost her up onto a hip and limped for the door with her astraddle, Tangerine protesting, "Aren't we going to have hot chocolate?" Outside, Tia let her slip to the ground and told Tangy to run on home, reentered Lou's place like a warrior, having learned a few things from the military men in her life.

"You know what it is, Lou? Me balling Fred, balling Jay, Freddy again. Right? You're jealous. Watching this lusty young woman balling every virile man in sight. But, you know what, find your own guy if you want to get laid. It's not my problem." She slammed the door; the vibration rang up through her wrist and arm. Had she really said that?

Tangerine was waiting for her at the cabin door. "Are you mad at Aunt Lou?"

"No...of course I'm not mad, a little annoyed is all."

"Lou was real sick last night, she kept going to the bathroom. We had to quit playing Scrabble because she got the shiver shakes."

"She did? My God! I hope she goes to see Doctor Bruce."

"I bet he's really busy. Mrs. Busker at school has it and Mr. Tibbs and whole lots of kids. Heather Peterson has been absent for three weeks. Everybody says she's dying."

Tia dropped to a knee and gripped her daughter's

shoulders. "Why didn't you tell me? There are lots of nasty things going around anymore. I'm going to keep you home until we know what this is. I want you to stay away from Lou and Lorna. Do you hear me, young lady?"

§

The moment Tia left, Louise started back up stairs—outlandishly steep, built by a Mendocino carpenter who defied conventions. Iconoclasm came with the territory, she supposed. Even the trees defied convention in size and grandiosity. She managed to navigate the first few steps standing up, then the shakes took her and she sank to her knees on a tread. What was it? Good Lord! She quickly discovered you cannot navigate a steep flight of stairs on hands and knees. She sat on a stair tread, sweat dripping off her chin, soaking hair, blouse, her under-wear. Good Lord! She slid off the stair lip to make a soft landing on the tread below, but there was no strength in her arms and she went down hard on her tailbone. Lying on her back, she found she could slip from step to step, belt catching tread lips and slowing her progress, feet acting as brakes. It took ten minutes to reach floor level again. Lord! She would crawl to the downstairs bathroom, somehow reach the thermometer in the medicine cabi-net, though knew already she'd never had a higher fever in her life. It wrung the strength and moisture from her.

Had she fought with Tia? Fever had burned the memory to mental ash. Something about Freddy perhaps? Designs on Tangerine, was it? Good Lord! Jealous that she did not have a daughter of her own? I had a son. Well, he was not my son, he was my sister's, but I raised him as my own, loved him, lost him as my own. What does Tia know of loss? The lovely man down south who must ship his son *over there* would understand. Teeth chattering now, she felt there would be diarrhea again. You must remember to hydrate, drink lots of water. The headache that had half-blinded her last night playing Scrabble with Tangerine had returned, finding the optic nerve and sending out pulses of pain that made her eyes bulge. Good Lord! This was no flu. Nasty ailments going around, things not seen before. Whom/what had she been exposed to? A passenger on that bus that had brought them north from SoCal? Something in the water? Since arriving home, she'd eaten nothing but canned things, veggies from the overgrown garden, Fred's goat's milk. If it's over 104 I must get in to see Doctor Bruce. Who would drive her now that Tia was alienated? Bearclaw? Freddy? Lorna? Though she understood the girl was sick, too. There it was! Good God. When was I exposed to Lorna?

It was a long while before she could read the thermometer, sitting on the bathtub rim, back against the tile wall, stripped bare-chested, hating the way her rayon blouse clung wetly to her skin. 105.4. Good Lord! Children sometimes...but not an adult! At what point does the brain fry? Then she was icy cold; she seized towels off the rack and wrapped them around her. A hot bath, she thought. Why was Tia so angry? Worried about Tangerine? Me, too...Listen, your daughter couldn't understand why I wouldn't kiss her goodnight. Are you angry that I favor that young man, Jay, over Freddy? Fred's over seventy, for goodness sake, old enough to be your grandfather. You need a fellow your own age, need a daddy for your little girl. Fred and his goats is horse piss hopeless. Then the trots hit her again, she just made it onto the toilet seat. Good Lord! Forty minutes later she was too exhausted to clean up, accordioned into herself in that stink, fearing she would slip through the shitter hole and be gone. Have you no self-respect, no dignity, Lou? You will do this thing. Make your way to the tub, wash yourself, cool off in cold water, clear your head, rise again like Lazarus from the tomb. You can do this.

§

Goddamn radio. First you get BBC World Service from God knows where. Then NPR from Houston–one of three NPR affiliates still broadcasting regular–then some fuckinay, sounds like a ham operator out of Idaho, fucking limpdick bleep doesn't understand the world has gone to hell in a wheelbarrow. Tina Junior kicks over her milk bucket just to be a bitch, and wouldn't you guess! Tia doesn't show up to help milk. Gone looking for work elsewhere, something with Tangerine maybe. She's spoiled that girl rotten. So it takes maybe ninety extra minutes to milk, last four goats bleating agony by the time he gets to them. That's a thing people don't understand: like having a full bladder and you gotta piss so bad it hurts. Blow that up to two gallons worth and you get the picture. Pissed off at her by the time he's finished. Finds her note tacked to the door:

> Really sorry, Freddy, but I don't dare be around sickness.
> I have my little girl to consider. She's home with me today.

"What damn sickness? What the hell?" he shouts. You can't come inside the shed and tell me in person, lover gal, for crissake? What kind of sleazy operation do you think I run here? I got to have sanitary; it's my livelihood. I got Lorna the hell out the moment I knew. And this Tangerine bullshit. Half the time she hides behind that little runt as an excuse. *Sorry, Freddy, can't do it tonight...Sorry, Freddy, I can't...*Bullshit.

Goddamn radio. Broadcasting some gook language... Chinese maybe. He kicks it off the hay bale, puts his foot through the back of it. Sinks down laughing. "Whoooeee, damn!" Wondering how he is going to live without news of our progress *over there*, latest death toll from London or Karachi, latest freaking disease become drug resistant— Typhus, they say, and the bleeping measles. Whooeee, death pox! Zoonotic diseases. Some freaking thing! Ain't that a bummer? Diseases crossing the border from animal to human, freaking wetback diseases. Some fish has liver pox, next thing you know it shows up in fishermen in the Antilles. Insect plagues that spread to plants. Go figure. Honey bees catch a stomach virus, next thing you know alfalfa has it. How's that work? Alfalfa don't have freaking stomachs. Watch out, girls, before I feed you stomach-virus alfalfa. Nothing the dweeb genetic engineers can do about it. There was that day some super-dweeb hacker of hackers, nerd of nerds, hacked into Wall Street computers and infected them with a data-eating virus in a cyberwar strike that knocked out the stock market in four hours. He'd gone outside and fired his M-16 in the sky in celebration like a damn Hamas nutjob. Whooeee damn!

What I am going to do, I'm going over and ask Tia what the hell! You can't spare me a howdy do? This bleeping Lorna business. Okay, I slept with her. Little christer sweetheart, hairy-legged angel (that's not all is hairy, I'm here to tell), natural, sweet-lovin' Jesus gal...little shy on the uptake maybe. Thing is, last time we make love she breaks out in one almighty sweat. Freaky. Stomach ache and her head about to split open, she says. Come on sudden the night before, she says. Me shouting, "I got a damn goat milk operation to run here, I can't afford sickness on the place. You're outta here!" How she better get in to see Dr. Bruce pronto, though he can't get any damn drugs most the time anyway. So she's crying, and I tell her I won't abandon her to the wolves. Twenty-four fuckinay goats to milk on my lonesome. Then I hear Tia's back in town. Whoooeee damn! Feel bad about not telling her I'd slept with a damn cholera victim...whatever, her with a little girl to worry about and all. Hoping it's not one of them drug-resistant diseases. Still, how can you worry about what you don't know? That's fucking crazy. Like we used to say over in Nam: *Cowards squawk, Marines walk*. Maybe nothing more than a bad case of woman sickness.

He listens through goats' bleating in the shed, ought to be hearing some fuckinay Brit announcer detailing the latest death toll *over there*, latest megastorm to wash away some chain of atolls, most recent resignation of a world leader–bleeping King Charles III last week. What's the world coming to without nobody sitting on the throne of England? Next they'll outlaw goats. He listens and can't hear a damn nothing. No reassuring murmurs of disaster. Goddamn radio.

§

Usually, it was a sweet luxury to have Tangerine at home with her. They might redo handmade wallpaper in the one-room cabin, play Monopoly, or go for a walk in the redwoods in search of chanterelles. Too hot for that: one hundred degrees in deep shade of the redwoods. Stuck inside the stuffy cabin all day. Tangerine complained that it was cooler at school. "You can't go to school, pumpkin, until we know what this sickness is going around."

"But the heat makes me sick."

"I know it does. Me, too."

Sick, too, that she couldn't help Freddy with the milking. She gave it some serious thought; might leave Tangerine outside the goat shed. Gave serious thought, too, to taking her along job hunting with her. But could not leave her in the car in this furnace blast. Wasn't, besides, in the mood to face the rejection she knew she would find out there, and didn't want to spend precious gas on a fool's errand. No, she had a job with Freddy. Just didn't feel up to it today. Most of all, she felt sick over Lou.

Come evening it had cooled off by twenty degrees. Like life pouring cool water back into your veins. As it cooled, there came a knocking on cabin walls. Tangerine lifted her head in wonder, eyes wide. "She never knocks in the daytime. She's knocking all over the place."

Tia shook her head. "That's not The Woman In White—" poltergeist, resident spook, whatever "–that's just walls cooling down."

"Are they happy?"

"Yes, I think so."

So they went out into the cool evening air, could feel an onshore flow breathing in from the ocean. Fog tonight maybe, that blanket of cool, reinvigorating moisture. Tangerine wanted to bring Aunt Lou out. "She needs to play, too, you know. She's not an old lady."

"Lou will never be an old lady. But, listen, I don't want you getting too close. Not until we find out."

Tia opened the back door of the great old pole lodge house and called: "Lou, it's lovely outside. Come out and play. Lou...?"

Nothing.

"Look, Louise, I'm really sorry about going off on you earlier. I'm an asshole, okay? I feel sick about it. Lou...?"

Nothing.

"We love you, Lou. Really we do. And it's so nice out. Louise?"

Baking hot. Waves of heat washed out the door over her and a complicated smell–partly pitchy white pine log beams, partly the smell of old ashes and domesticity, partly a beastly, foul abattoir odor, the stench of sickness. Tia pulled the T-shirt up over her mouth and went inside. Shattered glass crackled under her shoes in the kitchen.

"Oh, no!" She made her way up the steep stairs, calling Lou as she went. Her bed looked assaulted, covers torn aside, but Lou wasn't in any of the six cubbyhole bedrooms upstairs. The smell up there nearly gagging. The cavernous main room, with its twenty foot ceiling and great fieldstone fireplace, was empty, too. Deep shadows obscured far corners. The place felt like an ancient tomb filled with moribund air. Tia thinking Lou had surely gone for a walk. Then she saw the vaguest movement from the cot where Tangerine normally slept on nights when Freddy came visiting. Tia stopped short.

"Lou, is that you?"

Lou's claw-like hand, barely suspended off the counterpane, gave Tia a fright, her cheeks shrunken and mummy-like as Tia leaned over her. But most alarming was the weight of quilts thrown over her in hundred degree heat, yet Lou shivered, her teeth chattered audibly. Tia touched her brow and yanked her hand away as if she had touched a hot stove. Louise was burning up with fever.

"We are going to have to get you in to Dr. Bruce." Tia forgetting about the need to protect her child. A friend was dying here.

She sent Tangy running down the hill for Bearclaw, while she mopped Lou down, cleaned off filth, managed to slip on a clean gown. "You listen up, dear heart, you are going to live. You hear me? We are not going to put up with this nonsense."

Lou closed her eyes in assent. They carried her out to the Range Rover, Bearclaw talking nonstop. Cooped up with her own company day and night, the poor woman gushed when she had a chance—how it was typhoid fever, she'd heard all about it. "Like lots of people have it. Like there won't be nothing they can do for her. It's become like resistant to chloramphenicol and ampicillin, all like that. It like evolved or something...though I don't really believe in evolution, okay? They say if it doesn't kill you like within forty-eight hours, you'll survive. Lots of people don't."

"You want to shuddup, Bearclaw. Lou doesn't need to hear this. Tangerine either."

Bearclaw looked blankly from one of them to the next, shrugging as if to say, *Like what's your problem, dude?* She wore the same stiff buckskin skirt and vest winter and summer, a string of bear claws interspersed with shiny auburn acorns in a necklace around her neck. Fixed in space and time, it would have astonished her to learn the sixties were long over.

Tia drove into town, leaving her daughter behind in Bearclaw's dicey care. Dr. Bruce need only come out to the car and glance at sweat soaking Lou's hair and coursing down either side of her nose to drip off her chin. "It's typhoid fever, the extra-drug-resistant strain. Brought up from Mexico, some say. Not much I can do for her." His pursed lips nearly hidden beneath a bushy white moustache, his the saddest eyes she thought she'd ever seen, deep bags beneath; she had never seen Dr. Bruce smile. "Still, I want her in hospital quarantine. They'll keep her hydrated and give her something for fever. The halls are full of patients like her reclining on mats on the floor. Still and all, we're fortunate to have a functioning facility. So many places don't anymore. The good news is it's not ebola." Turning away from the car and lowering his voice. "We are finding a much higher incidence of mortality with this strain, especially in the old and young. What I worry about now is you, young lady, exposed as you've been. Though I suppose if you haven't shared food with her or been near her feces you'll be all right. We don't believe it's airborne."

"I have!" The abruptness of her reply startled Tia. "I cleaned her up before coming."

"Scrubbed your hands well, did you?" Incredibly, if it was possible, he looked even sadder than usual. Droopy, bloodshot eyes.

Tia both nodded and shook her head at once.

"Good! You don't want to get too cozy. Though some don't get it and some are silent carriers. You never know."

After dropping Lou off, Tia stood outside the old wooden hospital and gripped her elbows, rocking back and forth on balls of her feet. She had always loved this old main drag of Fort Bragg, washed by fog and sea breezes, the murmur of nearby surf, old Mendocino Brewing Company just down the street, beyond it lumber yards at the south end of town—redolent piles of newly-milled boards nearly exhausted now, few logs stacked in the yard, ready for cutting. What to do with Tangerine now that she had been exposed? She couldn't leave her with Bearclaw. Fred was out of the question. Really no one to care for her.

§

Corpses, might be, lined up along the walls, just haven't fully given up the ghost yet. Well, goodness. It stinks something prodigious: vomit, feces, disinfectant, death. Good Lord! They have hospitals like this in Africa, not America. They have brought me here to die. Although the fever has subsided some. She lifts her head to look around: hooked to an IV drip, the same stand serving four people, lying on the floor around her, tubes twining harum-scarum, twisting every which way from hanging IV bags, like tentacles of a dry land octopus. Saline solution, no doubt; they are trying to keep us from drying up inside and our souls blowing away. Good luck! How can you be this sick after only forty-eight hours? Hoping against hope she has not infected Tangerine and Tia. Where ever did I get it then? Suddenly she knows: Fred's goat milk, sick Lorna helping him milk. She raises a hand, hoping to catch the attention of a nurse hurrying by, makes a kind of incoherent mewling. The nurse stoops over her in a soiled white smock. "Do you need to use the bedpan, dear?" She asks, nearly in distaste.

"Catch her...please," Louise manages. "Tell her... don't...drink the milk." Just that small effort of speaking exhausts her. The nurse throws a dismissive hand and hurries off.

Let me die, she prays—not certain to whom, since she believes in no god (what pissant god would permit this), except the Earth Goddess, and not very assiduously in her—*Don't let them catch it, please*. Surely, so violent a fever would kill Tangerine. Someone moans in the hallway nearby, she hears teeth chattering. Good Lord! Altogether disconcerting to lie flat on the floor below knee-level of passers-by as if dead already. Goodness. A team of doctors and nurses gathers around a patient down the hall, working over her/him—plunging in needles, barking urgent orders, sounding frantic and hopeless. "Twenty c.c.s," a voice says. "Too late!" an authoritative voice contradicts. "We can't spare it." So that's it! Another soul stepped off this coil of tears. They pull the sheet up over the patient's face in that cordial ritual of finality, a shock of white hair protrudes above the sheet. Louise scarcely aware of orderlies who carry the corpse away. She is wracked with another bout of shaking and diarrhea. Two orderlies help her squat over the bedpan. She cannot believe she isn't dreaming: squatting on the floor over your own leavings in the company of strangers. Lord! Someone wheels a gurney past–actually drifts by in a rowboat on the lake where she squats buck naked on a dock, watching them pass. "It's some don't catch nothing," one of the men in the boat says. "Some do, some don't...maybe luck." True, some fishermen have no luck. Her sailor lover, Sammy, for instance, those many years ago. "I'll bring home dinner," he'd promise, then must stop at the fish market, bringing home his catch wrapped in wax paper. "Caught us swordfish steak today." His wreck-havoc grin. She holds up a hand to ask what is the secret, not of catching but of not catching. But, of course, she can't have held up a hand since she is clinging hold of the dock for dear life. Besides, she is naked and doesn't wish to call attention to herself.

"You finished now?" a voice barks.

Incredibly, with each diarrhetic spasm her fever seems to diminish, like she is shitting out fever. Can you do that?

"Got to get you cleaned up." The orderly turns to speak to a colleague. "I get a feeling this one gonna make it. Try not to breathe the fumes. Some say you don't catch it that way, but who knows for sure?"

I am an intensely private person, she wishes to tell them to set the record straight. You can't imagine what a horror this is for me–public exposure and humiliation.

My God!

"The way I see it, every human being on earth does it," says the skeptical male nurse, as if answering her. "Likely even Jesus Christ himself. It's our common humanity, eating and shitting."

"I'm not listening to this. Go ahead and lay down, dear. We'll check your tempature. I believe you may be graduating to a bed soon as one becomes available."

She must conserve her strength so that when the doctor makes his rounds this evening she can explain coherently about Fred's goat milk, how Lorna likely contaminated it with fever, and people must be warned away before it spreads further.

§

Goddamn Louise. Now they accusing my goats of spreading typhoid fever. Deputy Smoky Johnson drives out and wraps yellow "Don't Cross" tape around my goat shed. "How'm I s'pose to feed and water them?" I ask him. That ol' boy grinning like a damn mule. "Guess you'll have to crawl under. Thing is, Fred, we can't have you distributing milk until we get it tested."

"Tested where? All the labs is shut down anymore."

"You got you a problem then."

Like the bastard could give a damn. Come around a man's place and tell him he's out of business and tough luck. So what proof is Louise got? That woman never did like me, don't approve of me and Tia, whatever. They say she lost her boy over in Nam; she maybe resents them of us what made it back safe. No, ma'am, it's no picnic being a survivor. Sorry I couldn't of took his place over there. But bullets saw me and headed somewheres else. Anything got my name on it bound to come to nothing... now my girls.

Bleeping Deputy Smoky Johnson never did like me, sure. Believes if only I'd got lit up over there half the county's troubles would'a been solved. I got into it with Johnson once. Some dickwag down to Caspar Inn throws a glass of beer in my face and I throw him over the bar, broke his collarbone, then have to deal with his buddies. My blood is still up when Smoky Johnson shows up. I didn't give a damn he's wearing deputy green. Only thing saved me from doing hard time is he screwed up the paperwork. Whooeee damn! No hard feelings. Smoky just come out to shut down my livelihood.

"Maybe I could take my girls out and shoot 'em," I say.

"Don't get any ideas," he says.

"I got all kind of ideas. I like to see what you do if they take your family away."

"It's only goats, Fred." He got him a bottle of goat's milk to send somewheres for testing.

I tap a finger against his chest. "Every one of them

is got more personality than six of you put together, Smoky."

His hand goes for his holster. "Take it easy, Fred."

Me thinking how I'll have to dump my girls' milk in a ditch, maybe take it over to Skunk Sinclair's son to slop his hogs. Pigs can eat anything. Right after Smoky leaves, Tia shows up, her forehead glowing bright red. I know it's not the heat. "Where you been?" I ask.

She comes for me, a forefinger fixed like a bayonet. Goddamn! "You shuddup, Fred Schlepski. Don't you say a word. You have put my baby girl in peril and killed Louise."

"I didn't kill nobody. What in hell's the matter with everybody today? Old Abu Al Sharif mess with our drinking water?"

"You messed with our health, Fred. You and Lorna and your damn goats."

Well, I about lose it, grab her arm—though I never laid a rough hand on the woman before and don't believe in it—and pull her over to show her the "Don't Cross" tape, show her my big refrigerators full up with milk. I'm barking like a damn dog, just like a goddamn cornered pit bull.

§

Somehow she broke free and ran for the car. Nearly ran Fred down as he came into the drive, waving his arms, his face sagging apology. Oh, she knew the routine, that give and take of violence and regret. Returned to Los Angeles days when her husband came at her with blood on his knuckles, same grimacing mask, distorted by rage she couldn't comprehend. But not Freddy. She had never imagined Freddy.

Bearclaw and Tangerine were in the deep shade, just hanging, books drooped open across their laps. Too hot even to read; maybe 106 in the shade. "How's Aunty Lou?" Tangy coming for her across what passed for a yard; Tia backed away around the car. "Stay away, baby! Don't touch me! I may be infected, may be a carrier, Dr. Bruce is going to test me. Listen! you're right, Bearclaw, it's typhoid fever." A mother afraid to touch her child, imagine! There would be bruises, five blue fingers imprinted on each biceps. Freddy would be around, straw cowboy hat in hand–Fred The Goat Man trademark, brown with age and grime, leaving a permanent groove in his scalp– come to beg forgiveness. *No, Freddy,* she would tell him through the locked cabin door, *I don't know if it's the bashing or the remorse that gets you bastards off. I'm not going there.* Now Tangerine asked her if she never planned to touch her anymore. Tia sat in the dirt, hands over her face. Existential terror: her husband Syd smiling broadly as he let himself in the apartment and bushwhacked her with a roundhouse punch, then came for her around the bed. Not that! Never again.

Next day, she went back to visit Lou, fearing the worst. There she was sitting up in bed, smiling, fever not just broken but banished. "I survived," she cried cheerily. "I will be out soon. Good Lord, I must have shit out twenty pounds."

You didn't want to breathe in that place, the air unspeakably foul. Tia had blood drawn downstairs, and they said they would know in a few days. God knows how. Lou said she could take care of Tangerine when she got out: "I've developed immunity. Scrub down the house and start over. How's that?"

"About those nasty things I said to you, Lou—"

Louise threw a hand. "What nasty things? I can't remember a thing, feverish as I was."

Tia knew it was bullshit. Still, we can choose to forget (those bruises on her arms once they stopped smarting). Therapeutic forgetting. Any of us can act out of character; any of us can forgive such an act. She sat down on the edge of Lou's bed and told her that Freddy was devastated over his goats. "Not just the milk but the suspicion—" spreading hands to indicate the carnage around them, whispering, "–just think of all the people that drink his milk."

Lou gripped her hand. "You best get over there, dear. He may do them harm. God knows! He shot poor Tina in one of his fits, after all, his favorite goat."

Tia saw it clearly: Fred moving through the goat shed

from stall to stall, cutting down his girls, then stalking the neighborhood, hunting down others he loved, finally himself. Collective suicide. Wasn't it the method anymore?

§

He listens, an ear tilted up, the dead air still and heavy, no birdsong in the wilting heat, just one of his girls kicking her stall, stink of rotting mussels and starfish stranded in dried-up tide pools at low tide drifting inland from the coast, so foul he can near abouts hear it–high buzzing whine of carrion flies. Damn! No friendly chatter of his radio in the shed. Goddamn radio. Flat give out, like everything else. Sea level rising, drowning New York, Holland and such, though seem like it fell hereabouts and left dried-up, fish-stink mussel beds high up the rocks. Can it drop some places and rise others? They all betray you, every fucking one. Not Tia, for crissake. Sweet Tia. Come accusing me how I'm out to hurt her little girl and already killed Louise. I can't believe it. My girls condemned and "Don't Cross" tape strung around the barn and it's me the problem? Go figure. Got no choice but take out the bitch and her whining daughter–calls me freaking "Goat Man"– and Lorna who started this damn mess. Did she crap in the milk pail, for crissake? You couldn't never be sure with Lorna. All of them what come threatening. Or take out my girls. End of problem. Or both. There it is! 'Cause isn't nobody can make a choice like that. Fuckinay! All them nights spent loving in Tia's bed, sixties rock stars and longhair gurus watching from posters all sides. What's the girl know of the sixties? Bullshit fantasy. What's she know of Nam and crazies on the streets spitting on anyone in uniform? Still, sometimes he believed those nights in her cabin were all that kept him going. Plus rising at dawn to milk his girls. He loved that time of day: goats' steaming breath on the cool air, some jouncy Brit on the radio chirping, "This is the BBC World Service," rain playing snare drum on the tin roof of the shed, here before rains stopped and someone turned up the thermostat. One-hundred-fifteen degree heat in the freaking redwood forest, for crissake, bringing diseases nobody never seen before: typhoid fever, Marburg, and malaria. Equatorial death.

He caresses the hand grip of the M-4 carbine with the palm of a hand. No problem grinding that short barrel up into his chest beneath the sternum, aimed direct at his heart. Likely to paint that big drooping redwood over the house with blood and tissue fifty yards away. End of problem. Tell you what! Kill myself, leave the whole shitty mess to Deputy Smoky. No need to press the trigger with his big toe, any of that hokey shit, since he could reach it with his thumb. What the Cong tried to do and failed, I'll do it myself.

§

Tia heard a gun shot driving up Fred's long drive. She stopped and let dust drift in the open windows. Gas gauge on empty. Not likely she would find gas any time soon or could afford it if she did. She rested her forehead against the steering wheel and realized she could not go on to find whatever awaited her in Fred's compound. Call me a coward, I can't do it. Besides, what if he'd just shot the first of his girls, then turned and saw the target on her chest? Am I not another of his "girls"? Like hell I am. She drove straight back home. Tangerine down at Bearclaw's. Just as well. My lover dead maybe. Possibly both lovers. Jay, *over there,* might find death any moment. Maybe Lou is right: I am greedy. Didn't plan it that way, but I am. I may have to choose between them some day. Maybe the choice has been made for me already. It was this last thought that stuck and stung. How can such a loyal person be so disloyal? How can a man as gentle as Freddy be so violent? We are a creature of contradiction. It defines us.

A slamming on her cabin door shortly later, Fred's voice demanding she open. Come for me, Oh God! He could kick the flimsy door down, she knew. Maybe best he had come now when Tangerine wasn't home. She threw the door open to confront him. Blood soaked his T-shirt and cargo pants leg one side. He cradled his strong left forearm in his right hand—shreds of tissue and white splintered bone where the elbow should have been—his face ashen, riven with pain. "Can't let go," he said; "near abouts blew it off." Leaning against the door jamb. How he'd walked from his place she couldn't imagine. She wrapped a towel around the wound and got him packed into the car. Drove back roads at derelict speed, honking as she approached intersections, passing the few vehicles out on the highway at 100 MPH, terrified she would run out of gas before reaching the hospital; Fred had gone into shock, collapsed against the passenger door. She drove right up to the hospital steps and went inside, shouting. The sight of blood pooling beneath Fred's feet on the rubber mat as she exited the car more frightening even than Syd pacing inside that Los Angeles apartment years ago, while she huddled on the fire escape outside with her infant daughter.

They would leave the car parked on the brown grass before the hospital for months, out of gas. A symbol of defiance, monument to their collective condition, evidence that they would not give up. Someone planted flowers inside the trunk, watering them daily from their precious water supply.

§

They saved Freddy's life but not the arm. There I am in the superfluous wheelchair in the hospital lobby when Tia comes dashing in, shouting "Help," me shouting with her, thinking that Tangerine has taken ill. Half-relieved to hear it is Freddy until I know of his condition. At the last instant, he decided not to shoot himself and jerked the gun barrel to one side, old fool, and blew his arm nearly off instead. Lord, it goes from bad to worse, don't you know. Though it would seem I have survived. Tia learns she is not a carrier; the disease has passed over her house and left it untouched. But Fred is. They must use precious antibiotics to kill the bacillus in him, but must use them anyway to protect him from infection after amputating the shattered arm. He's quite cheery when we go in to visit him. To escape suicide is no doubt a reprieve: the simple joy of being alive.

"Only need one hand to milk, anyways," he says. "Two is handy, but only takes one. Don't need no arms at all to make love. So I'm all set."

"You are an original, Freddy, I'll give you that," I tell him.

"You're looking mighty fine these days, Louise, after surviving the sickness. I never noticed before what a fine looking gal you are. Must'a been a shitkicker once. When Tia dumps me, maybe I'll take up with you." He winks just as lewdly as you can from a hospital bed.

"Now that's horse piss, Fred. No woman alive would

find it a compliment to be called a 'shitkicker.'" Freddy
The Goat Man and me–now there's a radical idea.

So the sickness passes over and we wonder what's
next. Devastating rains, then drought, economic collapse, poverty and despair, disease and attempted suicide. Tia suggests we throw a survival party once Freddy
is out of hospital and Lorna back on her feet. We wait
two weeks until the fever has passed through the community and done what damage it intends–fourteen dead
on the coast, mostly elderly and infants, many more of
us badly shaken. Incredible what we have been hoard-
ing. Fred slaughters a goat and does a pit barbecue, and
Skunk Sinclair's son contributes a hog, I bring out my
coffee stash, Skunk Sinclair has a stash of Irish whiskey,
Bearclaw brings peyote, Jesus Alvarez does his cactus,
chicken and beer tamales (I didn't think there was a
chicken left on the coast or a beer), and lovely Lorna,
bless her heart, terribly wasted by the disease, brings her
Bible. "It's a damn feast," Jesus Alvarez says. "Might be
shameful if we wasn't so hungry."

All of us dancing and having a great old time behind Skunk Sinclair's whiskey, boogeying to the beat of
The Sinsemilla Braintrust, and Freddy makes a speech
about how much better a man it has made of him to lose
his arm. Hell, he might just marry and settle down–at
seventy-two is it?–lecherous old fart. Everyone looking at Tia. Three of the Barclay brothers openly make

passes at me. Actually, I find them charming, especially Cleve, who used to appear at Save The Earth meetings and curse us for anti-logging freaks who wanted to destroy his livelihood. Good dancer, too. He tells me how his wife died five years ago. "I'm still tore up over it." So I tell him about losing Jeff. He asks my forgiveness for being so wrong years ago. "I guess it's some of us want to keep insisting nothing will ever change, because we're flat scared it will." We sleep together that night. Maybe Tia's right: I'm hornier than I know. I about devour him and spit out the bones.

We get up next morning in that party litter, shards of the bunting Tia and Tangerine made drooped from tree limbs, Skunk Sinclair's son and band members sleeping it off under the trees. I make coffee. Cleve relishing it as he'd relished sex, closing his eyes and running his tongue around his lips. A man who knows how to enjoy his pleasures. "Where in hell have you been?" he asks. "Right here," I tell him. Tangerine asleep on the cot beside the fire, so I know Freddy is feeling well enough to rock that little cabin again, and I'm glad of it. I ask Cleve if he likes children.

"I like them well-behaved," he says. A large, gruff man, with a thoughtful heart.

"Tangerine is a delight," I tell him. And I ask him to spend the day.

For the first time in weeks a breeze blows in off the

ocean. Not the hamsin wind that carries on its parching tongue the smell of putrefaction and death but a vivifying sea breeze. "We just might of made it through," Cleve says. That party mess looks like the detritus of prosperity. Perhaps it is. Perhaps we will turn this around. Perhaps the fever has finally broken.

A Crack
in the Pavement

Bicycling home three days before his wife died, Gil
Ridley swerved around a deer carcass lying in the
middle of the road. He thought to race home for a hack-
saw and buck knife to butcher it while it was fresh, before someone else got to it. These were hungry times.
But, coming to a foot-dragging stop beside it, Gil realized
the cadaver was two-legged, naked and lying on its side
in a fetal position so he could not determine the sex, no
doubt run down by some big rig that had abandoned rut-
ted interstates and taken to back roads. Sonnabitch had
likely climbed down from his tractor, prodded the victim
with a toe and muttered, "Poor bastard is dead." Just left
it there. In his own driving days, Gil would have rolled
the body up in a blanket and wrestled it up into the
sleeper. Then, the damnedest thing! The corpse disappeared, sucked down into a crack in the pavement. Gone.

Gil dismounted the bike—no easy task with his arthritic knees and hip joints—kneeled stiffly down on the shoulder and sniffed the pavement. Sat up straight. "I seen mirages but, damnitall, I never seen that before." It had been there sure enough—what they called an "apparition," a forewarning of death maybe. Because, truth to tell, what he'd seen in that first instant was his own wife, Amanda Ridley, stretched out bare naked on the pavement (fine body for a seventy-four year old woman—used to be before cancer stripped flesh from her bones), and before his eyes she'd coiled up in a fetal position. "Can't blame you none, babe, exposed in a public place in your condition! No, sir." Doctors gave up on her five years ago when they closed the hospital in Haneysville after her last chemo, and she'd been living on borrowed time ever since. "Remission," they called it.

Walky Talky, passing silently on the far side of the road, glanced up at him; they exchanged a nod. Didn't bother old Walky to find Gil muttering to himself. After all, he himself walked the roads loudly reporting the news and weather from the transceiver they say Tommy Whitehead installed in his brain. But here lately Walky had stopped reporting; maybe his receiver was broke down or it had got too depressing reporting all that bad news. "That's the hell of growing old," Gil told Walky's retreating back, "trouble stores up over your natural lifetime to where you had about enough of it. I believe my Amanda's reached that point." Gesturing at that place on the pavement where her body had lay. "Life offers more problems than it does solutions. You can't blame a person for having enough of it. Still, I resent it. It's damn hard having your wife of fifty-two years ready to pass on you—ready and willing." Looking at the road again, Gil was certain it had been Amanda lying there. "Apparition," "premonition"...whatever you want to call it, scared the b'jesus out of him. Walky went silently on.

"How'm I s'posed to live without you, baby? How'm I s'posed to get by in this world of bad news without you? Answer me that! Good news either, for all that—if we ever got any! No one to share a damn nothing with."

§

It's what they called a "double-wide": two trailers stuck together along their lengths, so you got something wide enough to spit across. Recent downpours and wind fury had about done in the roof and carried off the aluminum canopy over the back deck, likely whooshed it up canyon to Lawr and Cora's place. From what Lawr said, half the town was deposited on his acreage in an airborne junkyard. *You're missing something, just come on up and dig through.* Amanda got a kick out of that; she itemized the various likely rained down on their heads: *Benson's bad temper, old Granny Whitehead's false teeth, Teensy Hancock* (who no one hadn't seen in a coon's age) *and the axe they say Judd Hancock sunk in his father's forehead, Melinda Haney's oversize bras* ("How about your own?" Gil asked), *and the crucifix what Hector Dario erected atop his house, along with them Xmas shiver lights adorning it.* Oh, she had a laugh over that. But now, as he approached the trailer, Gil could not tell if his wife was alive inside at all. How could that be, not knowing if your own wife was dead or alive? So was that highway apparition an actual vision of her death? "You wouldn't do that to me, would you, Amanda-Jean? Wait until I go off to die on me? Would you?"

Gil believed if only he could be there to hold her hand and walk her as far as possible towards the other side he might better accept her passing. It might give him a glimpse across the barrier, so to speak, so he could bring some of her death back with him. But he also knew it would be harder for her to let go with him holding onto her; she lacked the strength to wrench herself away from him, as she finally must. His desperate clinging would burden her all the more. What was best for one of them was worst for the other. No way around it. Here at the end of fifty-two years together they faced their biggest disagreement ever–nearly their only. Some damn irony! "You or me, baby," he told the trailer, "one of us is got to sacrifice. I flat know it should be me, goddamnitall. It's me the stronger party here, it's me the healthy party, it's me the so-called 'man of the house,' it's me the one needs to have a bold and sympathetic heart, since

I'm the one gets to go on living. There's the rub right there! Living without you won't be no life at all." Gil teared up so he could barely see the trailer, weeds grown up waist high around it, and was ashamed of himself.

They discussed endlessly how they might stage it: ritual-like, clinging and crying together, then he would leave her to go out and pace under the stars. Let her go. But that was predicated on knowing the exact moment of her death. Who can do that? Or he might return home after an outing like today and find her coiled up lifeless in a fetal position like that apparition. Gone. He would perform the ritual of clinging and crying then with her lukewarm corpse, as if Amanda still occupied it. "Kinda creepy, hon," he confessed. "Hate to admit so, but it is."

She wrinkled up her nose in her girlish way, sick as she was. "Yeh, creeps me out real good, too."

"Maybe I'll follow close behind you." Placing a finger to his head and cocking his thumb. "I've thought about it plenty."

"Why, you couldn't harm a mouse, Gil Ridley, let alone yourself. You know it. You'll stay on right here in this trailer and grow old surrounded by our memories."

"Old? Hell! What you think I am already? Old as I need to be."

"I mean *old*! For the both of us."

"Are you in there, Amanda?" he called to the trailer now, and thought he made out: *Where else would I be, you dummy?* But if apparitions can lie on the roads their voices can sure enough float on the air. Who was it mentioned seeing naked corpses lying in the woods and said it was over all the trouble they were having lately, perverse as things had gotten—*symbolic of our collective demise, so to speak?* Whoever it was, he thought them looney at the time. No longer. Open your eyes wide enough, no telling what you'll see.

Perverse wasn't half of it either. First the Missouri and Mississippi...all them rivers flooding so bad they took out Saint Louis and that country in there and drove people out and become swampland, then drought turned swamps into dried-up-bogs-like, half the world without potable water, the other half with too much of it, crops failing so at first grain prices went through the roof and no one could afford to eat, now there's flat nothing left to eat, even in places like California that were once bread baskets, markets and governments collapsing, sea waters rising to cover great cities of the earth—half of Europe and Florida and the Gulf Coast, what used to be—so any who lived on high ground considered themselves lucky, except, you know, thirsty and half starving to death and living in a state of perverse anarchy. Sluggards Creek—what was once hillbilly California—begun to seem blessed ground, civilized and full of decent people. Then, wouldn't you know it, he was losing Amanda. So even the joy of simple survival was denied them. Perdamnverse!

"I'm home," he called to the trailer.

Amanda wasn't dead, as he feared she would be, but lying naked in bed, like that apparition. She'd pulled off her clothes, finding them unbearable against her skin, eyes vague and distant, begun to retreat back in their sockets. Doctor Seathorne had warned she was likely to exhibit odd behavior—craving chocolate sometimes (wherever innahell he'd find it), or wanting to go for a swim in the pond (in her condition!), wanting sex in strange positions, when neither of them could manage sex at all anymore (his prostate had begun to just say no...half about pissing, too), or to see her dead brother, whom she never had any brother, or to clean the house middle of the night ("It makes me feel alive"). He got her comfortable as best he could, the painkillers gone long ago.

Amanda screamed agony through the days and nights. Gil pulled at his ears and begged God's mercy under the stars, beat his forehead bloody against the double-wide (left a dirty brown mark on the metal), took her in his arms and moaned with her; poor woman didn't hardly know he was there. You can drown in pain, like a river sweeping you along; observers on the shore see your pale face passing just under the surface—mouth wrenched open, eyes turned inside out—and they groan and coo for you. But they can't imagine, can't begin to goddamn imagine. Isn't nothing to be expressed in nifty scales from one to ten, but a swallowing completely up in a flood of agony. Still and all, drowning is quick panic. To drown in pain is horrible-slow panic, like the churchies' descriptions of hell and eternal burning. Mixed as such metaphors might be to the learned, it seemed to Gil Ridley that his wife was both drowning and burning at once—sinking in a river of flames far below the swirling surface. Close as they were, he sensed something of her agony; it mortified and enraged him—the unfairness of it. So that contention between them, which had seemed insurmountable just weeks before—whether to grant her permission to die or cling hold to ease his own suffering—evaporated. You cannot lie in bed next to someone you love and tolerate their consumption in a bonfire of pain. Not for long.

He pulled out the pistol he'd bought years ago because Amanda thought he needed a hobby, a silver-plated thirty-eight revolver, and stood shells beside it in a row on the bed table so she would know exactly what he was doing—could weigh them in her hand and become cozy with them. They didn't seem ugly or cruel or deadly or anything much, and he believed they were whatever you wanted them to be, as is so much of life in the end: cruel or merciful, foolish or wise. He was looking intently into eyes from which her soul had retreated—cornflower blue irises gone cloudy, whites grayed against pale skin, sexy-long lashes invisible now—and for a miraculous instant

Amanda sprang back into them in an act of mighty will, swimming up through that fire pond to the surface, and, though no one else would have seen it, he saw her nod assent, saw her right hand, which clutched the blanket, open and move ghostly up to touch her forehead then her chest to indicate she wanted it done properly.

Gil wrote out detailed instructions (because if you have a hard job needs doing, Amanda had taught him, write out just how you will do it; *That's half the battle won*): how he would send Walky up to Lawr Connery's place to bring him and Cora back, knowing the going and coming would give him time, then kiss her tenderly on all his favorite places and cherish the little pucker of thankfulness in her kiss, and promise her he was going to make it all right and bring an end to her pain, then pull the sheet up over her head—that hardest, like he was putting her down in the ground with his own hands—and, this had to be just so, find the fit of the barrel against her forehead. Incredibly, Amanda who could no longer move at all reached up to clutch his wrist with bony fingers and nodded okay. Gil looked out the window, caught a sob at his throat, and pulled the trigger.

Lawr and Walky must do the cleaning up.

§

He hung her Angels cap from the refrigerator door

handle. For Amanda the biggest grief growing out of *the troubles*, was that, first, they could no longer watch baseball games on TV, then major league teams stopped playing altogether. How would life be worth living anymore without baseball season? Sometimes he winged her cap across room like a Frisbee to land where it may, marking the place where her soul set down, and talked to her there. Plunked the cap down on his own head when they finished talking. Just weeks after Amanda passed, Gil started laying out an outfit for her on the sofa bed in the living room each morning–where he himself slept now he'd discarded the blood-soaked mattress–a different outfit each day, matched like he knew she'd like it. It comforted him to have her reclining there, legs and arms outstretched, baseball cap on her head, shoes where her feet would be.

Isn't none of my doing. It's your clothes, isn't it? Why innahell I'm gonna lay your clothes out on the sofa bed, Amanda? I ain't that nutty yet....Oh, yeah? What reason is that, hon?...The hell! The hell I'm lonely!...It's your cap, isn't it?...My cap? In the broom closet, I'm guessing. Haven't worn it lately. (Touching his head, realized he was wearing it.) Why innahell would I go for a bike ride? Why do I want to get outta the house? Isn't nothing out on those roads but corpses, apparitions and such. That's a threat to your mental health. I'm just holding on as it is....What would I want with your glasses? I don't know where you put them....The hell I'm wearing them. (Of course he was.)

In truth, Amanda lay in the side yard where Lawr and Cora buried her. Took them all day to dig her grave, hard as the ground was, the one who wasn't digging sat inside the double-wide with him and Amanda and talked rot, made them promises he knew there was no keeping. How her death would be a relief to him, a burden lifted. How they understood why he'd done it and would not inform authorities. How folks would come by to visit him. Baloney! Isn't no disease on earth people fear catching more than broken-hearted grief. Truth to tell, he was in a red fog and didn't pay much attention to their nonsense anyway. When the job was done, they outlined her grave with stones. All stood up over Amanda-Jean to say goodbye. No Bible verses or none of that. Though Cora read a poem and Walky talked about his mama's passing. Gil wept and muttered. Didn't seem like enough somehow. Now anymore, he went out weekly to rearrange the stones and add more, left her messages in stones, wrote backwards so she could read them from down below: *uoy evol I...uoy ssim I, ebab, nmaD*...all like that, knowing she'd get a kick out of it. Asked where innahell she'd put their marriage certificate and wedding photos, anyhow; went out early next morning expecting her to answer, rearrange stones best she could from below. No good. He'd just have to keep at it until he found a question she cared to answer. Amanda was like that.

But what he did with her ceramic figurines worried even Gil himself. Amanda made hundreds of the shiny little statuettes over the years, sold them at craft fairs before *the trouble.* Specialized in frogs and toads, salamanders you might find on Mars or somewheres, with stalk eyes and coiled tongues and intricate feet, warty as all-hell. Gave him the creeps. Plus politicians with popeyes and long faces like they'd been caught with their pants down, like most had. Warty, too. Nixon and Reagan and DoubleBush and TripleClinton and Obama and the rest. Amphibians and politicians, swamp creatures all. He removed them from packing boxes and lined them up along couch arms, guarding his feet and head, all along the back of the couch, circled up like half a wagon train on the nappy rug before it–hundreds of shiny little bug-eyed porcelain bastards. He cut out tiny napkin smocks for Chelsea–naked pubescent like Amanda made her, hair flying–some of the others, too (Nixon, for crissake, naked as a jaybird! Amanda was like that). Circled them up around his spot at the dinner table before he ate. Tiny sentinels. *See, there's this article I read once about this kid was a pyromaniac and he done the same thing around his bed: done rings of toy soldiers and superheroes and first responders with plastic squad cars and fire trucks around his bed at night—"to prevent anything bad from happening," he told the headshrinker....Well, goddamn it all, Amanda, I don't know what. Maybe I might shoot myself or light the*

place afire or swallow Drano. There's times I feel like it....
Get out where? What public events is that? Besides, I never
went to public events without you. Maybe I could walk the
roads with Walky; I'd cover local news, he could handle the
international scene: "Midge Talmadge's barn is set to be de-
molished today, news of Pete Seaver's death is greatly exag-
gerated..." like that. Lossa fun, right, hon? All old news, he
realized. Truth was, he had no idea what was going on in
Sluggards Creek anymore. He'd lost touch since Amanda
died.

You know, I can't call you 'baby' no more now you've
gone over. At some point in time we all have to grow up.
Even you, dear. And if you're not grown up before you die
you sure as hell are after....Them little bug-eyed bastards?
It comforts me, okay! What innahell else I'm gonna do with
'em? Whenever I got them weird froggies and droopy-faced
Richard Nixons goggling me, I feel like you're right here with
me. Isn't nobody else crazy enough on this earth could think
those up but you. So what you want for dinner, hon? Not
there's much choice. Oatmeal or dried up Wheaties or turnip
stew....Who says the dead don't eat dinner? Little as there is,
it's like eating nothing anyways.

Early on, Lawr and Cora and his neighbor Pete Seaver
stopped around to visit, but Gil slipped out the back into
the woods, not in the mood to see anybody–knowing he'd
catch hell from Amanda for it. *Maybe they mean well, but*
I don't want nobody poking around feeling sorry for me. I'm

doing just fine. Walky maybe. He either talked at you or didn't talk at all. But Walky had stopped walking. Finally they stopped coming. Just as well; his social self had died along with Amanda. Like she took a chunk of him with her. Every few weeks he heard Benson ring the big bell announcing community meetings. Once, he and Amanda would've been the first ones there. He could hear her admonishing him that he needed to get out of the house—six months now since her death and he hadn't hardly talked to nobody.

I don't need to talk to no one; I got you to talk to when I'm lonely, don't I?...Of course you answer, I hear you plain as day....Why isn't it the same thing? I'll tell you what, I miss the sex and I miss the way you made coffee—when we still had any—and I miss your peculiar habits: always checking under the toilet seat before sitting down for fear of black widows.... Sure, I knew! Shaking cereal boxes good before pouring out a bowl. What innahell for? How we had sex just about anywhere—community meetings before others arrived, for crissake. Half embarrassed me sometimes. But I don't miss your scolding one damn bit, Amanda. So don't you start.

The morning he ended her suffering he at first thought he wouldn't be able to do it. He hefted the pistol in his hand, pushed shells into the chambers and spun the cylinder, then set it back down on the night table and shook his head no. Amanda stared up at him, not blankly, though all the color was washed out of her irises and the inner light that had always illumined and shone out of her eyes extinguished...nearly. Just a tiny glimmer far back inside, like a candle glowing at rear of a cave. Her eyes held his, fiercely. The fist clenched tightly against her chest opened and inside was a scrap of paper with a crudely scrawled message: *Yes, you will, Gil Ridley.* The woman knew him, she flat knew him. How innahell had she managed to write it when she couldn't lift her hand off the counterpane? So he did it. Later, he discussed endlessly with her whether he had done the right thing. Begged her forgiveness.

Because often it is not the trouble we expect to have that is the trouble at all but another that grows out of it. Here he had struggled to decide whether to leave her side and let her die or to stay close and walk her to the other side, and the truth turned up neither and nowhere in between but some different and more terrible truth altogether. So after she'd gone he must resolve that earlier conflict on his own—whether to hold her close or walk away and let her go—found himself dodging back and forth between those options many times a day. Chiding himself, "You old coot bastard, can't you make up your mind at all?"

§

Gil stumbled out of the double-wide one chilly March

morning after a bitter session of self-recrimination which lasted most of the night, exhausted, legs aching, eyes numb and fuzzy. He had the awful feeling that Amanda had abandoned him, disgusted that he could not make peace with the kindness he had done her. However, making his way into the yard he saw signs of activity around her grave. Stones rearranged in a simple message: *Thank you.* The first one she'd left him. Gil collapsed on the spot and wept for gratitude. Who would believe such a thing? The dead do not move stones; they live among the stones but do not argue with them.

"But you are my wife," Gil was pleading with her as Pete Seaver approached the place. "How could I shoot my own wife, Amanda, the woman I love...whatever reason? Answer me that."

"You never shot Amanda," Pete called to him. "Lawr says she took her own life."

"She couldn't of, Pete. She lacked the strength for it. I had to do it for her."

Pete stared at him, likely not wishing to believe it. Surely, if Gil had killed Amanda, Hector Dario would have arrested him or he would have fled into the hills; he would not still be living here in this place where they'd shared a life together. Didn't make sense. But the stillness of certainty about Gil clearly troubled him. Gil's weren't the hard eyes of a murderer but liquid pools of pain and regret.

"The Lord has witnessed your transgression and has

forgiven you," Pete declared. "If he can forgive Cain, he can forgive Gil Ridley."

"What innahell d'you know about it, Pete? Anyways, it's not the Lord's forgiveness I need, it's Amanda's. Maybe you knew somebody once agreed to do a thing they truly disagreed with. Maybe you shoplifted with a high school buddy but disbelieved in it. All the worse when we get older, the things people agree to do. It's like that with Amanda's mercy killing. It's her suggested it, sure. She flat begged me to do it. But what sane person ever chooses to die, pain or no pain? Answer me that!"

"So it's true then? Murder is a capital sin, Gil Ridley. To murder your wife is an abomination before the Lord."

"So that's how it is? The Lord forgives me but you won't?" It's no wonder he'd lost all desire to converse with other people. Always went round in circles and vexed the spirit. But didn't with Amanda. Never. He threw a hand at Pete and went on digging up turnips.

Likely the man left after a time. Gil didn't give a damn. Next day he put up signs around the property: *Keep Out! Hermit on Premises.* He half expected Hector Dario to come investigating Amanda's death, likely arrest him. Half wanted it. But why would he? The jails were all boarded up, justice system broken down. Truth was, it wasn't God's forgiveness he needed or Amanda's, but his own. No hope there. That night he moved the couch cushions out atop Amanda's grave, fashioned a tarp into a crude tent above them. He would sleep out with her from now on. They could identify birds together at first light, as they'd always done: mockingbirds first (often carrying on with their antic mimicry half the night), early chickadees and grackles, cooing doves, a redtail hawk whistling high overhead. "Earth isn't done in yet, we still have birds." He knew she was glad to have him there, though wouldn't admit it, would scold him for sleeping out in the cold and damp where he was sure to catch his death. Maybe would. He just wanted to share a bed with her again, no matter if it was his deathbed. He arranged her ceramic frogs and politicians in droopy-jowled, bug-eyed ranks around his camp, hung her clothes on hangers from tree limbs in complete outfits like deflated scarecrows. Come next winter, the rain and weather would raise hell with them and leave them in tatters. What did he care? By then he would have clawed his way underground to join her. He felt less substantial every day, increasingly like the apparition he had seen lying on the county road, sucked at last down into a crack in the pavement.

FAMILY LIFE

My pops and me would siphon gas offn cars parked in their driveway and rest areas–where the driver's asleep inside–and swipe cans of oil whenever we could, 'cause that ol' chevy van is a hunka oil-drinking junk *Chevit-'r-leavit*. And Pop taught me how to pop out gas cap locks with a hammer 'n' punch, like poppin' a cork outn a wine bottle, and I got good at siphoning to where gas rushed up the hose from the tank about into my mouth to start the vacuum. Got me a mouthful now and then. Burns like tarnation. Come to be too dangerous, what with gas so rare to where people would kill you for it. Oncet this big ol' logger dude up to Idaho caught my pops siphoning gas and whupped the piss outn him, so I run back to the van and got the baseball bat–my mom and Krista hiding all sobby and scared inside–and come back and whumped that dude hard in the pit of his back, lain him out good, too. So he just lain there like a fat bug on its belly, twitchin' his legs and arms to where I'm scared I busted his back.

Din't feel good about it neither, 'cause we was stealing his gas and he got the right to protect what's his. But Pop said to get the fuck out! Afterwards, I couldn' decide whether I done good or bad. Still, it's him or my pops, and like my dad says, blood runs thicker than road tar. I useta think so oncet, anyways.

It got to be fewer and fewer rigs to siphon gas outn, what with people guarding it and rigging booby traps like they done. You'd see plenty cars just sittin' by the roadside with the gas cap popt off, flat empty—Mercedes Benzes and all—no good to anyone without fuel to run them. Twenty years ago, Pops says, he could'a made a killing offn all them abandoned rigs, just sittin' there rusting. So we give up on wandering and had to settle down.

A while there, we found us a nest in a abandoned house in Desert Hot Springs, California (what useta be): real nice, big and fancy, this heart-shaped swimming pool what had turned swampy and mosquito confested, and Mom blamed it for giving her West Nile virus. But soon Pops says we gotta move on, it's too many scumloads squatting in all them abandoned houses. But what I think is my pops ripped off some dude what got after him. So we move outn there to this mesquite canyon offn a dirt road in the desert. Real isolated, no scumloads nor mosquitoes neither, lotsa night sky. I liked it. But Mom is bad sick and my sister's sick-bored, Pops, too, I b'lieve.

Worries me plenty when my pops gets bored to where he lets out his mean side on anyone in the vicin'ty—usually me. Sometimes, happy as we are in the spot where we landed, he says we gotta move on just outn meanness, I guess. He's pissed off, anyways, at Mom for being sick. Won't admit it, but he is. Pissed, too, when she complains about his cooking.

"Well, that's all we got to eat, Starr. Rabbits we snared and a itty bitty rice." (What we grind up and mix it in a soup with cactus limbs and yucca fruit—desert scrub soup.)

"Go out and find us more," Mom says. "Ain't that y'r job, Alf? I'm ill, I need nourishment. Can't you see I'm ill?" We rigged up this hammock for her outn a blanket tied by ropes between mesquite trees so she's up offn the ground, anyways, away from ants and such. 'Cause my mom plain hates insects. She's lyin' up in there.

"Why'd we come out here, Dad?" my sister bitches. "I hate it here! It's boorrrring."

Pops eyes her sideways. "Yeh, okay! I'm not having a big ol' time of it myself, kiddo. Still, it's people safe. We got it to ourselves...except that crazy ol' coot up the road, and she's no bother." The thing about Pops, he don't never get mad at my sister, says they're birds of a feather and all. Don't never raise a hand to her. Where if it's me complains, wachout!

My sister makes a face in the ol' coot's general direction. "Smelly, dried up old witch."

"Why'nt you go see what she's got," Mom says, all weak-like. "She must have something to eat."

"Just eggsactly what we planning to do. Right, Les?" Pops winks at me. "Soon's the moment's right. Eggsactly what we have in mind here."

First I heard of it. I got this uncomfor'ble feeling, like when I hit that dude with the baseball bat and other times I could mention. The ol' coot don't seem so bad to me, not even that old, works in her garden under the hot sun and all, 'cause we been spying on her from a mesquite thicket.

"It's prob'ly alots to eat out here if we look," I say. "The Indians lived out here, din't they?"

"Puhhh-leeese!" My sister gives me a rolling-eye frown. Krista useta be timid and scared of everything. But then, whenever we stayed with Mom's sister in Bakersfield, she got in a posse with our girl cousins and neighborhood kids and cut her hair butch and dyed it green and got what Mom calls her "puberty attitude." Not scared no more, just obnauseous. Pop says she "got her hormones up," and I b'lieve it, too. Super-obnauseous. He seems to enjoy it.

So Pops goes scouting the ol' coot's house, and I go looking for desert veggies. I cook up lizard stew one night, which my sister won't eat it but the rest of us three do. And get so stomach sick we swear we will die, ter-

rible pinching cramps and the trots so bad it runs down
our legs. Makes Mom all the sicker. So Dad slaps me silly–this nasty way he got of whumping me up one side
the head with the flat of a hand and catching it with the
other, sos y'r head snaps back and forth and near jars y'r
brains out. Mom tells him, "Stop!" before he breaks my
neck. He says, "Maybe I wanna break it!"

"He only wanted to help, Alf. He didn't know it would
make us sick."

We liberate water from the ol' coot's water tank
nights, anyhow, else we wouldn' be out there atall, and
my dad's trying to decide whether to walk in bold and
demand food offn her or sneaky-freak and take it while
she's asleep, 'cause it's a big ol'-timey wood house, all the
paint peeled off like it got sandblasted and a zillion ways
to get in. "Made to order," Dad says. "The thing is, Lester, if you read y'r scripture, it says right there in black
and white that the righteous shall enjoy the fruits of the
earth. The Hebrew people walked into the Land of Ca-
naan and took what they required, because they were
chosen of God." My pops was raised on religion and gets
it whenever he needs it most.

"How d'you know y'r chosen?" I ask him.

My dad hard-eyes me like he's about to to be pissed
off for me asking such a dumbass question, his pupils
shrink down to little black BBs. "Them who can take;
them who can't contribute. That's God's law, boy. Old

people is done their taking, it's contribution time."

So that night we snatch a chicken from the ol' lady's coop and make chicken soup for Mom. She feels so much better behind it, I decide it's cool. The ol' coot is got others. Even Krista develops a better attitude. Me and her sit under the stars that night, and she tells me her dream of living in a mansion like what we had in Desert Hot Springs some day—with a heart-shaped pool and huge 'frigerator full of food instead of dried-up, moldy stink-rot—and our cousins living next door. "My husband like invented a climate machine to save the world, and he's famous, and we're rich and happy. Mom and Dad live upstairs, and you can come visit us sometimes, numbnuts." I don't want to tell her none of that stuff is ever gonna happen. She has her heart set on it.

So there's this devil sandstorm. It's like the earth and sky get mixed up together, as much gritty dirt in the wind as under y'r feet; it invades y'r eyeballs and the crack of y'r ass, and this big ol' wind-weak salt pine falls down acrost the ol' coot's house. Early the next morning we go in to see what we can scavenge, 'cause Pops says she abandoned the house and moved into the trailer beside it; everyone knows abandoned places is fair game. But Dee—that's the ol' coot's name—hasn't abandoned and isn't dead neither. She points a shotgun on us and throws us out, half-crazy maybe, but I like her for it.

Long story short: Dee and me become friends, Pops

and me cut up that tree what fell on her house, Dee gives us food and lets us stay in the trailer beside her house, Mom gets better quick, I mess up and Dad beats crap outn me, and Dee gets all upset about it, she fronts us a tank of gas and throws us out—I like her for that, too—and says I can come back anytime I need to. Whenever we're leaving, Dad wants to go back and rip off her food stash and fill up the jerry cans with gas from her reserve. I know it ain't right but don't dare say nothing, 'cause my dad's in a evil mood. But Mom refuses to go back there. She's scared of this demon Tawk-witch what hangs out in the desert and eats kids' souls (Dee says, though I know it's only her ol' friend Tripp what we seen, dressed up as Tawk-witch). It's complicated, anyways.

Question is whether we go back to Bakersfield or to Wanderer City, what they call, offn I-15 near Escondido. Whenever we Wanderers run outn gas and have to stay in one place, a bunch of us congregize together in a neighborhood of broke down RVs and rusty vans—in the parking lot of a abandoned mall maybe or some park what the state give up—and share whatever we can scavenge. There's times we commando a market what's going outn business and seize the stock before landholders can. There's all these nasty-lookin' Wanderer dudes armed with knives and baseball bats forming a ring around it, while the women and us kids clean out the wares, usually not much: moldy oatmeal and split peas full of rat turds. They say we're like Gypsies over to Europe, but I never seen Gypsies. Anyways, Mom and us kids prefer Wanderer City to camping out on our own. It's safety in numbers–from vigilante landholders and kidnap traders who steal kids. But Pops says isn't no one on this earth you can trust less than a Wanderer. "Isn't no blow to a restless wind," he says.

So we go back to Bakersfield, and my sister has her posse again, but I wish we was back in the desert–even angry as my dad was out there–where I helped my friend Dee weed her garden and counted shooting stars at night. Mom's sister, my Aunt Macy, isn't so glad to see us neither. She says, "I thought you wouldn't get back here again unless you walked."

Pops laughs. "Meaning never! We thought you could use you a couple men about the house." 'Cause all the cousins is girls, and Uncle John is *over there* in the war.

"I can't afford to feed extra mouths," Macy says. "There's little enough for us as is, given paltry Army checks and nothing in the stores to buy anyways. They'll be even less now."

"I don't catch y'r meaning," Dad says.

Macy don't answer, just stands in the doorway blocking us from entering her house; don't never invite us in. I never seen her look so sad and meanly.

"Nice attitude when I been deathly ill," Mom snaps. "I'll have you know we got our own, Macy. Still, if it's you and yours come to us in trouble, we would take you in...

no matter. No matter, hon!"

I got to think a minute how adults say things what they don't b'lieve just to score a arguing point. Fact is, I can't never remember one single time we ever shared nothing with nobody. Macy or nobody.

"Forget it!" Macy says. "You all can stay in the Cedars next door. They abandoned it. It's not very big, but it's cozy."

Just then a man, listening from inside the screen door, steps out (I b'lieved I seen a shadow in there). "I can fix you a shunt to bypass the meter and get you folks' water turned on."

"Who inna hell's that?" Pops asks Macy–just like the dude ain't standing there.

"*That* is Roger Jones Hernandez-Habib."

Pops snorts and looks the dude up and down, real impolite. "How many last names you got?"

"Just the one. You can call me RJ." The man don't take no offense; maybe y'r big enough you don't got to–maybe six-four, two-fifty, built like a D8 Cat. Dark-complected like he might be a Gypsy hisself. My pop's a little dude, he takes offense at most anything. RJ extends a big hand to shake, and Pops looks at it like he don't wish to, finally kinda brushes his palm acrost it.

"You the new man in the house, I guess?—" Pops grinning in a way what worries me "–Y'r the *Jack in the box...Piggy in the poke*...whooowwee!—" Pops slaps RJ on the back. "Woops! Hey, I forgot, ragheads don't eat pork. Sorry, dude. Guess he's the new *lead in y'r pencil*, girl?"

"All right, Alf, you made your point," Mom snaps.

Dad winks at Macy and laughs. "What's my point got to do with it?"

All of us staring at Pops—like what's it all about—even Krista. But RJ is got a puzzled frown to his brow, like he can't figure Dad atall or don't wish to. So I dunno if he's plain dumb or Christly or what. Or maybe them sand-worshipper Muhammeds take offense slow. Aunt Macy is flat po'd, so mad she starts crying, like my mom does sometimes. "You have an ugly mouth, Alf Minor. A filthy, ugly, nasty, sewery mouth." But RJ puts an arm around her and smiles. "No harm done." Maybe he's the type what explodes all at oncet. Big dude like him! But Pops says the bigger the tree, the more fun it is to chop down.

"What I'm saying, y'r a married woman, Macy. I'm saying y'r husband's *over there* and got no chance to defend what's his back home. Maybe I got to defend it for him."

"You got to mind your own business is what you have to do, Alf, you lousy bastard."

"So now it's me the bastard?"

I can't figure why Pops is so po'd about who Macy's hanging with. He ain't like that. Or why he wants to pick a fight he sure to lose. 'Cause, on second thought, RJ don't look so easy-natured: hard high Indian cheekbones and a biker's fat face, got a purple scar acrost his right cheek what pulls his eye down toward it; he studies my dad at a slow, watchful smile. Meanwhile, the cousins' heads looks over each other like meerkats inside, motioning at my sister. So Krista ducks past my aunt on into the house before Macy slams the door in our face. Not that I blame her.

So we go next door to set up, and my mom says we better move on if there's going to be trouble. "Won't be no trouble," Pops says. "I got it offn my chest. It surprises me you don't give a damn some raghead is got his hands all over y'r sister while y'r brother-in-law is *over there* dodging bullets. Don't it about make you sick? John fighting them bastards *over there*, and they're wife-buggering him *over here*."

Mom studies him peculiar. "How d'you know what they're doing at all?"

Pops shouts a laugh. "How in hell do I know...Well, hello!"

"Anyways, he's no more Arab than you are."

Dad looks at her hard, like he about to lose it. "What you call him then?"

"Why is this so important to you, Alf? Why do you give a damn?"

Dad don't answer but turns and goes right out to unload the van. I can't decide if it worries me more to have him mad at me or mad at someone else. At least I'm used to it. Maybe I better tell RJ it don't mean nothing: put a flame under a pan and it will boil. My dad's got a flame lit under him which he lit it himself. Mom's always saying, "He isn't really angry at you, Lester, he's just angry." About *the troubles*, maybe, or cause we run outn fuel, or he got it in his blood. So I ought to be madder than hell myself, but I can't get mad for beans—except at my sister.

§

I seen some weird stuff. I seen this dude oncet died of cancer in Wanderer City, so they killt his baby girl and put her in the ground with him for to keep him company. Pops says that stuff ain't s'posed to happen in the US of A; it's against our principles. Maybe it might happen *over there* somewheres. But here anymore anything can happen.

RJ makes good on his promise: he's out there before we wake up next morning rigging a shunt line for our water. Bare-chested, all sweaty when my dad goes out, built like a frigging brick shithouse—all abs and biceps, no fat on him, covered every inch in faded tattoos. This fice dog dead center to his chest with its fangs bared, like a message to my pops: *Don't mess with me.* "All ready to go there, Alfred," I hear him. Then my dad: "Listen up, sand pilgrim, we don't need y'r Arab charity. We ain't gonna drink y'r filthy water." Then–I plain can't b'lieve it–Dad is thumping a finger at his chest, up in his face, so RJ is got to tilt his head back and look down past his nose at Pops, lips clamped tight. And I hear Pops say, "poozle-doozle..." something nasty about my Aunt Macy, something about Uncle John, and it's "raghead" and "sand nigger" every other word, so I'm thinking, whoaaa up! Ashamed-like Dad is using all that kinda language, when nothing po's him more but someone calls us "Gypsy pissheads." RJ does a weird-like little smile. "I'm Mexican, Alf, if it makes you feel better." His voice so deep I'm trying to communicate real hard to my pops: *This is one tree too big to chop down.* No use. Dad yanks off his shirt, like to say: *I'm a skinny runt but I'll whup y'r ass.* Got himself up in a lather. He lands a fist in RJ's belly. Like the dude don't tense up or nothing. Slow-like and deliberate, he whumps Dad atop the head with a fist, and the air goes outn him and he slips to the ground in slow motion.

I charge out, yelling, swinging Dad's machete over my head, ready to defend my pops, 'cause *blood runs thicker than road tar.* Mom behind me, screaming, and Aunt Macy and the girls, who musta been watching from next door. "Doooonnn't!" But too late. I'm slicing at RJ–not even hardly noticing that he ain't kicking Dad or nothing–and bring that blade around at his head. RJ catches my arm and grips my head to his chest, hugs me a minute, like I'm caught in a steel vise. I feel the blood moving inside him through my cheek, like it circulated from me through him and back into me again, and I can hear his heart bumping ('cause I got him a bit exercised). Kind of moaning-like, like there's a pipe organ in his belly playing a long-low note. Weird as it may sound, it calms me right down; I just want to stay there. I can't remember my dad ever hugging me like that since I was a baby. "Okay," he says, "okay now, *primo.*"

Then my mom and Macy and my cousins and my retarded sister is crowding around talking all at oncet, and Mom drops to a knee to make sure Dad is alright, moaning, "You bastard, wha'd you do to him?"

"Real sorry, ma'am. He should be all right."

And my smart-ass sister saying I'm the biggest crapass simp she has ever seen. "So what you gonna do, genius, cut his head off or something? You retard."

"Well, I...Pops was...I din't..."

Her and the cousins laughing and mimicking me. Dad kinda like blinks and looks around like he just got religion; looks up at RJ and you can see he's puzzled sure enough.

"Are you happy now?" Mom asks him, flat po'd. "You deserve every bit of it."

After that, Dad won't let Mom visit her own sister or nothing (but she sneaks over on the sly anyways), won't so much as look at their house next door to ours, won't let us use the water what RJ turned on—so we got to sneak water offn the neighbors, including Aunt Macy, which don't make no sense atall—which is my job. Still, the cousins and my sister is in and outn our house like no one cares. Pops says it ain't the cousins' fault that their mom is a slut whore.

My mom says if a person falls hard enough it's likely to knock sense into them. Not my Dad! It only makes him the madder, and I know he's layin' for RJ. So early one morning, anyways, when I'm getting water at an outside spigot, RJ comes outn the back door, he cocks a finger at me and laughs. "Gotchou!" 'Cause right along him and Macy knew I'm taking water, can hear it from inside splashing into my bucket. Besides, my sister's sure to tell them; she don't keep no secrets where I'm concerned, especially if it gets me in trouble. RJ sits down on the porch stoop.

"Your pops said he wouldn't use your water I turned on. Right, *primo*? He always keeps his word where it comes to matters of personal principle, even when it causes him a heapa' trouble. Am I right?"

"Yessir," I mutter, knowing I shouldn't be talking to him, 'specially not about my pops.

He looks off at what useta be the chicken coop where Aunt Macy kept her chickens before they got stole. Oncet, she had the prettiest yard you ever did see, lotsa roses and lilac bushes and red-leafed hawthorne and lawn thick as a sponge, what all dried up in the drought, gone brown now. RJ nods his head, like it's something we could agree on, all that dead and brown. "Your pops stays angry most the time, don't he? Nobody of you knows why. Neither does he." I won't answer. Still, he goes right on. "Yeah, I know, *primo*. I useta be angry all the time myself. You looked at me wrong, I wanted to kill you. Right?"

He got me interested now. "What happened?" I said.

He sits there, shaking his head like he won't say or don't want to go there. "Grief and trouble happened. Grief on top of trouble until it wasn't worth it. Maybe you heard of the Mexican Mafia?" RJ thumps a thumb to his chest. "Tha's me, *primo*. Drugs, contracts, vendettas... you name it. I made it to Decision Maker before I bailed. They likely be after my scalp still if *the troubles* didn't end it." He looked up at me slow. "I've killed men, Les, until I couldn't no more."

"You plan to kill my pops?"

"No more killing, *primo*. I'm done with that." Slapping his jeans thighs, he stands up.

"How'd you get so strong, RJ?"

He smiles, easy. "Lifting weights in Vacaville mostly. Your pops won't be a happy camper if he sees us talking. Am I right? Yeah, I know the dude, *primo*. I was him once myself. I know."

We get friendly after that. It's like talking to RJ is like talking to my dad in a different lifetime, except he don't whack me. I ask him how he stopped being angry.

"I looked at myself in the mirror one day and didn't like what I saw, *primo*. The anger went right out of me like someone pulled the plug, right? Just like that!"

Wow! I'm thinking, how can we get my pops to see himself in the mirror? Still, I don't dare let on I am talking to RJ; that's a worse betrayal than becoming friends with ol' coot Dee in the desert. He'd prob'ly kill me for it.

So I go for a walk with my pops a few days after, 'cause he wants to get to know the neighborhood better, he says. Gives me the long-eye as we walk–like blood-shot from lack of sleep–what scares the b'jesus outn me that my dumbass sister told him about me and RJ be-ing friends. 'Cause her and the cousins know everything. So it's this ol' dried up golf course give over to foxtails and stickery weed what crunches underfoot, reminds me how we walked into the sage at ol' coot Dee's before he kicked my ass.

"Why'nt we walk on the road, Pops?" I ask him.

"We're walking here–if that's all right with you?"

"Yessir." My voice quivery-like, what I can't control.

He flicks the back of my head with his fingernails, and it stings, too. "I dislike when you call me 'sir.' We ain't in the military here, boy."

So I begin bitching about my sister Krista, how bossy she gets around the cousins, treats me like dirt and makes fun of me to where it gets them all laughing, knowing I shouldn't but it just spills out. All unexpected,

Dad whumps me with the heel of his hand.

"You sound like a freaking little girl with y'r squawky, high-pitched voice, boy. Byaaaah-byaaaah-byaaaah! Jesus! Just like a gawdamn tattletale girl. Near about to make me sick."

"I'm sorry, sir."

Pops whacks me again. Don't seem fair: my voice is broke, so I can't help it. He starts in on what a "sand-bitch fairy" RJ is, how he'd whup his ass if they ever got in a fair fight where Dad wasn't caught by surprise and din't have his guard up (I don't remind him who started it), how he'd do it for Uncle John. "I never heard of no Mexican raghead...Jeezus!" Shaking his head. "What? You don't believe me? You don't think I could take that fat Mexican fairy? Huh?"

"Yeah, you could, Dad. Sure. Easy. I just know you could."

He looks at me a minute, kinda nodding his head, like he's trying to decide. I'm in for it now sure. We're standing on this little knoll, like a stage, what useta be a green, gone dry and brown, and there's this sand trap like a big ol' kidney wrapt around one side, full of leaves and milk thistle, a pole still stuck up outn the putt hole, but the flag only a hank of threads. Dad pulls out that pole, he gives a whoop and heaves it like a javenlin spear offn the green. Then wants me to try. My throw's about half to what his is, and he rags me about it, says I throw like a girl. So I try again and do better, and Pops puts an arm around my shoulders, like he never does. Scares me; I freeze right up. "Okay, boy...okay." He got his moustache trimmed back so it's just a thin line over his upper lip. "Pussy tickler," he calls it. Then he's charging off back home, carrying that spear on his shoulder and me behind. I feel like I dodged the bullet this time. Just barely.

I seen Dad hanging around Macy's house one night soon after. I'm sitting out under the stars in our yard, and seen this figure step offn the back porch next door and reckanize Dad by his walk, that metal spear perched on his shoulder (he sharpened the end good and plans to use it as his "equalizer" against RJ's size advantage), like the cut out of a African tribesman against the sky. It sends this jolt of terror through me. Like that time we thought electricity was turned off in this house we was scavenging, so I seize hold of copper wiring to pull it outn the wall for salvage scrap, and it knockt me on my ass half acrost the room. What'm I gonna do? Dad's my dad, sure, but RJ's my friend. Shouldn't you warn y'r friend if he's in danger? Thick as blood may be, I don't want neither one of them getting hurt or killt.

§

What it is, I go in through a living room window, dropt down on all fours like a cat. Real dark inside, but I got it mapped out in my head from all our visits. Useta smell smoky-sweet from Uncle John's pipe tobacco and cinnamony from Aunt Macy's bread pudding. Now it's a dusty smell, fruity from the cousins' cheap cologne. Not a sound. What if Pops is upstairs right now, outside Macy's bedroom door, about to rush in and jab that spear through RJ's heart? Scares holy hell outn me. But I gotta warn RJ: he's my friend, he's cool, he never done nothing to us. Warn him my dad's layin' for him even if it does betray my own blood. 'Cause it'll betray them both if Dad kills the dude. It ain't right besides. Sometimes a person is got to be stopped from theirself.

So I take the stairs on tippy-toe, stepping near the wall so they won't creak, but they do anyways–like a soul torn outn someone's chest in the night. Gotta wait a long time between steps. Finally upstairs, I do a sneak-a-freak past cousins' bedrooms–wonder which one my creep sister is in–and remember how oncet I seen cousin Shannon undressing for bed through the door crack (real breasts, too, and pussy fuzz); she looked up and seen me, and she's screaming and carrying on. Boy, I caught hell for that. But I don't see my pops. Don't see nothing but the empty gray inside of a cave. I hear the cousins breathing and wonder how I'm gonna do it–din't figure that out–just go in my aunt's closed bedroom door, I guess, and

shake RJ awake. Flat out warn him. I would'a done it getting water, but he isn't come out lately. Like he knows my
pops is layin' for him and he don't want no trouble. I'm
standing there outside the door, hands stiff at my sides,
working up courage. It's a grunting inside and Macy
saying, "Shhhhh-shusssh up!" So first I think it's fuck
noises, then b'lieve I only made it up. Reaching for the
door handle when someone grabs my biceps. It's like all
the piss and vinegar freeze right up inside me and I can't
move. Just knowing it's Pops, and he knows eggsactly
what I come here for.

But then I seen cousin Shannon's blond hair glowing
phos-fro-escent. "Damn!" I whisper, "you scared the living pee outn me." We go on down the hall to negotiate.

"You little sneak pervert," she whispers back, "I
caught you! Playing Peeping Tom again."

"No, I ain't. I never come for that. I come to tell RJ
something important."

"Yeah, I bet. I know exactly why you came. Maybe I
should scream right now."

Somehow I convince her not to, and we sit there in the
hallway, our backs against the wall, fast whispering, and
Shannon agrees to only tell my sister; not bust me right yet,
only bust me later. It gets to where I completely forgot what
I come over for atall, only thinking about the shit I'm gonna
be in oncet Pops finds out.

Dad's all like pissed off quiet next day, watching my

every move with little angry slit eyes, picking his teeth with a twig; he's got what Mom calls his "sullen face" on (*his I'm-in-for-shit face*), and I just know Krista snitch told him I was in Macy's house last night, and he knows egg-sactly why. I'm thinking I will run off right now, pack up some rice and a cooking pot, my jacket and spare socks, and take my chances on the road, try to get back to Dee's in the desert. Only question is: Do I tell Mom I'm going? My sister is more uppity than perusual, knowing she got me nailed up by the tail feathers this time. Nailed up good. I catch her hanging clothes on the line in back and stick my fist in her face and tell her I know she told Dad I was in Aunt Macy's house last night and told him me and RJ is friends. She laughs all-dissful-like and pushes my fist away.

"I never told him nothing, you numbnuts jerk. I wasn't even sleeping over to the cousins' last night. Like everybody knows but you, widget. I would'a scratched your face bloody if I was. Besides, RJ isn't at Macy's no more, genius. He went to stay with his mother."

"That's a lie. He would of said goodbye. I heard him...I heard him and Macy last night."

"Wha'd you hear?" All suspicious-like, watching me.

"Nothing, okay! I din't hear nothing."

She curls her fingers to scratch me. "Wha'd you hear, numbnuts? You better tell!"

"I told you...nothing! I din't hear nothing." I walk

away. Krista calling after me:

"I'm gonna tell Macy you're spying on her. I'm telling Dad."

For oncet, I wisht I had a mean streak, wisht I could find my dad in me, just a bit, wisht I could shut her up from telling.

But it's my mom takes up the anger slack, beats us all to it.

What it is, I go in to confest to my dad: not knowing what I'm gonna tell him about RJ and last night, only knowing I gotta tell him something before my sister does, so he don't beat me for what I done and for being a sneak-a-freak about doing it both, knowing that sure. 'Cause Dad don't respect much but he respects a man being a man about the things he done.

But I guess she beat me to it, 'cause I'm about to knock on their bedroom door at end of the hall when Pops grips my arm from behind–like Shannon done last night–and swings me around, right up to his face. His breath smells of pepper, and the gaps between his top teeth seems like caverns, and he's asking what I ever heard at Aunt Macy's last night. "Nothing, sir," I say, "I din't hear nothing." He don't hold nothing back but punches me right acrost the mouth and splits my lip open against my teeth. "You sneaky little bastard, don't you dare lie to me. What you sneaking about y'r Aunt Macy's house for? You spying on me, boy?"

"You? No, sir. No...I ain't...I never..." Truly, I don't know what he means. I close my eyes and tilt my chin up the other way for him to slug me again. Blood runs down my chin. Not whimpering or nothing, knowing this is the one I always been dreading–this is the bad one–when I hear Mom furious-voiced, "Leave him alone, Alf, you bully sunnabitch. Don't you touch him." So he rares back–I never seen so much anger in his face and eyes: red as bloody rare beefsteak and black as pebbles–about to whump her, too. But Mom don't cower, don't flinch away; she gets right up in his face and says something. It's like all the air deflated outn his inner tube and the fury-color with it, and he gone white-dry like he just seen hisself in that anger mirror.

Mom tugs him into the bedroom and shuts the door. I got my ear up against it, listening: how her sister Macy confest all, just now when Mom went to visit her, confest how last time we was here Dad and her slept together, and now they done it again, and she hated it, she felt sick about it, she couldn' live with it and din't want it no more. But she was all tore up about Uncle John dying *over there*, then RJ leaving her, and she lost track to herself. She was terrible sorry. What's amazing, the more Mom talks the calmer her voice gets, so it's like she's discussing the weather or something. I stand there, my back against the door, listening, my mouth hung open, I s'pose, like Moses before that burning bush. Awed. Bloody-mouthed.

My ears on fire.

Pops saying, "You can't trust a word that whore says," his voice creaky-weak. "She's a slut. Sorry to say it about y'r sister, but she is, Starr. Woman like that might say anything."

"D'you hear me, Alfred Minor? John is dead. A road-side bomb. Couldn't even find the pieces of him. D'you hear? Can you imagine what that does to a wife? I don't wonder she needs comforting. But you, asshole...you! What you need you don't get at home?"

"I'm not listening to this bullshit. You gonna listen to that whore? Sleeping with some Mexican raghead, her three little girls down the hall, John's daughters! Y'r own daughter over there. Don't you give a damn, woman? Maybe it runs in the family. Maybe you got you—"

"Hush up, Alf! Sit down! Don't you dare threaten me."

"Can't you see," he shouts, "the woman's jealous, she wants to wreck our marriage."

My sister appears down the hall; I wave at her to bug off. But she don't. She come right up to listen, and–weird as it is–I wanna cover her ears, wanna protect the little rat snitch. Her buzz-cut hair, stood up like crooked, un-cut grass, makes her look like a little kid, my baby sister.

"Sit down, Alf," Mom repeats, quiet and stern. "I knew it was something going on, the way you cut into RJ. Like a jealous lover, I thought then, but wouldn't let

myself believe it. Now I do. My own sister! Yes, her three
little girls sleeping in their rooms down the hall, that's
right! Your nieces! It's you the whore, Alf."

A loud, hand-open slap sound! Mom shrieks. Krista
looks at me, her eyes huge and scared. "You bitch!" Pops
snorts, low and growling-cruel the way he gets. Another
slap.

It's like a ol'-fashion flashbulb explodes inside my
head. Like that electric bolt what knockt me acrost room
is entered my veins and all the blood vessels scream inside me at oncet. Like I swallowed that burning bush
what sets my stomach afire. I rush through their bedroom door, not even thinking what I might do, not guessing. My dad's hand raised up to hit Mom again; she's in a
cower down on the bed, her mouth saying, "don't." Pop's
mouth dropt open when he seen me. I jump up and grab
his hand, kind of keep on going and pull him down to
the floor. Wham! Momentum, I guess. Not like I meant
to or nothing, just want to stop him. Dad so astonished
he just lain there a minute and can't move, watching as I
leapt up and grabbed the bat what's in the corner beside
the bed and raise it up high above my head, legs spread
wide, over top of him.

"Don't you never hit her. Don't you never touch my
mom. Don't you never again."

He grins, looking up with his little BB eyes. "Or
what?"

"Or I'll kill you."

Like it's some argument to his face, like the top and bottom half disagree, and his mouth works to make a compromize, and his eyes narrow and his forehead all wrinkles up. Like he has a small fit. When it's done and passed, there's tears leaking outn his eyes. His voice is different from what I ever heard it. Kinda squeaky high and crackly, like mine when it broke. He boosts up and leans against the bed. "All right...son. Okay! You're right, boy. You're right. I won't never raise my hand to y'r mother again. You c'n put that bat down now."

"Yessir." So I do.

"If you don't mind, I'd like to speak with y'r mother alone."

I walk out then. There's Krista right outside, looking at me like she never seen me before. Like it scares her some to see me now. "Wow, Lester," she says. Inside Dad is telling Mom how sorry he is and hopes she'll forgive him and knows it's anger took hold in him lately and he wants to deal with it. Though I can't see it, I b'lieve he is got his head in her lap and she's stroking his hair and kinda cooing, saying it'll be okay. Maybe, just maybe, he seen hisself in that anger mirror. And maybe it's me held it up for him to see. Though it was crackt, it hadn't broke all to pieces yet. Maybe, just maybe, it never will.

WILLIAM LUVAAS has published two novels, *The Seductions of Natalie Bach* (Little, Brown) and *Going Under* (Putnam), and a story collection, *A Working Man's Apocrypha* (Univ. Okla. Press). His essays, articles and short stories have appeared in many publications, including *The American Fiction Anthology, Antioch Review, Carpe Articulum, Confrontation, Epiphany, Glimmer Train, Grain Mag., North American Review, Short Story, Stand Mag., The Sun, Thema, The Village Voice* and *The Washington Post Book World*. He has received an NEA Fellowship in Fiction; his stories have won *Glimmer Train's* Fiction Open Contest, *The Ledge Magazine's* Fiction Awards Competition and *Fiction Network's* National Fiction Competition. He has taught creative writing at San Diego State University, The Univ. of California, Riverside and The Writer's Voice in New York. He is online fiction editor for *Cutthroat: A Journal of the Arts*.

SPUYTEN DUYVIL
Meeting Eyes Bindery
Triton
Lithic Scatter